THE

LIGHT

BEYOND THE

SHADOWS

Also by Peter Santos

Everything I Wanted to Know About Spirituality but Didn't Know How to Ask: A Spiritual Seeker's Guidebook

The Little Book of Spiritual Growth: A Straightforward Primer on Energy, God, Spirit, Soul and Ego

Little Gifts: A Collection

For Children

Little Gifts: The Adventures of a Pigeon-Angel

THE
LIGHT
BEYOND THE
SHADOWS

BOOK 1

A TALE OF AWAKENING

PETER SANTOS

Spirit Speaks Publishing

The Light Beyond the Shadows: A Tale of Awakening

Copyright © 2023 by Peter Santos.

Published by Spirit Speaks Publishing
www.spiritspeakspublishing.com
Berlin, Vermont

ISBN-13: 978-1945705076

Library of Congress Control Number: 2023933969

This is a work of fiction. Names, characters, places, businesses, organizations, events, and incidents are a product of the author's imagination, and any resemblance to actual persons, living or dead, organizations, locales, and events is entirely coincidental.

Cover design by Peter Santos. Cover tree by powensby on Pixabay. Old Paper Texture by nevermoregraphix on DeviantArt, altered and edited by Peter Santos.

"You will understand why . . . someday."

BOOK 1

A TALE OF AWAKENING

Prologue

The old man looked over the golden, sun-kissed fields from the covered porch of his old farmhouse and smiled. It was time. His story needed to be told, and he was the only one who could tell it.

He walked inside to his desk, pulled out some blank pieces of paper from a drawer, and dipped his quill into the small container of ink recessed in the wood. This was to be his last piece of expression, an account of the end of his farming life and what had felt like lifetimes of struggles before he had awakened to the truth. He never once thought about who would read it; he only knew that it needed to be written.

Pausing with the black point of the quill almost touching the page, an understanding washed over him, one of the many he frequently experienced that came infused with a level of certainty that made doubt impossible and the perceived outcome inevitable. He now knew that only one person would ever see the finished manuscript, despite the past calls for it from many who had listened to his lessons. Only one, but she would be enough.

She would know when she happened upon the story, know that it was something different, something that would speak to her young but incisive mind more deeply than anything she had read before. Even though it would take her years to fully understand it, she would quickly see, feel, and accept the profound connection she had to him, the author and subject, one that was both realized and unrealized at the same time, dancing in a never-ending partnership that served them both. In one sense, their past and future together had already been written.

He wrote the first words in large letters across the page, a title that he knew would help grab her attention, *A Tale of Awakening*. He thought for a moment about adding his name below it as most writers did, but he wasn't that person anymore. That man had died long ago. Besides, with only one reader, did it really matter?

He closed his eyes.

When he opened them, a smile again spread across his face. He dipped his quill in ink, brought it to the page, and chuckled as he wrote, *by Erich Evepret*. It was a name that some might understand if they were to have the opportunity to read the story and reflect on it, but alas, the one reader of the tale would not comprehend it, at least not initially.

He often communicated more than what the spoken word could convey, and those who had attended his talks could often discern those deeper symbolic or layered meanings, if they were ready to recognize and experience them. Most, however, were not in a place where they could understand, despite their desire to. The words on the page before him held more significance than simply the name that the letters formed.

He knew his one reader would be open to these subtle meanings, even if she were not able to fully grasp them when she read the story he was about to begin. But she would be ready. She had to be, as she unknowingly was a part of what made his transformation possible. Because as much as this was his story to tell, it was also hers.

The old man flipped the title page to the side, uncovering a fresh, blank sheet. Pausing but for a moment, he began to write, and his tale about friendship, love, life, mystery, and the extraordinary experiences that led to his death began.

It was a beginning, but also the beginning of the end.

Anna

Walking home from school, Anna's eyes darted to a man pushing a cart of pots and pans on the cobblestone street. The uneven surface rocked the cart erratically, and the resulting clinking and jangling of metal stood out against the muted sounds of conversation as the city's residents and merchants went about their afternoon business.

With his heavy boots, scorched trousers, and leather topcoat, Anna assumed he worked at the forges located outside the city on the southern road. She had never been there, nor much outside the city at all, but the man's rough appearance reminded her that there was so much more than what she had experienced in her young, sheltered life under the watchful eyes of her parents.

Behind the man, over the slate roofs of the low, timber-framed buildings that lined the street, she could see the Grand Wall in the distance, the massive, impenetrable barrier that encircled the city and surrounding lands.

She normally didn't register the Wall's presence, as it was leagues away and an accepted background to daily life within the Territories, but today was different. Something about it drew her attention as its lengthening shadow reached for her across the city in the waning afternoon light. It looked different, *felt* different, and she didn't understand why.

Distracted thinking about it, she barely heard her friend, Melissa, talking.

"It'll just be us, and maybe any boys you want to invite," Melissa said, giggling. Their friend, Laura, was walking with them.

"Um, what?" Anna said, bringing her attention back to her friends.

"Your birthday. Tomorrow, right? Thirteen?"

"Yeah, right," Anna said. "Uh, let's just make it us." She wasn't interested in boys, and she liked spending time with her two best friends.

Switching topics to voice what she was thinking, she said, "Hey, does the Wall seem different today?"

"What do you mean?" Laura asked.

"I don't know. It seems different in some way."

The three girls stopped and looked into the distance.

"Looks the same to me," Melissa said.

"Me too," Laura said.

"Why? Do you think it moved?" Melissa said under her breath as they began walking again.

"I don't know," Anna said. "It doesn't look like it did. Maybe I'm just seeing things."

"Well, at least it keeps us safe from the crazies," Laura said. "I don't want to go through what my grandparents went through."

"Yeah, me neither," Melissa said.

Anna's grandparents' generation had experienced an attack on the Territories from the foreigners who lived in the wasteland outside the Wall. The assault was unsuccessful, of course, due to the strength and size of the barrier and the valiant fighting of the Grand Army that repelled the invaders. Since then, there hadn't been any attempts by outsiders to breach the Wall, and it remained a protective fortification that kept the residents of the

Territories safe from external dangers. Anna hoped the foreigners had learned their lesson from the defeat.

As the girls continued their walk home, Anna thought about the mysterious origins of the Wall and its occasional, inexplicable movement, or so the rumors went. The government had banned talking about it, so Anna only knew what she had overheard from the hushed whispers of others. Apparently, the last time it had miraculously expanded was the night before she was born, somehow enlarging the realm of the Territories. No one understood how or why, and because it was forbidden to discuss, citizens within the Wall eventually accepted its new position and went about their lives as before, except for the occasional murmurs about it.

One such rumor was that it was subject to the magic of the Ancients, a tribe from long ago that supposedly knew how to mysteriously transform physical objects, so either their magic had been discovered or the Wall itself had been enchanted at their hands, causing its movement. But not having experienced anything strange about the barrier in her lifetime, she only really knew it as a fixture in the landscape that offered protection from outsiders. Besides, magic was only possible in the fantastical stories she liked to read, and in her imagination.

"Okay, so, your party," Melissa said, bringing the conversation back to Anna's birthday. "How about three o'clock? I'll make sweet biscuits."

"Yum!" Laura said.

"Yes, yum!" Anna repeated. "I'll definitely be there."

"Me too," said Laura.

"Uh," Melissa said, looking at Anna and making a face, "don't you have to check with your parents first to make sure it's okay?"

She was right, but Anna didn't want to acknowledge it. It was embarrassing enough that her friends knew how controlling her parents were.

"It's not a problem. It's *my* birthday, it's a Saturday, and I can do what I want," she said, almost convincing herself with her tone. But underneath her words was the familiar, unsettling feeling she always had when she had to ask her parents' permission for something. However, because it would be her birthday and she would only be with her close friends, who her parents already knew, she felt somewhat confident that she would be allowed to go. If any boys were to attend, though, she was sure she'd have to stay home.

The girls took a shortcut off the main road near the marketplace down a street known for its inns and taverns. Although Anna's parents had told her to avoid certain places like this, she and her friends often shortened their walk home from school this way. She risked her parents' anger by defying their directives, but she felt this was a minor infraction and her parents hadn't yet found out, so she and her friends continued to do it.

Most of the buildings on the street were similar, displaying white walls that contrasted with the dark, exposed timbers that framed them. A woman in an older, shabby dress adjusted her bonnet before linking arms with a man in a wrinkled suit, and together they proceeded through one of the entrances. A boy in a cap followed, carrying two suitcases. A few pairs of eyes in the windows lingered unpleasantly on the girls as they passed, their owner's hands gripping drinks like they were extensions of their bodies. Walking past a small alley next to one of the taverns, Anna could see a large cart delivering barrels through a side door, the casks marked with the symbol of the main whiskey producer in the Territories.

Before crossing the next intersection, she glanced up at the funnel-shaped device sitting atop a pole on the corner. It was a loudspeaker, a strange piece of equipment that somehow increased a person's voice so that it spoke louder than even the loudest orator. They were located all over the city and throughout the Territories and were supposed to be the way the Territory Governors warned residents of dangers coming from outside the Wall, but they hadn't been used for that in years. Consequently, she rarely gave them notice, except for when they occasionally and inhumanly screeched to life with test announcements, which sent their deafening messages across all the land within the Grand Wall. Only then did she pay attention. But her gaze now lingered for a moment on the device.

"What about tonight?" asked Laura. "What are you doing with no school tomorrow?"

"I'll check with my mother but can probably do something," Melissa said.

Anna knew that asking her parents to spend time this evening *and* tomorrow away from home would be too much. There were limits to their permissions. "You know me. I've got to study," she said.

"Even though it's the weekend?" Laura asked.

"How do you think she keeps getting perfect scores on tests?" Melissa said.

It was true. Anna was a good student and always aced the exams. Some of it was her natural smarts and some was the rigid study structure imposed by her parents. At times she was thankful for the intense, forced schedule, but lately it had begun to feel overly burdensome and stifling to her newly-budding desire for independence, a sense of freedom that beckoned to her from behind the shadows of chores, studies, and obedience to her parents' and society's rules and regulations. She hoped her parents would let up and allow her to do more of the things *she* wanted to do as she got older, maybe even once she got past this birthday, but she wasn't holding her breath given past experience.

"I wish I had better study habits," Laura said, looking down. "I want to do better in school."

"Do you want to study tonight?" Anna asked, hoping for the company. "I'm sure it would be okay for you to come over."

"Are you kidding? No way! It's the weekend!" Laura said, holding her arms out and skipping a few steps down the street. All three laughed, and Melissa and Anna followed, skipping as well. Anna played along, but she hadn't been kidding.

They continued joking and talking about their plans for tomorrow for the next few blocks until they came to the street where Laura and Melissa lived. Although the two girls were in different lodging houses, they were close enough to be able to hear each other yell from their balconies. Anna wished she lived closer to them to be able to do that. She wished a lot of things were different.

Melissa and Laura said goodbye to Anna and promised to see her tomorrow for the party. Anna continued home alone—only a few minutes away—glancing once again at the enormous wall in the distance.

Having paid such little attention to it previously, she now felt her skin crawl slightly as she observed it, and it wasn't because she found it annoying that it put the city in shadow more than she liked. It reminded her of being confined, the same feeling she experienced from spending so much time in her small bedroom studying when she wished she could go out to explore the city and surrounding farms and forests. All within the Territories, though, as there was no way to go beyond the Wall even if she wanted to. It was said to be impossible to pass and that those who had tried were never heard from again.

With her robust imagination fed by the many fictional stories she liked to read, she began fantasizing about how the immense barrier might have been constructed, envisioning great beasts carrying the enormous boulders and wizards magically levitating the stones to stack them to heights never before reached, finishing just in time to stop the advance of the terrible, disfigured army that lived in the harsh, inhospitable environment outside the Territories. She visualized herself there at that time, approaching the Wall and miraculously passing through it to see the barren world that existed on the other side. In front of the terrifying army, with a wave of her hand, she transformed the landscape into a lush forest teeming with life, and the army realized they didn't have to fight anymore and dropped their weapons, for the resources they had been fighting for were now abundant around them.

She often took a brief excursion like this to another world, painting imagined excitement into her overly-structured life, which provided a taste of the limitlessness she wanted to believe was possible. These internal journeys, as well as knowing she would eventually be out from under her parents' stern supervision, helped her get through her busy and outwardly uninspiring days.

She followed her usual route home, a left by the bakery that had the most delicious sweetcakes, a right by the tailor shop, then a few blocks before another left onto the street where she lived. Several whitewashed, two-story houses lined the lane, as well as some shops, and because it was on the shortest route between the marketplace and one of the main streets that led to the city center, it was a common pedestrian thoroughfare. She could see her mother on the balcony beating a rug hanging over the railing, the coif on her head whiter than the grubby apron that mostly covered her brown dress.

Anna lived with her parents in a lodging house, like her friends and many in her school, an old, exposed beam, wood and plaster structure consisting of two apartments on the second floor, hers and another family's. A shared, single washroom down the hall held a washbasin and pitchers of water brought up from the communal kitchen on the first floor. Next to the kitchen was a combined sitting and eating area, and out the back door was the privy.

Anna was fortunate to have her own bedroom, as many of her classmates did not, and she wondered if it had anything to do with her father working for the government as a constable. Friends at school sometimes talked about wanting a government job when they got older because it carried a higher standing than many other professions, and anything that was closer in status to the Territory Governors was respected and valued. And as the Governors created and enforced the laws of the Territories through their council, they seemed to be able to influence the distribution of extra benefits, like better living spaces and access to more refined goods. Those they trusted and employed were most often the recipients, so Anna wasn't surprised at her classmates' desires.

Several people walking on the street glanced up at Anna's mother with irritation as they passed through the dust cloud descending from the beaten rug. Anna waved to her mother, held her breath through the cloud, and entered the house. She could still hear the thumping of the stick against the rug as she climbed the stairs to the apartment's main door, which was open. Throwing her satchel of books on the bed in her room, she joined her mother on the balcony.

"Hi."

"Hi." Her mother waved her hand to try to clear the lingering dust in the air in front of her. "How was school?"

"Good." Anna leaned on the railing and looked into the distance at the faraway Wall. The uncomfortable feeling from before lingered, and she wanted to wriggle out of it but didn't know how.

"Ma, why can't we talk about the Wall?"

Her mother stiffened. "Why do you ask?"

"I don't know. It just seems strange that it's not allowed."

"Well, whether it's strange or not, it's the law."

"I know. I guess I'm just curious about it. What did you think when it moved?"

"We're not talking about this. You know better." Her mother's voice had that clipped tone that indicated Anna was approaching a line she shouldn't cross. Her mother turned to go inside but not before saying, "And what did I think? I wasn't thinking. I was giving birth."

Alone on the balcony, Anna thought that it wasn't a good time to ask about going to Melissa's tomorrow.

A blaring tone suddenly screeched from the loudspeaker on the street corner, causing Anna's body to jolt in surprise. Two more tones rising in pitch quickly followed as her mother returned to the balcony. Anna hadn't heard the higher-pitched sounds before—usually, three even tones preceded a test message—but she knew from school what the rising tones meant: the government was issuing a warning.

Anna froze in place, staring at the loudspeaker, her mother behind her with her hands on Anna's shoulders. The sound of the tones echoed across the city before a loud, heavy voice crackled to life.

This is a Level 1 Warning by the Council of Governors. We have discovered an enemy force assembling outside the Grand Wall. Do not panic.

Currently, it is many days away, and we are doing what we can to prevent any attack, but we are preparing the Grand Army as a precaution. Please see your zone's manual for the necessary steps you must take for your designated area. This is a Level 1 Warning.

Anna's mother had moved to Anna's side and was holding her tightly, although Anna wasn't sure how tightly because she was firmly holding onto her mother as well. They looked down at the people listening in the street as the declaration repeated two more times. The message closed with three rising tones.

Worried but oddly excited at hearing her first ever warning, Anna asked, "What does it mean?" and looked up at her mother, whose abnormally crinkled forehead expressed a combination of surprise and concern.

"Just what it says, dear, that the government is looking out for us." Her words didn't seem to match her look.

"What do we have to do? What's in the manual?"

"We just need to be aware of anything suspicious going on and to stay alert for the next steps, if any, but we can ask your father when he comes home."

Anna nodded. Being a constable, her father might have some idea about what was going on.

Her mother gave her a squeeze and they walked back inside. "I'm sure it'll all be fine, dear," she said. "There's never been anything beyond a Level 2 Warning, at least not in my lifetime, and we were never in any danger. And don't forget, we have the Grand Wall to protect us, and it's never been breached."

Her words reminded Anna that they were indeed safe within the Wall, but hearing her first warning coupled with her uneasy feeling when glancing at the barrier on the way home left her worried, and she wondered if things were going to be different this time.

~

Anna's father didn't come home for their scheduled dinner, which was unusual, so her mother kept the family's meal warm in the kitchen while the occupants of the other apartment—a middle-aged couple with no children—ate quietly at the downstairs table. When the pair finished, they went upstairs to their apartment, barely having spoken a word. They never seemed much for conversation, and Anna found them a bit odd.

As it was getting late, Anna and her mother decided to eat without Anna's father. This gave Anna an opening to ask her mother about the party tomorrow.

In between slurps of chicken and vegetable soup, Anna asked, "Ma, Melissa and Laura want to have me over tomorrow afternoon for my birthday. Is that okay?" She filled her spoon again.

"Will it be only you three girls?" her mother asked. "Anyone else? Any boys?"

Anna swallowed the spoonful. "No, we talked about it and agreed it would be just the three of us."

"How long will it go for?"

"I don't know, maybe an hour or two."

"Do you want to have them here?"

"No, that's okay. Melissa's excited to have it there, and to make sweet biscuits."

"Sounds nice. That should be fine, but we need to check with your father when he gets home."

That wasn't exactly the resounding endorsement Anna was looking for. However, if it was good enough to satisfy her mother, then maybe she would help Anna make the case to her father.

"Do you think father got delayed because of the warning?" Anna asked.

"Probably. You know he's occasionally late. I'm sure he'll be home soon."

As if on cue, the heavy thumping of her father's boots in the entryway declared his arrival. He lumbered inside with a big sigh, his nightstick swinging from the belt around his dark blue, square-shouldered, constable's coat that filled the doorway. One hand clenched what looked like the evening paper. As he entered, he removed his constable's cap with his free hand.

Saying nothing, Anna's mother immediately rose and scurried to the kitchen to get him his meal as he tossed the paper and cap onto the table and took off his belt and hooked it over the back of an empty chair, the nightstick clapping against the chair leg. He stared at Anna's mother in the kitchen while he unbuttoned his coat and threw it over the back of another chair. Walking to the head of the table, he sat next to Anna.

Anna looked up at him. His messy red hair framed his lean face, sharp jawline, and tight-lipped mouth. He seemed distracted, as he often did when he came home, but there was something different about him this time. He usually at least acknowledged her when he came in.

Anna's mother brought his meal and placed it before him. "Honey, I didn't know when you'd get home, so we started without you."

He mumbled thanks and looked down at Anna. "You said a prayer before eating, right?"

Anna nodded. They had, albeit a brief one.

Her mother sat back at the table and her father extended his arms to hold their hands. They all bowed their heads.

"Perceiver, Grand One, we thank You for the creation of the world," he began, "and for Your wisdom and guidance, without which we would be lost. We thank You for creating the Grand Wall, which protects us from the immoral heretics who wish to do us harm. We thank You for the Territory Governors, who ensure we stay safe and ordered during the dangerous times we are entering. And we thank You for this meal and how You guided it to our bodies to sustain our ongoing battle against those who wish to undermine Your cause. Amen."

Anna and her mother said, "Amen," and her father let go of their hands and began eating.

After his first mouthful of soup, he looked down at Anna, reached over, and gave a tug on her red-haired ponytail. "How ya doing, child?" he said.

"Good," Anna responded, breathing a sigh of relief. She sometimes didn't know what to expect when he got home. At least he wasn't in one of his irritated moods, which could escalate easily and make her want to hide in her room. Tonight, he seemed to be reflecting on something, and his prayer included "dangerous times," which she hadn't heard him say before. She assumed it had something to do with the warning. Still, his playful tug on her hair gave her hope about getting permission to go to the party tomorrow.

They continued eating in silence. After a few spoonsful, he asked, "Did you hear the warning?"

Anna nodded while her mother said, "Yes, what's it all about?"

"Well, I can't really talk about it, but at this stage, we need to be on the lookout for anything out of the ordinary."

"Like what?" Anna asked.

He glanced down at her with a blank expression that reminded her of how she had seen him on the street as a constable. It was intimidating because it seemed to strip away any humanity from whomever he was looking at, and it sent a chill down her spine. "Anything that looks different than usual," he said and turned back to his bowl.

Different than usual. Anna thought of the feeling she had when observing the Wall earlier and wondered if that counted. She couldn't convey what she had seen or felt, except that it *was different*, so she quickly dismissed the thought.

"Are we in danger?" her mother asked.

Anna's father swallowed and said, "No, not yet, but this isn't like the previous warning." He then looked directly at Anna's mother, holding her gaze for a few seconds, before continuing to slurp up soup.

Anna knew well enough that that look meant that her mother shouldn't ask any more questions about it. Still, Anna wondered what he meant.

They continued to eat in silence, with Anna and her mother finishing before her father. Anna gave him a few minutes to fill his belly further before asking her big question.

Swallowing heavily, she braced herself and asked, "Can I go to a birthday party tomorrow afternoon that Melissa's having for me? Laura will be there too. No one else."

"Oh, is it your birthday tomorrow?" her father asked, angling his head to look at her. His slight smile gave away that he knew the answer. Anna was happy to see it and smiled back, nodding. He had remembered after all.

"Have you asked your mother?" he said.

Anna nodded again. Her father looked at his wife, who dipped her head in acknowledgment.

"Okay, but you come home immediately if anyone else shows up, especially boys," he said, pointing his spoon at her.

Anna eagerly nodded again, trying not to display too much excitement. She had passed her biggest hurdle and would be able to go.

"Do you still not want us to do anything for you here for your birthday?" her mother asked.

"No, thanks," Anna said. "It'll be enough to go see my friends."

"Well, why don't we take you out for a gift in the morning," her mother said, looking for confirmation from her husband, who nodded while scraping the bottom of his bowl. "How about the bookshop? You haven't gotten a new book in a while."

Anna nodded enthusiastically. "Yes, thank you!" She loved to read but had consumed all the books on her bookshelf at least twice and could use a new story.

"You'll do some studying tonight, right?" her father said, more of a statement than a question.

Anna nodded.

"Including your faith studies?" he added, looking down at her. Again, it was more of a statement, and it implied that she wouldn't be able to go to Melissa's if she didn't obey.

She nodded again. She would study, at least some, but then probably switch to a fictional story and read late into the night, something she had been doing more and more lately. And she could stay up later than usual and sleep in tomorrow because it was the weekend, and her birthday. She actually didn't need to study that hard or that long anyway because she learned things quickly and retained them well, so extra study time often meant that she could either get ahead in her lessons or pretend to study and instead read one of her books. Her parents wouldn't know, and she was fine with that. It was one of her few consistent acts of rule-breaking she felt she could get away with as long as she did well in school. On the few times they caught her not studying when she was supposed to, she just said she had finished and was taking a break with some reading, so it hadn't been an issue anyway.

With dinner over, Anna and her mother cleared and washed the dishes while Anna's father stood and collected his constable's gear and paper and headed upstairs. Anna could see the banner headline across the front page of the paper in his hand, *Governors Issue First Warning in Over a Decade!,* before he climbed out of sight.

Finishing the dishes, she went to her room to study, at least that was her intention. But as she stared at her school assignments and tried to focus, she couldn't help but think of the Wall, the warning, and her father's words about dangerous times.

Christopher

The midwife handed the freshly-swaddled newborn to the young mother sweating on the bed. The father leaned over and adjusted the feather pillow behind her head, then crawled into bed beside her and wrapped his strong arms around her and their son.

The child had come early, and it was fortuitous that the midwife had stopped by the old, log farmhouse to check on the mother just when her contractions began. The father had been working in the vegetable garden when he heard a shout from the second-story window, and he ran into the house and held his wife's hand throughout the relatively brief ordeal, as the baby arrived after just twenty minutes of labor. Once in the world, the newborn cried for only a minute before locking eyes with his mother and giving her a silent smile. The midwife said she had never seen such an easy delivery, nor a baby that calmed down so fast.

It was the couple's first child, and as much as the father had some idea of what to expect, it didn't prepare him for the level of stress he had experienced these past few weeks knowing that so much could go wrong. He had known of women who had died in childbirth and so had become increasingly uneasy as his wife's belly swelled. He was now able to take a few deep breaths seeing that both his wife and son were healthy after such an experience. The midwife's comment also helped soothe his anxious mind and emotions.

"He's beautiful," the mother said, cradling the baby's head in her hand and gently caressing his wisps of hair with her thumb.

The father nodded and reached over with his finger to stroke his son's cheek. "He's perfect." He kissed his wife on the head. "You did great."

"You too. Are you happy it's a boy?" She looked up at him and smiled.

He grinned and brushed her hair back from her face. "Yes, but it wouldn't have mattered. I'm happy you both got through it."

As soon as they had married, she had moved in with him and his parents to the homestead that had been in his family since his grandfather had built the house and began tilling the land. The family grew fruits and vegetables and sold the harvest in the marketplace in the city as often as they could. Her additional hands were a welcome addition to their efforts, helping share the responsibilities in the household and the fields, and the farm prospered. They both looked forward to raising a family there to sustain and grow the farming business.

Although the father's parents wanted to be home for the birth of their first grandchild, they were in the city selling what had been harvested the previous day because they thought the baby had at least a few more days before arrival. They would be thrilled to hear the news when they returned home though, his father especially, because he felt a strong boy was a better asset to the workings of a farm than a girl.

The midwife collected the soiled sheets and bowls and left the room, returning soon afterwards with a fresh pitcher of water and two glasses. She had thankfully also changed the stained apron over her dress to a fresh, clean one. The room now felt different without the harsh sounds and lingering smells of birth.

"How are you feeling," she said, pouring a glass for each new parent.

"Wonderful but tired," the mother replied while the father took a large swig of water. "Is it okay to take him out of this?" She tapped the swaddling cloth.

"Of course."

The mother gently unwrapped the baby, freeing his chubby arms and legs, which began to jerk about randomly. Reaching down, the father put his finger in the palm of one of the small hands, and the tiny fingers instantly closed around it. The baby's eyes left his mother's, and he cooed as he looked around and then locked onto his father's face, his little legs kicking.

"He has a strong grip," the father said.

"Like his father." She put a finger in his other hand, and the baby gurgled. "I know we talked about names. What do you think about a name now that he's here?"

"Christopher," the father said without hesitation. For some reason, the name came to him quickly and strongly.

She glanced at her husband with a raised eyebrow. "That wasn't on our list."

"Yes, you're right. I don't know why I said it, but that's just what seems right for him."

"Christopher . . . Christopher . . .," she repeated. "I like it."

The midwife sat in a chair in the corner, observing the family but leaving them the space to have this first stretch of time together with minimal interruption. The new parents laid there, basking in the radiance of this wholly complete, new being that had come into the world.

Christopher's movements slowed down and his eyes began to close. The parents removed their fingers, and his mother wrapped him in the swaddling cloth and yawned. Sleep had been difficult for her the past few days. The father, too, was feeling the exhaustion that appeared after holding on to so much stress for so long. It felt like they could all finally rest now.

"He's going to grow up to do great things," Christopher's father said softly and slowly. "I can feel it."

Christopher's mother yawned again and nodded. "As do all who come into this world so loved."

She closed her eyes and immediately fell asleep along with the baby.

The father smiled with a love and contentment he had never felt before, reflecting that this was what life was all about. Christopher was the future, and his father made a commitment right then and there to do whatever he could to the best of his ability to make sure that his son could reach his highest potential as an adult, an embodiment of the perfection he now saw in him as a baby.

The miracle of life had begun.

Anna

Anna somehow knew she was dreaming.

She was sitting outside in the front row of an assembly of people listening to a man speak. It was a gorgeous day with just a few wispy clouds interrupting the expanse of the crisp, blue sky. The man sat on a large rock with the crowd scattered about the grassy, slightly rising hill in front of him. A few people had strange symbols tattooed on their arms, and similar symbols seemed to be coming out of the man's mouth as he spoke, hanging in the air like shimmering soap bubbles blown by a giggling child. He was teaching, and she and the crowd were rapt with attention.

Even though it was a dream, it felt real, which put her in the strange space of feeling between two worlds, or rather having one foot in each. Finding she could switch her focus from being the dreamer, an outside observer of the scene, to being completely consumed by the setting's vibrant textures that tingled all her senses, she chose the latter, her awareness settling softly on the grassy hill where she sat.

The shine behind the speaker's piercing, brown eyes evoked something vague inside her that had no name. After just a slight hesitation, she plunged headfirst into the feeling as the man spoke, her body humming strangely among others in the group of listeners who also seemed enthralled by him. Even though he hadn't yet looked directly at her, she was his captive, entranced not just by his eyes but also by his speech and whole state of being. It was a willing imprisonment, as she had stepped freely and enthusiastically into his domain, his words now spinning around her and lifting her up and out of the world she knew. Any resistance she may have had to the open feeling coursing through her body only sharpened her awareness of what was occurring.

She felt incomprehensibly light, as if suspended inside the iridescent bubbles before her but without feeling confined. In the sparkling spheres it was exquisitely warm and welcoming, expanding in her chest like the aftereffect of that sip of whiskey she had tried once, a jar of it snuck into school by a classmate who had convinced her to have a taste. But there was no harsh entry like the liquor, only a gentle resting in the cozy, loving feeling that enveloped the crowd, as if they were also contained within the magical bubbles. She noted that it seemed like the speaker, at the center of the energy, was both the source of and invitation into the floating, kaleidoscopic globes, the symbols being the doorway and his words the key.

As he spoke, the man made eye contact with each person in turn, slowly sweeping his gaze across the listeners as it made its way to the front of the group. Already captivated, she could see and feel the power behind his eyes coming toward her, and the anticipation buzzed her with excitement tinged with a hint of apprehension.

When he finally directed his gaze to meet hers, the visual connection conveyed a timelessness beyond words that shot her out of her body and almost caused her to fall over in the grass. She felt buoyant, elevated in her core, and the buzzing she was already feeling escalated as a dazzling light quickly flooded the landscape, wrapping her and everyone else in its intense but refined arms. The combination of the heightening vibrations and the brilliant light became too much, and she blinked, breaking the connection. Time had slowed, and what she had thought were minutes was instead barely seconds. She blinked again, and the scene disappeared as she stirred in her bed. She was back to her life in the Territories.

The sun's morning rays had snuck silently into her bedroom, illuminating both her face and the dust floating peacefully above her. She squinted open her eyes and turned away from the window, the movement under her blanket causing the dust above to violently tumble in the disturbed air. Sighing heavily, she realized she had forgotten to close the curtains again last night.

She rolled onto her stomach and buried her head under her pillow, grumbling to herself for once again having forgotten to cover the window. Awake past her normal bedtime and deeply engrossed in one of her fictional stories, she vaguely remembered the dim light from the thin, crescent moon coming through the glass, the glow from the heavenly body normally a reminder to close the curtains to prevent the first light creeping over the Wall from waking her if she slept in. Now, it was too bright for her freshly-awakened eyes, and she wanted to reinsert herself back into her dream.

Tossing and turning as the cross of the windowpane's shadow slowly moved down her body as the sun rose in the sky, she struggled to doze again, so she resigned herself to groggily meeting the morning light. Unfortunately, she was one of those who had difficulty going back to sleep once awake, so instead she lazily gazed over at the shelves full of books on her wall and tried to remember a title she hadn't read in a while.

With nothing coming to mind and not feeling the urge to get up and travel the short distance to the shelves, she looked around at the rest of her sparse room: a simple, wooden desk and chair below the bookshelves with her schoolbooks on it; a slatted chest at the foot of her bed with a few clothes and stitched, straw-stuffed animals on top; blue curtains bunched to the side of the solitary window; a drawing she had sketched in school a few years ago hanging next to the window; and a small, wooden side table within arm's reach with a recently-finished book and wrought iron candle holder. Since last night, the formerly vertical candle had turned into an amorphous puddle, its rigidity transformed into a beautiful, white, formless shape that contrasted its simple, black stand.

She tried to shake off the increasingly confining feeling of the only bedroom she had ever known, the same four walls appearing to move closer to each other with each passing season. Now, on her birthday, she took note of how static and boring the room had felt for so long, which brought to mind her frustration with the limits on her activities and expression.

As her father basically controlled the household, she was constrained by how he wanted her to behave and perform. It was the same with school, where her teachers imposed their planned studies and activities, replicating the feeling she had at home of not having any control over her life. Despite being one of the school's top students, which she thought would convey some freedoms, instead it brought only more attention and work, which steadily built resentment as she carried, successfully, the many commitments thrust upon her. The teachers, and her parents, seemed to feel that because she *could* do something, it meant that she should, without ever checking in with her to see if it was what *she* wanted. Standing up to her father and her teachers wasn't something she knew how to do, yet.

She sometimes wondered if her father was simply replicating his own strict, religious upbringing and trying to make her just like him, but she knew she was too different, both in personality and physically, as she felt he wished he'd had a boy instead of a girl. At this point, it seemed the only thing she had in common with him was the same thick, red hair.

The only other item on the walls was an old painting depicting a scene from one of the religious stories she had grown up with, something her father had insisted remain hanging in her room. She never liked it. It was old-fashioned and ugly, portraying a larger-than-life man speaking to a group of people sitting on a hillside.

Looking at the painting now, she realized that the scene depicted on the small canvas was like the setting in the dream she had just had. Perhaps she had created the environment in the dream to reproduce the familiar painting, which had been hanging on her wall for as long as she could remember. Recognizing the similarities, she was drawn back to the free, buoyant feeling from the dream and breathed out any remaining stale, night air from her lungs, closed her eyes, and tried to recall the dream's details.

She couldn't remember many, but the speaker's eyes were there, and they seemed to enhance the warm, uplifting feeling in her body, which felt both strange and familiar at the same time. As she struggled to recollect the scene, she saw something she didn't remember from it, or it was something new: a flat, round stone in the center of a clearing, buried so the top was level with the ground, with a carving of three spirals coming together in the center. It looked ancient, like it had been there for centuries, the dark lines of history marking the rough surface like an uneven spider web. She recognized it, or thought she did, but couldn't place where she had seen it before. In her vision, she hovered over the stone, then fell into it with such speed that it jolted her eyes open when she hit it.

That was different, she thought, now quite awake. The original uplifting feeling lingered, but the surprise of the sudden, visual impact disrupted its warmth. She wondered if there was some meaning to the imagery, or to the scene with the speaker that she couldn't fully recall. She could sense there was something there to understand, but whatever it was remained elusive, like much of the dream. Somehow, though, it left her feeling as if something important was going to happen.

She sat up and stretched her arms out to her sides, inhaling and exhaling deeply. Picking up the finished book on the side table, she stood and walked the few steps to the bookcase to place it back on the shelves next to the familiar titles that stared back at her.

The stories were her escape, as they took her outside herself on grand adventures to landscapes full of daring explorers, mythical beasts, magical kingdoms, and romantic engagements. She immersed herself completely when reading, imagining being carried on the wings of the words that soared skyward, taking her up and away from her familiar, rigid surroundings as she followed the exciting journeys to magnificent and satisfying endings. The tales painted pictures of worlds different from her own, ones she could wholeheartedly dive into and lose herself in, creating at least some temporary freedom from the one within which she lived her days physically. Running her fingers across the spines brought back memories of those fantastic lands.

Lately, her vivid dreams reminded her of these stories as they took her to realms where anything was possible. She always felt better in these other worlds compared to how she felt going through the mundane and stifling routines of her ordinary days. The dreams, and the stories she read, helped her feel the freedom and independence all too often absent at home and in school.

Once, years ago, inspired by one of the tales she had read, she had drawn a small circle with a piece of charcoal high up on the white, plaster wall in the corner of her room and had labeled it "to another world." She would stare at it before reading and as she fell asleep, imagining crawling through the portal to a realm where she was free of the world she knew. There, she could *be* in the stories she read, released from the constraints of her structured days, at least for a spell.

But when her father had seen she had written on the wall, he was furious.

"What is that?" he bellowed. "What have you done!?" Anna cowered on her bed with her blanket pulled up to her eyes. At the time, she didn't understand why he was so angry.

"Why are you so irresponsible? he yelled. "You don't draw on the wall! What's wrong with you?" He was staring at Anna, his eyes raging.

He turned and went to the writing on the wall, reached up, and rubbed it vigorously with his palm, smudging the charcoal into an unidentifiable, gray cloud. "Now look at this mess!" He held up his black palm for Anna to see. "You're going to clean all this up."

Anna's mother stood at the threshold of her room, silent but watching. Anna's father sometimes worked himself into an intense, barely-controlled temper, and it appeared he was on his way there. He wiped his palm on his pants and started to undo his belt.

"So thoughtless. I raised you better than this! Apparently, you need to learn some discipline." He pulled his belt out. It hung down from his hand like a dead snake as he glowered at her.

Anna was crying, wanting to disappear under her blanket, but she couldn't look away from her father. Experience told her that that just made it worse. It wasn't often she saw this side of him, but it terrified her when she did.

Anna's mother stepped into the room and put her hand gently on her husband's arm. "Honey, I think she knows."

He spun around, and her mother flinched, and Anna thought he was going to hit her, but he just glared. Anna was thankful for his focus to be off her for a moment.

"You'll clean it off, won't you, dear?" her mother continued.

Anna nodded through her tears.

Her father spun back around and stared at her. "You better. And wash all the walls in here while you're at it. They're dirty." He leaned in closer to her, his face flushed and contorted under his mop of red hair. "And don't you *ever* deface my walls again."

With that, he stormed out of the room, leaving Anna quivering on the bed. Her mother watched her father leave and then sat beside Anna and gave her a hug, but it wasn't that convincing or comforting.

"You'll be fine," she said. "You know how your father gets. It'll pass. I'll put the brush and a pail of soapy water by your door. Make sure you do all the walls. You know your father's going to check."

Anna nodded and wiped away her tears, and her mother rose and left the room.

Anna appreciated her mother's role in these episodes, often intervening at the last moment, but it wasn't enough, and she suspected her mother knew it. That's probably why Anna found a new book on her bedside table the next day. It wasn't the first time she had received one after one of her father's angry outbursts.

Since that incident, Anna was careful not to do things that she thought might trigger her father's rage. She didn't want to go through anything like that again, so she kept her head down and conformed to her structured life, only venturing outside the lines in her imagination, like when she looked at the Wall yesterday.

Both her books and her internal stories offered a way out, a place where her mind—and indeed, spirit—could roam free. She couldn't wait until she was older when she could legitimately escape the binds of her current life for the beautiful and extraordinary unknown. That future beckoned to her more strongly as the days passed, a reality almost tangible in its hope. In that sense, her portal "to another world" still existed, though only in her own mind.

Detecting the aroma of a delicious breakfast wafting upstairs, Anna rose to sit on the edge of the bed and remembered that her parents had promised her a trip to the bookseller. Excited, she got up and quickly dressed, tied her red hair back into a ponytail after a quick wash down the hall, and skipped downstairs, the dream now a distant memory.

Her father was already eating at the common table, but her mother had waited for her, and she had made her favorite: griddlecakes with slices of apple mixed in.

"Happy birthday, honey!" her mother exclaimed with a false flourish.

"Yes, happy birthday," her father mumbled with his mouth full.

"Thanks!" Anna said, "and thanks for this." She sat down as her mother brought over a heaping stack of griddlecakes covered with butter and honey.

She quickly devoured half the tower of sticky goodness. In between bites, she asked when they could go to the bookshop.

"After we eat and clean up, okay?" her mother said, directing the statement and question more to her husband than to Anna.

Anna's father looked first at his wife, then at Anna before nodding.

Anna ignored his apparent indifference. She wasn't going to let his lack of enthusiasm affect her own.

She smiled at her mother, side-eyed her father, who was too focused on sopping up the remaining honey with his last griddlecake to notice, and turned her attention back to the quickly diminishing pile on her plate.

~

When they finally left their lodging house, a heavy shadow from the Wall cut a distinct line low across the buildings on the cobblestone street. From their darkened doorway, Anna's father took the lead, marching with purpose, while Anna and her mother followed and did their best to keep up without running. Although Anna's father sometimes had to work on weekends, he didn't have to today.

It was Saturday and a beautiful day, and the streets bustled with the typical, mid-morning, weekend activity of residents getting outside to shop and see the city. Anna overheard some anxious chatter about the previous day's warning, but it was fleeting and didn't seem to affect people's normal behaviors. Either people weren't that worried or they didn't want to be caught talking about it. Strangely, Anna hadn't thought about the warning at all that morning until hearing about it outside.

She walked with her parents down the street they lived on, turning left at the end of it to take the main route toward the marketplace. The bookshop was located on a corner at the end of the wide thoroughfare, opposite an antique shop that Anna also enjoyed visiting when she could. There was something about seeing old belongings from a bygone era that appealed to her. The pieces expressed real stories, ones she reconstructed in her mind as they spoke to her from a time past. Because the two shops were close to each other, she sometimes would go to both in the same outing. She assumed it would be okay with her parents to do so on her special day.

"Can we stop in here first?" Anna asked as they approached the antique shop. "Please?"

"Of course, honey," her mother responded, glancing at Anna's father with a determined look. He stopped, stood still for a moment, then nodded and walked into the shop ahead of his family.

An ancient bell above the door rang as they entered, and the shopkeeper looked up from examining a small item on the counter, peering over his prehistoric glasses at the visitors. Anna waved, and he smiled. She had been to the store many times and was a familiar face to the owner, a friendly, pudgy man who always sported spectacles that looked older than most of the items in the shop.

"Good morning, my dear! Nice to see you again."

"Nice to see you too," Anna replied before skipping over to the tables to browse the vintage items. Anna's father walked to a side room filled with old furniture, and her mother began slowly wandering the overstuffed aisles.

The main room of the shop was deep and wide, and there seemed to be little rhyme or reason to how the items were organized. Along the walls were the taller stalls and bookcases, which surrounded tables in the center arranged mostly perpendicularly to the front door but with a few smaller ones placed horizontally seemingly at random. A slight musty smell pervaded the space, something Anna had initially found off-putting but later came to tolerate and even embrace as it indicated she was entering another time period.

The number of objects overflowing the tables and shelves appeared endless. It was almost as though a new section of the store would magically appear each time she visited, so she could always find something novel to grab her attention. And today, she would hopefully be able to take home more than just the little trinkets she had bought in the past with her meager allowance.

Drawn to a tall bookcase toward the back of the store crammed with old dolls, she bounced over and picked up a few, only to quickly put them down again. They felt boring and devoid of life, as if sitting for years on the shelf in the shop without attention had slowly extracted their spirit until there was nothing left. With no one to love them, and for them to love, they withered into dry, empty husks of their former selves. Anna couldn't sense any story from the lifeless forms.

She crouched to look at some of the books and papers on the lower shelf, pulling out a few dusty volumes for inspection before replacing them, uninterested. She rarely found books she liked here, as most of them were academic, historical, or filled with boring, dated stories that simply didn't interest her.

About to stand up to search elsewhere, she noticed a dark brown binding at the far end of the shelf, mostly hidden by a large, encyclopedic title. Enthusiastically, she pulled it out.

It was a book with a leather covering tied shut with thin rawhide straps, and on the cover were three barely perceptible, faded, embossed spirals that came together in the center. The hair on the back of her neck stood up, and she gasped as she remembered the carved stone from her attempt to recall her dream earlier in the morning. Her mind wobbled, and she felt like she was in between sleeping and waking, with her mind in two different realms that she couldn't quite define. With a light, buzzy feeling in her head, her instantly-scrambled brain tried to make sense of the coincidence of seeing the same odd image twice within an hour in different places, but it couldn't complete even one logical step toward understanding why or how. Whatever the case, something about what she now held took her breath away.

Standing, she turned it over in her hands, wiping off the dust and feeling the warmth of the aged material under her fingertips.

She placed it gently on top of an old, wooden box on a table next to the bookcase, carefully untied the fastenings, and opened it, her heart beating loudly in her ears.

Inside was a stack of loose papers, with the top sheet showing a title and author's name, *A Tale of Awakening by Erich Evepret.* Slowly leafing through the pile, she found it was a handwritten story, and her excitement grew at seeing the old, cursive style infusing the pages with personality and life. This was a story in its pure form, one she didn't have to create herself like with the other dated items in the shop. And she absolutely knew that seeing the same image earlier and the connection she now felt deeply in her bones meant that this was for her and that she needed to take it home.

"Ma, instead of going to the bookshop, this is what I want!" she exclaimed, calling her mother over. *"Pleeease!"*

Her mother sidled up to her and looked at the papers with a dour expression on her face.

"Really? Some old papers? I thought you wanted to get a book for your birthday?"

"I did. This is a book. It's a story, just on loose paper instead of all bound together."

Her mother turned one of the pages and shrugged. "Why not?" she said to Anna's delight, then turned to walk to the front of the shop.

Anna carefully straightened the papers, folded the covering over, and tied it back together. Pausing to examine the faint image on the cover, she suddenly remembered where she had seen the design before. It was one of the old, pagan symbols she had been warned about in school. One of her faith studies classmates had shown it to her along with several other so-called taboo symbols in a pamphlet last year during recess. Her friend said that he had found the pamphlet hidden in a drawer in his father's desk and that studying it would enable her to perform the magic of the Ancients, otherworldly feats that the mystical group from long ago were supposedly able to do.

The teachers had warned the students about viewing such pagan signs, as not only were they illegal to possess, they would also drive one mad because they violated the dictates of the Church. Even though the teachers didn't reveal any of the actual banned symbols, they had given the students an idea of what to be on the lookout for. When Anna saw the designs in her friend's pamphlet, she didn't want to get in trouble, or go mad, so she turned away.

Later, Anna found out that the teachers had harshly disciplined her classmate with the pamphlet, and the constables had arrested his parents. Apparently, the boy had shown it to another student, who had told one of the teachers, who had reported the incident.

Now recognizing the design on the cover, Anna was nervous. She looked over her shoulder at her mother, who was browsing some trinkets on a table near the front of the shop, and didn't see her father, who was probably still in the adjoining room. Anna didn't want to get in trouble, but she also knew that something about this book spoke to her and that she had to read it.

With her parents distracted, she took a deep breath, clutched the book to her chest with the cover facing her, and walked to the front of the store. She hoped the shop owner wouldn't see or recognize the symbol.

Nervously placing the item on the counter, cover down, Anna stared at the owner, looking for some sort of revelation.

"What do we have here?" he asked, picking it up and turning it over in his hands. His eyes flipped from the cover to Anna, then back to the cover again. Anna swallowed and clenched her jaw, awaiting her fate.

Anna's mother came up behind her. "How much would this be?" she asked.

The man held the book with the cover facing him. "Oh, I haven't seen this in ages," he said. "Where'd you find it?" Anna wanted to think he was intentionally holding it so her mother couldn't see the spirals.

"Over there," Anna said, pointing to the bookcase with the dolls.

The man glanced over in the direction she pointed, put the book face down on the counter, and looked at her over his low-slung glasses. "Did I hear that it's your birthday today?"

Anna smiled broadly and nodded.

"Then no charge. Consider it my gift to you," he said, smiling.

Anna's eyes widened and she slid the book off the counter and hugged it to her chest, again with the forbidden symbol facing her. "Thank you," she practically squealed.

"Are you sure we can't give you anything for it?" her mother asked.

"No, it's my pleasure," the shopkeeper said. "I didn't even know I still had it."

"Where'd it come from?" Anna asked impulsively. She was curious, but as soon as she asked, she immediately regretted it, wanting instead to take all attention off the likely banned item.

The man indulged anyway. "Oh, I believe it came from an auction maybe twenty years ago outside the city. I got a bunch of things in the bundle—furniture, old farm tools, books, papers—and this was one of them. I don't know anything else about it."

"Did you read it?" Anna asked, cautiously wanting to know more.

"No, my dear. I only opened it to see what it was. Then it found a shelf so it could wait for you." He winked at her.

"Looks like a story. I can't wait to read it!" Anna said, trying to act normal in her excitement, but this was anything but a normal book, and she knew there was a risk in taking it home.

"Well, then I'm sure you'll enjoy it," the shopkeeper said, this time looking at her intently with less of a smile and with a gleam in his eye that told her that he knew more about the item than he had let on.

Anna's eyes widened and she suppressed a grin. They now shared a secret, a dangerous one.

Anna's father emerged from the adjacent room and came back to the counter. "Did you find something?"

Anna's demeanor stiffened. "Yes." She held up the leather-bound book momentarily, the spiral cover still facing her. "There's a story inside."

"Okay, if that's what you want . . ." He trailed off. As much as Anna was a reader, her father was not, and he never cared to engage with her about her books. "What do I owe you?" he asked the shopkeeper, digging into his pocket.

"No charge, sir," said the man. "My gift to your daughter on her birthday."

Anna's father stared at him as if he had some ulterior motive for giving his goods away for free to Anna. Apparently not sensing any, he said, "I insist," and he held out some coins.

"Not necessary, sir," the man said, keeping his hands to his sides. "I'm just happy to see young folks take an interest in old things, which can find new life in their hands."

Anna's father paused, then put the coins back in his pocket and nodded thanks. He turned and headed out the door. Anna's mother followed while Anna hugged the book to her chest again and mouthed "Thank you" to the shopkeeper, who nodded and smiled, before she trailed her mother out of the shop.

Outside, her mother asked Anna, "So, no bookshop then?"

"No, thank you. I'm happy with this," Anna said. She wanted to get home. The longer the symbol was out in the open, the greater the chance of it being seen, and she didn't want any repercussions from that. She was also tremendously excited to read it.

Once home, Anna isolated herself in her room with the door closed, giddy and nervous in anticipation of reading the story. Something about the item spoke to her, a feeling of knowing it was no accident she had stumbled upon it. She turned it over in her hands, slowly drawing her fingers across the slightly raised, spiral design. It was faint, as the leather was old and worn, and she wondered what would happen if her parents found it, or the Church, or the government. If discovered, since her father was a constable, she didn't know if he would turn her in to the constabulary for questioning because he followed the laws, punish her privately because she was his daughter, or something else. For now, she was fortunate her parents hadn't noticed it. The shopkeeper had helped with that, at least she thought he had.

She wondered if the book contained secrets related to the stories of the Ancients she had heard about, whispered accounts from her classmates who had somehow learned of them. The rumors were that there existed sacred texts that were revered by followers of that obsolete culture that supposedly contained the secrets of the mystical past of the Territories and the Wall. *Was this one of them*, she thought.

Whether true or not, the unmistakable feeling she had holding the book and looking at the cover made her feel as if it were written specifically *for her*. How could it not be, when she had a vision of the cover design that very morning?

Flushed with the thrill of having such a forbidden treasure in her possession, Anna delicately untied the straps that held it closed and carefully opened it to reveal the pages inside.

She slowly flipped through the papers. The handwriting was in a script she had learned in school, but it really wasn't used much anymore. It was definitely old, and the author's writing style made the pages seem to dance with inspiration. Noticing that the last page was different than the others—creased, worn, weathered, and having just two faded words in the middle of the page—she wondered if it had been tucked into the back of the book by accident. She left it in place just in case.

Going back to the cover sheet, Anna recited in a whisper, *"A Tale of Awakening by Erich Evepret."* Barely able to contain her excitement, her heart pounding in her chest, she took a deep breath and turned the page.

A Tale of Awakening

by
Erich Evepret

Commencement

With the rising sun come shadows, long yet ephemeral, in their endless dance with the light that both creates and destroys them. The light knows nothing of this, participating only because the shadows insist on the masquerade.

~

Pulling his cart filled with crates of fruits and vegetables, Christopher's boots dug into the firm earth with each step forward, the cadenced sounds beneath his feet disappearing among the footfalls and creaking wagons of the many merchants traveling the same route into the city to sell their goods.

It was fall, his favorite time of year, the period of easy weather before the arrival of the ferocious storms that signaled the end of the harvesting season. He knew the high winds and driving rains were coming soon, though, so he took advantage of the calm, mostly sunny days to make the trip from his farm in the southwest rural territory to the marketplace on the outskirts of the city to sell his goods. In the afternoon, he would return to his farmstead with a lightened load and a pocketful of coins, ready to pick and prepare what he thought he could sell the following day.

As he strode forward, pushing against the wooden crosspiece that extended in front of his cart, worries about the farm that had been in his family for generations dominated his thoughts. He was the sole owner of the property after his parents had died, and he felt pressure to take care of the homestead and business as well as they and their ancestors had, but he had already failed. Not yet having a family of his own nor able to find workers he could afford, he had done the best he could on his own, but it wasn't enough. The farm was in decline, as evidenced by the overgrown gardens and neglected orchards that had once been immaculately maintained, as well as by the lower yields they produced, not to mention this season's taxes he hadn't yet been able to pay.

His mother had succumbed to the fever that had ravaged the Territories when he was a child, taking almost one in ten people before their time, so Christopher grew up mostly under the tutelage of his father, a kind and complex man who taught the curious boy everything he needed to know to be able to take care of all the various concerns that came with running a successful farm. But when his father died accidentally five years ago when Christopher was in his late teens, the shock and grief left him barely able to accomplish even some of the most basic, necessary tasks. In addition, he couldn't be in two places at once, selling produce in the city while also doing what was needed on the property to maintain the homestead and crops. Consequently, the farm suffered.

After a difficult period of transition, he was able to take his mind off his swirling emotions by throwing himself fully into the operation of the property, and the business persevered, although greatly diminished from the abundance of its previous years. Juggling all the responsibilities continued to remain challenging, however, especially through the heavy rains that flooded the Territories the last two seasons and lowered the yields far enough that he couldn't pay his taxes this year. This put the farm in jeopardy of being confiscated by the government, a possibility he couldn't even begin to fathom. He had recently received an official notice that the payment was overdue, with a warning and grace period until the end of the season to pay, but he wasn't sure he'd be able to make enough in the marketplace to cover it with what little time was left before the rains came. He was trying though, going into the city daily to sell what he could before heading home in the afternoon to work the land and harvest the next day's produce for the market.

The stress of trying to stay on top of everything bore down on him. With an increasing number of sleepless nights, Christopher knew something had to change. The farm's future, and his livelihood, depended on it.

Traveling in shadow, Christopher looked up as the sun's morning rays peered above the Grand Wall to the east, illuminating the faraway spire of the cathedral in the distance. In the center of the city, the highest point of the church was taller than everything but the Wall, so it received the first and last sunlight of the day, and he loved seeing the dazzling reflection of the early light off the gilded trim of the steeple while on his morning journey. It reminded him of the great heights man could attain.

The city stood out prominently compared to the surrounding farming areas, as it was situated on top of a broad hill roughly in the center of the Territories, the land inside the Wall. The hill began rising, on all sides, from about a forty-minute walk away from the farm, with the first collection of low buildings along his route—a series of blacksmiths' workshops—appearing soon after his effort increased with the slope. Seeing the smoke begin to rise from the early-lit fires in the forges indicated to him that he was about halfway to his destination, still some distance away from the more congested urban territory. Far ahead, at the highest point on the hill and soaring above the adjacent government buildings, was the cathedral, a visual focal point around which the inhabitants of the Territories orbited.

Like a recurring pattern, as the cathedral was in the center of the city, the city was in the center of the land within the Wall. Christopher thought that if he could rise up and view the Territories from above that it might look like a giant, all-seeing eye, with the Wall providing the boundary within which the colorful iris of the city floated amidst the more evenly-colored, rural fields and forests. He wondered if the pattern repeated, if he could travel even further up and see the Territories as just a dot in the center of the landscape that surrounded it, but his vision was limited to what he knew, and that didn't include what was rumored to be dangerous and inhospitable land that lay outside the Wall.

Stepping forward assuredly with his loaded cart balanced on its two large, wooden wheels, Christopher passed the smokey furnaces beginning to glow with the energy that would transform the blacksmiths' rough, raw materials into their perfected forms. The echoes of hammering hadn't yet rung out but would soon. He sometimes heard the irritating reverberations as he headed up the long hill to the city, but knowing the fine work being accomplished by the skilled craftsmen lessened their annoyance.

He remembered when he was a child and used to see horses and oxen pulling many of the carts and wagons on the road, but those days were over since the livestock disease that preceded the fever that took his mother had decimated their numbers. Now, only wealthy landowners or those higher up in the government owned horses or cattle, and they seemed to selfishly control their breeding, as the farm owners Christopher knew hadn't been able to acquire any to help with their farms or with travel to and from the city.

Past the workshops and up the slope he continued. His journey to the city was almost effortless at this point, as his lean, muscular physique was so used to the trip that he could let it find a way forward on its own while his mind disengaged and drifted to other things. He did that now, allowing his body to go through the motions while he began thinking about what he had experienced last night.

Lying in bed contemplating how he was going to make enough to pay the farm's taxes, he had felt an abstract feeling of longing, a sense that he was missing out on something important as he went about his days working the land and selling his goods. He tossed and turned trying to get to sleep as his mind tried to make sense of the expanding feeling that seemed to challenge the practical needs to reverse the fortunes of the farm. It felt like his accumulated stress and all he did to try to lessen it—like vigorously selling his produce in the city and working hard in the fields to try to increase the declining yields—were somehow distractions to keep him from something greater. The feeling of yearning made everything about his physical life feel immaterial in comparison.

He had had glimpses of this before, but this time it had a sense of timelessness that put his current difficulties into a broader context, reducing their significance. But his troubles *were* important, to *him*. His ancestors' and his own life's work were at stake, and he didn't know what he would do if the farm were seized. Who was he if not a farmer and a steward of his family's land? His mind wanted to continue to fret about the real-world issues of the farm's struggles and to figure them out, but the *feeling* of coming from this higher perspective minimized those matters, leaving him sleepless and confused.

Finally, after staring at the ceiling for some time in the dark trying to reconcile the opposing concepts through brute mental force, he gave up and tried to shut off his thoughts, closing his eyes and diving into the feeling instead. There, his head stopped spinning and his body relaxed, and he realized that perhaps there was a way to help the farm and calm his anxious mind through *not* attempting to figure out a solution in his head. At this point, he had to try something different, because mentally tackling the problem as before hadn't worked. Perhaps it wasn't something to *figure out* with his mind but rather something to understand from the different perspective he was now *feeling*. He didn't know how to do that, and it didn't make sense to him, but lying there in bed he decided to be open to ideas he normally would dismiss out of hand. His livelihood was on the line, as was the farm and his mental and emotional well-being, and he just couldn't continue as he had in the past.

And before his mind could worry about or question his resolve, he fell asleep.

Now, walking along the dirt roadway up the hill toward the city, his head was muddled thinking about what he was going to do differently and how he was going to perceive solutions he hadn't been able to see before. Realizing he was still *thinking* about it, he took a deep breath and sighed, baffled by the seemingly impossible task.

Feeling a little lightheaded amidst the long line of merchants snaking its way into the city, he stopped and lowered the handle of the cart, which anchored its load onto its two front supports. Something strange was happening. He felt different, outside of himself, as if he were observing his thought process for the first time. Anything similar he had experienced before paled in comparison as the feeling struck him with a power that took him to the heights of something unknown yet distantly resonant.

As he stood there trying to make sense of it, the energy quickly ramped up to a dizzying peak, culminating in an audible snap with an explosion in his awareness as if the long, crooked fingers of lightning had cracked open his skull to reach in and stab his brain with its poker-hot nails. The impact and brilliant flash took him out of the physical world and blinded him as it shocked every part of his body into a discordant buzzing that made him stagger to stay on his feet. He closed his eyes and desperately held on to the handle of the cart to prevent from falling.

But his physical body was the last of his concerns because his mind, his whole being, was detached from it, witnessing himself as a mere shadow of something beyond comprehension. The concept of time and space left him as he felt himself expand to the far reaches of the universe, only to collapse back in an instant with all his senses ablaze. Even blinded and with his eyes closed, his vision felt more comprehensive, real, and authentic than what he had ever imagined possible.

He was between two worlds, or rather was in more than the one world he was intimately familiar with, struggling to stay conscious in the center of the unbearable, disconcerting convergence of his mind, physical body, emotions, and . . . something else. There was no word, nor anything in his life's experience, that could describe its presence.

It didn't last long. Although physically stabilized by the cart's handle, his body continued to vibrate as the intensity of the experience slowly diminished and his senses began to stabilize. He struggled to lift his head and managed to crack open his eyes. His sight had returned.

Standing in front of his cart like a lost, disoriented child, he peered into the distance at the sun's rays now reached the tops of the buildings that surrounded the cathedral. The waves of energy gradually subsided to a manageable, low-level hum as other merchants hauling their goods passed with irritated glances as they maneuvered around him. Christopher wasn't there to notice their looks; he was there physically, but the experience had left him mentally elsewhere, everywhere.

It took a bump from a passing traveler to snap him out of his daze. He blinked and looked around, realized where he was, and instinctively picked up the cart's handle to begin to move forward, becoming another walking shadow in the line of people and goods heading into the city.

~

The marketplace was a long, wide, cobblestone street just inside the city limits where vendors of every kind came to sell their goods. Almost everything could be found there—fresh food, pottery, household items, clothing, fabrics, trinkets, etc.—and it was known that if a product existed in the Territories, some form of it was sold in the square, as it was often referred to.

Christopher arrived and maneuvered his cart into his usual place near a side street, pulling it in next to his short and stocky friend, Martel, the spice seller. Martel was a jovial sort, always in a pleasant mood and ready to engage in good-natured banter. On the other side of Martel was where Ariana usually sold her freshly-cut flowers, whose fragrance was always a welcome scent over the often strong smell coming from Martel's goods.

Christopher had known Ariana when he was younger but hadn't seen her consistently since his father's passing. However, since she had taken over selling flowers for her aunt a few months ago after her aunt had become ill, they had reconnected, and he enjoyed engaging with her. She had a bright, airy energy and a lightness in her step that seemed to disregard the heaviness of the city that so often afflicted the attitudes of others. She and Martel were familiar figures and friends, as were all the regular merchants in the market, and their presence always helped take his mind off the issues with the farm.

"Good morning, my friend," Martel said with a smile as Christopher set his cart into position. Ariana hadn't yet arrived with her bouquets.

"Good morning, Martel," Christopher said, setting down his load and brushing the dust off his clothes.

"And how are you this fine morning?" Martel asked.

"I'm well, but I had a strange experience on the way in."

The intense energy of the morning's bizarre incident had slowly dissipated as he had made his way to the city, so his mind was back and able to have a conversation, but his sight remained slightly altered. He was looking at everything around him in a new light, as if the haze within that was beginning to lift was also revealing something new about the city that had previously gone unnoticed. It was, perhaps, the start of finding a way to save the farm, although he knew not how. Regardless, without yet knowing what, if any, steps to take, he could feel a change coming, and he wondered what it meant and where it would take him.

"Do tell!" Martel said. He was always one for stories. Their talk helped pass the time during the slower parts of the day, but now they were getting ready for morning customers, and Christopher didn't even know how to describe what had occurred anyway, so he did his best to simplify it.

"Well, it was like I was taken out of my body and saw the world differently, like from a higher perspective."

"Interesting. And what did you see?"

Christopher paused, thinking of how it had temporarily blinded him. He felt different after the incident, with his responsibilities and the physical world fading behind something intangible but more important, bringing in some sort of all-encompassing perspective that he couldn't yet comprehend. It was the feeling he had had last night but experienced more physically and intensely.

"I'm not sure how to describe it, but it was more of a feeling, like there's more to the world than what we see and do here . . . a whole lot more."

"Like we're safe in the Territories and there's a big, bad world out beyond the Wall?" Martel said. "You don't want any part of *that*." In addition to his humor, Martel had the ability to bring a lightness to more serious conversations. Christopher wondered if he was the same at home with his wife and two young sons.

"No, it's more like there are more important things than me worrying about being able to keep the farm going, which sounds crazy, because what would I do? What's more important than that?" Martel was familiar with Christopher's struggles, but Christopher hadn't shared the full extent of them, that he now was on notice about his taxes.

"Good question," Martel said. "I don't know. Obviously, that's important."

"Maybe it can give me ideas about what to do, a way to look at things differently." Christopher had thought about borrowing from his friend, but his pride wouldn't let him.

"I know it's been difficult, brother," Martel said, using a term of endearment he reserved for close friends. "We all miss your dad. If you ever want to bounce any ideas off me, you know where I am. I think at this point there's a Martel-shaped shadow on the wall here." He pointed behind him.

Christopher chuckled and nodded. "Thanks. You may regret you said that."

"Ha-ha, never!" Martel said smiling. "I'm always up for sharing my infinite wisdom."

Christopher nodded. "Like the time you encouraged me to flirt with that woman who I didn't know was married?"

Martel laughed. "Yeah, well, except that one. Boy, her husband was angry."

"Yes, he was," Christopher said, chuckling. "Let's try not to repeat that."

"You got it."

They both returned to setting up their goods, but a moment later Martel snapped his fingers in surprise. "Wait! I think I know what it's all about, what's more important!"

"Oh, really," Christopher said, expecting another witty response from his friend.

"It's all about love!" Martel said, opening his arms wide. "Love makes the world go round! Speaking of which . . ." His eyes shot over to Ariana, who had just arrived on his other side carrying her baskets of flowers.

Seeing Ariana in the morning was one of the best parts of Christopher's day, as her beauty and smile lit up the street before the sun's rays directly hit the marketplace. It was no different today. Her golden hair cascaded below the multicolored kerchief that held her hair from her face, framing wide, blue-green eyes, high cheekbones, and a small, slightly freckled nose above full lips on a mouth that was grinning at him. She wore an olive-green skirt held up by a leather belt and an off-white shirt with sleeves to the mid-forearm, something most would consider common and plain, but Christopher found it the opposite. Whatever she wore he found perfect, for her clothing couldn't contain who she was, or how he felt about her.

He could feel color rise to his cheeks. He and Ariana had rekindled their previous flirting once she had started coming to the marketplace in place of her aunt. It was something that had been interrupted by his father's death and its aftereffects, when he was overwhelmed with taking care of the property and had intentionally withdrawn from others, even those who had offered to help. Prior to then, he and Ariana seemed to be at the beginning of the winding path towards a betrothal, with the encouragement of both of their families.

Now, seeing her almost daily, the old feelings for her had stirred, and they began to overcome the resistance he felt at not being able to offer appropriate courtship due to the struggles with the farm. So, he connected with her innocently enough as a friend but with the undercurrent of picking up where they had left off years before. Martel was certainly aware of it, and his comment was a bit more than Christopher was comfortable exposing right then.

Christopher smiled and waved at her, and she put down her baskets and smiled back. "Good morning," she said.

"Good morning," Christopher said. Martel gave her a half bow.

Christopher looked at Martel and said with a grin, "Maybe you're right."

Martel burst out laughing. "Finally, someone said it!"

"I'm going to deny it later," Christopher said, laughing along with him.

"Right about what?" Ariana asked, stretching her arms.

Both men looked at her, then at each other. Martel gestured for Christopher to answer, giving him the opportunity to keep what they were talking about private.

"Oh, nothing," Christopher said. "His being right was so fleeting that it's like it really didn't happen anyway."

"So nice to be surrounded by people who respect you," Martel said. He and Christopher both chuckled.

"Uh huh, I get it," Ariana said, smirking. "Boys will be boys." She turned back to arranging her bouquets.

"And men will be men!" Martel said in a deep voice, puffing out his chest.

Ariana turned back and said, "Really? Where? If you see a *real* man, I'd like to give him these." She held up the flowers in her hand.

Martel feigned being hurt by her comment, but all three laughed.

"She gives as well as she takes," Martel said to Christopher.

"Indeed," Christopher said.

He liked this banter the three of them had, and he missed having it at home as time passed. Tired of his solitary living situation, he had recently begun thinking about a future family and all the wonderful benefits that accompanied it, but he didn't feel that pursuing a partner was appropriate until his struggles with the farm changed for the better. Having had the curious event on the road that morning, however, he now wondered if the incident was trying to show him how to put desires like these into context. Perhaps they were somehow linked, that his longing for family *and* for better fortunes for the farm came from the same place or were inhibited by the same obstacle, whatever that could be. And maybe that even applied to *everything* in his world, that all of it was connected, and the experience on the road had simply given him a brief glimpse of that grand, all-embracing perspective.

With his first customer of the day stepping up before him, he put these thoughts aside to attend to business, but he couldn't shake the strange feeling that he was now perceiving everything around him with just a bit more clarity.

~

Christopher always brought a small wooden stool with him when he traveled to the city to sell his fruits and vegetables, nestling it snugly in his cart among the crates of produce so it wouldn't fall out on the sometimes bumpy, dirt road. He used it during the slower times when the marketplace activity waned. Otherwise, he would stand and engage with his customers, many of whom were regulars.

Selling was easy for him with his natural and friendly conversational disposition, especially since buyers often already knew what they wanted and what things cost, so the interactions were as much a chance for a brief conversation as they were for purchasing his goods, and today was no different. He engaged in the enjoyable, light banter during the morning rush, effortlessly selling, making change, and conversing with his patrons as usual, even if the early morning event on the road had left him a bit distracted.

Now, sitting on the stool behind his cart after things slowed down, he had time to pause. He took a deep breath and absentmindedly looked over at the closest loudspeaker that stood attached to a tall pole in front of the antique shop on the corner at the end of the street.

The innovative device had been invented, or perhaps discovered, in his grandparents' time, and the government had installed these voice amplifiers across the Territories, leaving no area outside the speakers' reach. It was groundbreaking, and it hinted at the magical. The rumor was that the government scientists in their fortified research building had figured out how to build and operate the equipment from some ancient texts, but there was no way for the public to know the truth. Some gossiped that the Territory Governors kept all sorts of novel inventions hidden from the populace to have them for defense of the Territories. A few even said that the Governors could somehow miraculously move the Grand Wall themselves for reasons that remained unknown. But even in the days of his grandparents, it was hazardous to talk about the government's innovations, the Wall, or question anything related to those in power, so people spoke little about it. Times hadn't changed.

Other than test announcements, Christopher had heard official proclamations from the loudspeakers before, but only a few times and never when in the city. In his experience, they were used exclusively for warnings about threats to the Territories from outside the Wall, which hadn't occurred in years.

With the market relatively empty and no customers to wait on, Christopher's eyes left the loudspeaker and drifted over the buildings that lined the marketplace to the far-away Wall, which stared down on him and the city like an intimidating, ever-present parent. There was something about it that now grabbed his attention, and it brought to mind what he knew about the barrier that protected the Territories.

The Grand Wall, as it was called, had been around for as long as anyone could remember. Countless generations had been born, lived, and died within the tall, imposing structure that encircled the Territories.

It was enormous. Its height was fifty men high, was of an undetermined thickness, and its length was, quite literally, immeasurable. It enclosed not only the city and surrounding towns but also the forests, fields, farms, hills, and valleys further away from the city. Some had tried to follow the Wall around its entirety but could not, as there were sections that were impassable due to natural obstructions such as steep canyons and treacherous rivers that passed under the barrier, not to mention its less physical attributes.

It had some qualities that could only be described as supernatural, as a few times the dawn had revealed it having expanded, with new land inside the Wall that had previously been on the other side. Because that had only happened during

Christopher's lifetime, it was a relatively recent mystery compared to the unexplained origins of the aged structure itself.

No one had seen the Wall move, be built, or disintegrate and rematerialize in a different place, or even understood how its transformation could come about, save for some kind of secret magic the Governors might be privy to. Or the Ancients, the mystical group from hundreds of years ago who supposedly could perform alchemy and transform matter as the tales allege. Nonetheless, the Wall's movement had intermittently grown the Territories.

The first time the Wall ever moved in all its history was when Christopher was seven years old. He remembered because it coincided with him also experiencing another first: the first day since his mother's death that he truly recognized that she really wasn't coming back. This was something his father had talked to him about, moving on without her, but not until he had run through a field of tall grasses with his arms stretched wide, feeling the freedom that only a child playing in nature could feel, did the continuous grief and sorrow he had been experiencing since her death the previous year dissolve. The next morning, the Wall had mysteriously moved outward.

Before that day, even his parents and grandparents had only known the Wall as an old, fixed structure that they and the rest of the population accepted as part of their lives. So, when the citizens awoke the next day to the Wall having inexplicably expanded, many panicked, and the Territory Governors issued a warning throughout the Territories about a potential attack by the dangerous foreigners outside the barrier. Only the standing Grand Army had ever seen the invaders from beyond the Wall, but old stories recounted occasional attacks on the Territories, and the government had prefaced those attacks with announcements to warn the population to ensure it was prepared and could get to safety in case the Wall was breached. But the Wall, as everyone had experienced, was unbreachable, so the foreigners were never able to get within to terrorize the populace.

If the barrier was impossible to understand before, once it had moved it was even more so. Some had attempted to figure it out, but any efforts to try to go beyond it, or even to survey or map it, were met with failure. The Governors had made such talk and actions illegal for some reason, and they bid the constables to search for and arrest those who conversed about it or tried to discover its secrets. In addition, Christopher had heard of people getting thrown in prison or having their land seized if they were caught speaking against or even about such government dictates. Even though people were allowed to get close to the Wall, it seemed the Territory Governors wanted to keep talk of its origins and mysteries out of all conversations. So, over time, in order to avoid harassment, arrest, and imprisonment, most people simply regarded the Wall's presence and mystical qualities as a part of their daily lives without giving them a second thought. At least that's what Christopher tried to do.

But despite it being illegal to discuss, he sometimes heard whispered stories in the market about those who attempted to travel outside it. The few who undertook such actions were said to have either died trying or were never heard from again. He didn't know why, but he was always enthralled with these tales. He couldn't stop thinking about the brave souls who seemed to have risked everything. *What were they looking for? Why did they attempt to leave? Does anyone ever succeed? What is really outside the Wall?* Because people didn't, or couldn't, talk about it, he didn't know how many others had the same thoughts, but he took comfort in knowing that at least a few had tried to figure it out; he wasn't alone with his questions. He liked to think that perhaps everyone contemplated these things as he did, but he couldn't know that without risking the forbidden conversations, which he was too law-abiding to engage in.

Discussions about it were one thing he could control, but his thoughts about it were another. They frequently popped into his head uninvited as he observed the immense structure on his travel to and from the city, just as they did now as he gazed at it.

He felt a sense of guilt and betrayal of the edicts of the Governors when his thoughts drifted to the barrier. He trusted the government, just as he had trusted the system of instructions and chores his parents had set that worked to make the farm a success over the years. Rules and laws were in place for a reason: to ensure the smooth and successful functioning of whatever they related to. In the case of the government and the Wall, that meant protection from outsiders but also accepting that discussions about it were forbidden. Consequently, Christopher did his best not to think about the massive, mystical barrier, internally pushing the questions and thoughts down into the shadows where they hid, at least temporarily. And when they inevitably reentered his mind, he engaged them until his internal, rule-following conscience kicked in once again to force them into hiding.

Gazing at the distant barrier, these thoughts and questions once again tumbled around his head. This time, however, they had a more tangible, visceral power that was different from his familiar, abstract musings about them that he could usually successfully repress, and they mixed in with last night's grand feeling of perspective and what had occurred to him on his morning journey.

He was confused and desperately wanted *not* to be confused. He needed to understand all of it—how he could pay his taxes and save the farm, how he could resurrect the farm to its former grandeur, what the higher perspective from last night was trying to show him, how he could get answers to his questions about the Wall, why he experienced the incident on the road that morning. The disparate thoughts swirled around his head looking for cohesion but found none. He thought if he could put his life on hold for a spell and crawl into a hole to escape to another world, it would at least temporarily relieve him of his difficulties and give him the time and space to figure everything out. But he also knew that wasn't possible.

Complicating his attempts to understand it all was that the hope of actually finding answers to his questions made him physically uncomfortable, like he was wearing an itchy second skin that he wanted to squirm out of. The more his mind tried to think through his mental confusion, the more unpleasant his body felt. Not until he was successful in slowing his spinning thoughts did the feeling dissipate, but it left him exhausted.

As he sat in the market awaiting customers, the only thing he was able to wrap his head around was that change was coming. Whether it was bad or good or whether he was ready or not, he knew his life would be changing very soon.

~

The slower morning time was a period when vendors often had time to wander about and converse with each other, although they all kept an eye out for customers and helped each other if needed. Martel was talking with a merchant across the street, and Ariana seemed to be trying to rebuff the attentions of an older, gentleman in a rumpled suit.

Like Christopher, both of Ariana's parents had passed away, hers many years ago when she was a child, so her aunt and uncle had raised her as their own. Christopher's parents had known her relatives during his youth, and they were a good family. And although Ariana and Christopher had only seen each other on occasion back then, his childhood encounters with her were visions etched into his memory, like the permanent, stone carvings in the cathedral in the center of the city.

He remembered the first time he saw her. He was twelve and she was a year younger. There was a town fair outside the city that her family and Christopher and his father attended, and he saw her come bounding through a field of tall grasses next to the road and enter the fairgrounds ahead of her aunt and uncle. She was beaming and giggling, with the morning sun filtering through her long, straw-colored hair. He couldn't take his eyes off her. She was so perfect and free, at least to a twelve-year-old boy. And when their families met and spoke soon afterwards, he couldn't help but make funny faces at her just to hear her laugh.

"How are you doing?" Ariana stood before him with her head cocked slightly to the side. "You seem a little out of it." She had evidently been successful in rejecting her admirer.

"Uh, I'm fine," Christopher said, his response coming out more curtly than intended. And he was, kind of. There was a part of him, however, that continued to ponder the questions and issues before him, although now in more of an abstract way instead of concretely and logically.

Ariana stiffened and looked at him with a mixture of surprise and concern. "Okay then," she said and turned to walk away.

She had barely pirouetted in place when Christopher said, "Wait." She spun back around. "Sorry, I'm a little preoccupied. It's been a strange day."

Ariana stepped toward him "Strange in what way? Was that what you and Martel were talking about earlier?"

Christopher took a deep breath, glanced down, then looked back up at her. She reminded him of a wildflower, so beautiful and feminine but at the same time hardy with a grounded practicality. Her experiences in the city and time with her pragmatic aunt had clearly influenced and shaped the innocent girl he used to know. He liked what he saw, and what he felt.

"Well, something happened this morning that made me feel a little strange, like I'm being made to reflect on something."

"Sounds interesting," she said, clearly wanting to know more. "What is it? What's going on?"

Given her interest, he proceeded to tell her what he had told Martel about what had happened to him on the road that morning.

She listened attentively. When he finished, she asked, "So, what do you think it means for you and the farm?" She also knew about his difficulties, but not about the unpaid taxes.

"I don't know," he said, "but it's something I think I need to keep looking at. For some reason, I feel I'm supposed to trust where it takes me."

"And where is that?" she asked.

Christopher chuckled. "That's what's bothering me. I don't know. Maybe that's the grand joke of it all. I've got enough on my mind with the practicalities of the harvest and preparing the gardens before the fall rains, and I'm now supposed to devote time and energy to something like this with no definable actions to take? It doesn't make sense."

"Maybe it's not supposed to," she said.

Christopher paused and looked at her. *Maybe it's not supposed to.* Something about the phrase resonated within him and evoked the buzzing feeling he had experienced on the road. He stared at her awkwardly for a moment before slowly repeating, "Yes, maybe it's not supposed to."

"So, like Martel this morning, I'm right?" she said with a smile that cut through his pondering.

He smiled back. "Shh. Don't tell him."

Switching to a more serious tone, she said, "And maybe there's something right in front of you that you're not quite seeing clearly, something you need to trust and act on." She stared at him intently.

He nodded slowly, thinking, and looked across the marketplace at a blind beggar sitting on the cobblestones. "Yes," he said, "maybe."

Ariana turned to see what Christopher was looking at, then faced him with a discernable look of disappointment on her face. "Well, let me know if you figure it out." She promptly spun around and walked back to her flowers.

He caught her expression before looking again at the blind man across the square. "See you later," he said, sitting down once again on his stool.

Christopher knew the beggar, in a manner of sorts. The man had occupied the same space on the cobblestones for as long as he could remember, and always in the same spot. He was one of several panhandlers that sat scattered along the less busy walls of the marketplace. The government tolerated the presence of these mendicants if they weren't too aggressive in their solicitations. So, they mostly didn't accost people but rather plead their case with imploring looks and cupped hands, the adulterated prayer position that seemed to work better than the conventional one seen in the cathedral and at the foot of children's beds in the evenings.

One of Christopher's daily pleasures was giving a piece of fruit, usually an apple when they were in season, to this particular blind beggar who sat across the street from where he set up his cart. Christopher didn't know the man's name, but he was different from the other panhandlers, not actually appearing to beg at all. He just sat quietly with no hat or plate in front of him, and people gave him food or a spare coin as they passed.

Whatever he received during the day, he appeared to always have enough.

What also distinguished him from others of his sort was his clothing and demeanor. His simple, linen trousers and tunic appeared old but not as old or as sullied as the other beggars' outfits, and they matched his calm and unassuming bearing. He looked peaceful and grateful all the time, offering a slight nod and smile to acknowledge when something was given to him. Despite lines of indeterminate age on his face, there was no anger, desolation, mental confusion, or the stress of the streets reflected in it as often expressed by the other beggars. He was like the monks Christopher had read about in the forbidden tales who were said to have exuded a peace that would've seemed out of place in the bustling, frenetically-paced, city environment.

When Christopher had been going through the throes of adolescence, he had stumbled upon an old, leather-wrapped book beneath a loose floorboard in the corner of his room. He was cleaning his space—as if organizing his external environment would magically help structure and calm the anxious, pubescent thoughts that ricocheted around his head—and he noticed the end of a board pop up when he bumped his bed. Curious, he pulled the bed out from the wall so the entire floorboard was exposed, and he lifted up the end that had risen. Beneath it was a boxed space that looked like it had been specifically constructed as a hiding place, and the book was lying neatly in its center.

The leather cover had a dark circle inked and embossed on it with the raised edge of part of a lighter one next to it, like the dark one had moved slightly from its original position leaving a ghostly arc behind. He remembered looking out his window that night and seeing the same image in the night sky, the thin crescent moon silently looking down on him from above, it's wholeness largely hidden by shadow.

The book contained pages of handwritten parables about the mysterious monks from long ago, stories that were prohibited because of the government's and Church's view on old, pagan beliefs. He wondered who had hidden it there and if his grandparents or parents had read it. He suspected his father knew about it, but Christopher never mentioned it to him because at Christopher's age and at the time it felt like a special gift just for him. Even though he followed the laws of the Territories and he knew this type of book was banned, it was something that gave an outlet to his adolescent need to challenge authority, and he could do that by studying the tales in the book while safely keeping it to himself. It was his secret, and no one needed to know about it. Still, he felt uncomfortable as he read it, the poisonous venom of guilt snaking into his awareness as he read the sacrilegious pages.

In the parables, the monks lived in monasteries and villages in a land that was magically hidden from those who didn't have the appropriate perception or ability to see it, which protected them from persecution by those who didn't understand their ways. They used their otherworldly powers to help others and gave lessons on how to live well in a sometimes-challenging world, all of which Christopher assumed were teachings from the old, sacred tribe known as the Ancients. The tales were simple yet magical for the young Christopher and his curious mind, and he at the time wanted to believe that such a place existed, in part because the mysterious Grand Wall was conspicuously absent from all but one of the stories, and in that one the characters in the story could transcend the Wall.

The monks had all but disappeared centuries ago, but a few times he had heard that someone had caught a glimpse of one deep in the woods northeast of the city. The speed at which the government investigators questioned the talebearer and swarmed into the area to search for evidence was impressive. No trace of a monk or any dwelling was ever found—only the pristine forests of that region—and the accounts quickly became more about the mental state of those who had reported the sightings than what they supposedly had seen. It was yet one more thing that stuck in Christopher's mind that added to his reflections about the Wall and the government.

But if the blind man wasn't one of the mysterious monks—which he didn't appear to be based on his appearance and compared to what was described in the old tales—he was certainly someone unusual. When Christopher was a boy and his father was training him in the family trade, his father told him to bring something to the very same blind man across the street every day, and it was time for him to do that now.

He plucked an apple from his cart and walked across the street to where the beggar was sitting. Approaching him, Christopher held out the apple and the blind man's hands opened to receive it. Christopher placed the fruit gently in his cupped hands like he had done countless times before, and the man gave a slight nod. Christopher turned and went back to his cart.

This was how it always went, a simple gift and small acknowledgement. However, there were two times when the blind man's response to receiving the offering was different.

Christopher could remember the first time his young self gave something to the man, a fresh apple he had stretched his small, six-year-old body heavenward to pick that same morning. His father had bid him to bring the apple to the beggar sitting cross-legged on the cobblestones across the square, who looked surprisingly peaceful and strangely the same age as he did this day. Young Christopher nervously walked across the market and stood before the man, who gently turned his hands upward, which contrasted to the despairing begging motions he had seen in the other panhandlers. The young boy placed the apple in the beggar's hands, and the man looked up at him with his cloudy, half-closed eyes, smiling with a kindness that made Christopher forget he was looking at a simple blind man on the street.

It should have been easy to give the gift and go back to his father, but he couldn't turn away. The man's obscure and distant gaze was like nothing he had ever seen, and it mesmerized him. It took a shout from his father to jolt him out of his gawking stupor, and he realized he had been staring at the man, who had never wavered in his compassionate expression. Young Christopher immediately turned and ran back to his father, looking over his shoulder as if the blind man had gotten up and were chasing him.

Back and safely comforted in his father's strong arms, both looked across the street at the beggar. His father's voice dropped into his serious tone, and he said, "Every day that you come to the city, you must bring that man some food, no matter what. Okay?"

Christopher didn't understand. "Why, father?" he asked, breathing hard from the false fright and sprint across the street. He understood the idea of helping others but didn't understand why this specific person and why every day.

His father turned him around and kneeled so they were closely facing each other. "Because you must," he said. "You will understand why . . . someday." There was a finality to his last sentence that indicated no more questions were to be asked. And that was that.

Whether it was because he was a rule-follower or because his father's seriousness in that moment had thoroughly impacted his young self, since that time, day after day, year after year, when in the city, Christopher brought something to the blind man occupying the same space on the cobblestones in the square. He even occasionally did it on days when he wasn't selling his fruits and vegetables. On those rare instances when he found himself running errands in the city, he would inevitably find a reason to stroll to the market to give the beggar something.

The second time the blind man's response had been different was directly after Christopher's father had passed away. Once Christopher was able to return to the market, he walked over and placed an apple in the man's open hands, and the beggar grabbed Christopher's hand and held it. Surprised, Christopher's initial reaction was to pull back, but he immediately relaxed when he felt the kind, soft, leathery hands of the man, not holding him in fear or wanting but rather silently offering what felt like compassionate understanding and condolences for the death of his father. *How does he know?* Christopher thought. Then he realized that for the first time in all the years he had seen him that the blind man's eyes were wide open and had changed color from milky-white to deep black with almost mirror-like surfaces that reflected the rising light illuminating the street. They were like dark pools of water that had no depth and infinite depth at the same time.

In those few seconds, Christopher felt something open inside, a distant, caring feeling brought forward to conflict with his present, grieving state, something impossible to express. The man released his grip, and Christopher turned to walk, dazed, back to his produce cart. Not until he was back behind his fruit and vegetables did he notice the tears streaming down his face.

From that day onward, Christopher's gift to the blind man took on far greater meaning. Even though the man's demeanor and expression had barely changed over the years—in fact, that was the only time Christopher had ever seen his eyes fully open and a different color—there was now something indescribable between them, or at the very least Christopher felt different because of what had occurred that day.

As he reflected on that feeling and on his father's words from so many years ago, he looked again across the street at the blind man and wondered. *Someday*, he thought. *Someday*.

~

Christopher usually left the marketplace mid-afternoon to get home to do the required work on the farm and prepare his goods for the following day. During these last few months, Ariana accompanied him on occasion, as they shared the road for part of the way back, and she often finished earlier than other vendors because of selling all her limited inventory. Christopher glanced over and saw she was down to her last bouquet, so he began organizing his remaining unsold produce for the trip home, hoping they could walk together.

Focused on arranging his goods, he heard, "Here you go, Martel. For your wife." He looked up and Ariana was handing her last bunch of flowers to Martel.

"Oh, Ariana, thank you so much!" Martel exclaimed. "These are beautiful!"

"You're welcome," Ariana said. "Tell her I said, 'Hi.'" She glanced briefly at Christopher.

"I will," Martel said. "Thank you."

Ariana collected her empty baskets and walked briskly past Martel and Christopher, who said, "Hey, if you want to wait a minute, we can walk together."

"No," she said, not stopping and barely making eye contact. "I need to get back. Maybe see you tomorrow." She floated down the street and out of sight around the corner.

Christopher looked over at Martel. "Did I say something to offend her?"

"Oh, Christopher," Martel said, "are you really asking to understand what women think?" He laughed, and Christopher chuckled. When his laughing subsided, he continued, "It's not about understanding them here"—he pointed to his head—"but about connecting with them here," and he tapped his chest.

"Yeah, I'm working on that," Christopher said, and he meant it. He wanted to open up to Ariana more fully, to share more about himself beyond what she already knew about him. Like with his conversations with Martel, there was much he kept to himself, like the overdue taxes and the circumstances and effects around the death of his father.

He had made peace with his mother's death from the fever, which at the time had spread quickly and lethally through the Territories, but his father's passing years later was a freak accident, or so Christopher had told himself. The two had had an argument about their allotted responsibilities on the farm— oddly, Christopher couldn't remember any specifics—and directly afterwards, his father was bringing some jars of pickled ginger to the cellar when he tripped and fell down the stairs, dropping and shattering the jars and hitting his head on the post at the bottom of the steps.

Christopher had gone for a walk to let off some steam after their quarrel and had found his father upon his return, unmoving, unnaturally contorted on the cellar floor amidst the broken jars and the pungent smell they released. Even though Christopher knew in his gut there was nothing he could do to revive him, he first fetched the neighbors and then the local physician, who said it appeared as if his father had had a heart attack because the head wound wasn't major enough to have caused a fatal injury. Christopher wasn't surprised that his father's failed heart was the cause. He knew it had been compromised since his mother had departed them both.

His passing didn't just deprive a son of his father. All the things his father was ever going to do, ever going to be, had been extinguished, leaving holes in a tapestry that could now no longer be woven. Threads of kindness, laughter, love for his family—even of discipline and occasional anger—had been unceremoniously cut from Christopher's future, and after his death an uncertain outlook loomed over Christopher as he struggled to weave his own path forward alone.

It took a year for him to come to terms with his father's accident, or rather bury the feelings of it. He thought he had experienced, released, and moved past the shock and grief over that time, as well as the succeeding guilt and anger—at himself mostly—and had emerged on the other side with his emotions under control. However, just like no longer cultivating ginger after that fateful day, whatever curative actions he undertook could not heal the deeply-embedded, emotional wound.

He was always able to outwardly keep himself together when around others, but these lingering, self-destructive emotions occasionally rose to color his thoughts. Despite attempts to dismiss them when they surfaced, they continued to operate in the background like irritating pebbles in his boots.

How could he share this with Ariana, or Martel? They were his closest friends, but this was so deeply personal that he didn't even know *how* to talk about it. He also didn't want to jeopardize the easy rapport they had.

He finished arranging his remaining goods for the trip home, bid goodbye to Martel, and stepped forward, the cart starting to creak into motion. He took one last glance across the marketplace at the blind beggar, and a chill ran across his skin. He froze. It was long enough for Martel to notice.

"What's the matter? You okay?" Martel said, turning briefly to look around the market.

"I'm okay," Christopher said, regaining his composure. He presumed Martel had not seen what had grabbed his attention. "See you tomorrow."

"Yes, see you tomorrow."

Lost in thought, Christopher continued forward, the large wheels of the cart wobbling on the cobblestones. Just before he turned the corner to exit the square, he took one last look down the street and saw Martel looking at him with mild concern, and Christopher could see that across from him through the remaining people milling about the market was the blind man sitting in his usual spot and staring intently at Christopher, his eyes wide open and as black as the darkest night.

~

Christopher stepped uneasily along the dirt road, his typically natural physical movements feeling unsettled as he traveled the familiar path home. The beggar's altered gaze remained in his vision until he was close to his farmstead, which left him recollecting about the period directly after his father's death, the only other time he had seen the blind man's eyes opposite their usual milky-white color.

He didn't fully comprehend or appreciate the beggar's compassionate understanding that time long ago, nor did he now, but he felt it tenderly washing over him with the same softness as before. Something about it made him feel as if it were trying to carry away old emotions that no longer served him, but it was confusing because he could also feel himself resisting it, wanting to hang on to what had become so familiar. In some ways, the emotions were helping keep the memory of his father alive. Whatever was happening, it just added to the strange day he was already experiencing.

Approaching his homestead, he attempted to dismiss these various thoughts so he could focus on what he needed to do to prepare for tomorrow's market.

He pulled the cart to the front of the covered porch of his old, log farmhouse and removed the one crate of unsold vegetables, thinking he might try to can them later if he had the energy and will to do so. After bringing it inside, he grabbed three empty crates from the cart and walked up the hill behind the house to the orchard where he picked apples until the crates overflowed. One at a time, he brought them back to the front of the house and placed them in the cart for tomorrow.

Heading to the shed, he grabbed a wheelbarrow, hoe, and knife, and proceeded to the gardens. There he dug, plucked, and picked for a few hours, filling the wheelbarrow with carrots, potatoes, turnips, broccoli, and other vegetables, then going to the well hand pump by the house to wash any remaining dirt off the items. He picked and hauled two loads, each time rinsing the vegetables and laying them out on the porch to dry. Finished, he returned the tools and wheelbarrow to the shed.

He glanced over at the overgrown blueberry bushes behind the low, stone wall made of fieldstones his great-grandfather had originally cleared from the land, but he didn't have any energy left to pick the delicious berries as well. Instead, he went back to the farmhouse and up the porch steps to sit in the old rocking chair to try to relax for a few minutes and enjoy the view.

The covered porch had been a favorite place over the years for his family, and the families before his, to sit, talk, and play with the children in the evenings as the sun went down over the West Wall. Porch time served as a way for the labors of the day to drain away with the sunlight so everyone could reset themselves for the next day. Christopher had found that to be true and did his best to continue that tradition, even while living on his own.

But the porch no longer rang out with the energy of conversation and the cheerfulness of youth, just as the shed—which used to store excess yields but now kept only the cart and his great-grandfather's old wheelbarrow and farming tools—felt empty and devoid of life as well. Regardless, Christopher tried to uphold the custom of sitting on the porch as it likely kept him from feeling completely overwhelmed. It was a thread to his past that brought back the memories of more joyful and peaceful times, allowing him to escape the reality of his burdens, if only for a short time.

He knew that having others around to help with the property—namely a wife and eventual children—would be a tremendous help to the farm and its future. Throughout the generations, wives and children had been essential to the operation of the homestead, providing consistent care of the household, the land, and the men who toiled the fields and sold its yields in the city. Since his mother had died, Christopher had begun to appreciate all of what she and the women before her had done to sustain the farm. He even felt that without the women's support and hard work over the years, the farmstead would have had its troubles long before now.

But he didn't feel ready for a family. It would be unfair and inappropriate to partner with someone while the farm was in jeopardy, even though a wife might be able to help him turn things around. Maybe it was pride, but he felt he needed to get a better handle on the farm's finances before starting a family.

The strange day had confirmed this and had given him glimpses of something more important yet undefined that he felt he needed to accomplish, or at least understand, first. That is, unless it was all tied together in some way as he had thought earlier in the day. In that case, maybe there was just one solution that could answer all his questions and concerns and pull him out from under the constant stress of never being able to do enough.

He sat with these mental musings while watching the sun go down. After a bit, with work still to be done while there was still some light, he rose to collect the vegetables that had been drying in the cool breeze, filled one empty crate at a time, and brought the full ones down to the awaiting cart. Once the porch was clear and the crates secure, the cart was ready for morning, so he pulled it to the shed to stow it for the night.

His late-day tasks completed, he returned to his chair on the porch and looked out over the shadows stretching across the fields in the waning light. Feeling exhausted from the day's efforts, he began to worry about how long he could keep up the work and what he could do that he hadn't already thought of to prevent the farm's eventual failure, or seizure.

Perhaps the farmstead's decline was related to his not being as religious as most residents in the Territories. Having been a more regular churchgoer when younger, his attendance wavered after his mother passed away, as it depended on his father's attendance, and it dropped to barely twice a year after his father died as farming responsibilities took over his life. Christopher sometimes felt guilty that he wasn't doing enough to fully satisfy the Church's obligations, which promoted frequent attendance, a controlled familial and societal structure, and strict adherence to the Church's and the government's dictates. Despite his perceived moral failings, however, he still occasionally visited the cathedral because he enjoyed sitting in the presence of the first known sculpture of the Perceiver, the visionary upon whom the

Church and the Territories were founded. That, at least, helped him feel better about his dwindling faith.

At least he was still contributing to the functioning of the Territories by fulfilling his given role as a farmer. That mattered to him, even though his contribution seemed minimal at this point. It was a way for him to participate in something bigger than himself, which was the perspective he had been experiencing since last night and was now feeling more intensely. But managing the farm and making a living from it had become increasingly unsustainable, and he knew something had to change. He took comfort, though, in knowing that it was better than being born outside the Wall where the ravaged wasteland saw endless danger, conflict, and death, or so he had heard.

In the distance, Christopher watched the sun begin to hide itself behind the Wall that had been a part of his family's life for as long as anyone could remember. Indeed, the enigmatic barrier had always been a part of everyone's life in the Territories. It was now further away from the farm than it had been when he was a child, its evening shadow taking more time to cover the greater distance to the house, allowing the light to linger later into the evenings before it fully descended below the Wall.

It was that time now, and the enormous shadow quickly crept across the land and ascended the farmhouse steps as the sun dropped below the top of the barrier, winking at Christopher with its last light.

He remained sitting for a few minutes, relishing the anonymity of the dusk, feeling like he could disappear in the darkness that made differences diminish. But even the blackest shadow couldn't help him hide from the likely appropriation of the farm, nor could it erase the thoughts that troubled his mind or the emotions that unsettled his body. He was hanging on, barely, and not just physically. Like during the incident on the morning road, he was frozen in place with no control over what was happening, and he didn't have any idea how to escape what was surely coming.

~

"What do you want to know?"

The voice was clear and resonant, sounding more like a command than a question.

"Ask."

Despite the imposing tone, there was a warmth to it, a surety, like a favorite teacher challenging students to find the answer they already know but have trouble retrieving.

Christopher couldn't think of what to ask. He felt blind to his surroundings, and the sensations of the situation washed over him with such intensity that words failed to form. He tried to look around, but it was dark, belying the buzzy lightness he was feeling in his head and chest. He somehow had the feeling of being in a tunnel, but it didn't feel confining, and he reached out to touch the walls, but his hands met only the empty darkness.

"What do you want to know?" the voice repeated.

The words crashed down on him, infusing his form with an uncomfortable confusion. *I don't know! Why is this happening?* He felt as if his brain was running on sand and going nowhere.

He knew he had questions, but they weren't forming in his mind. There was so much he wanted to know—the Wall, the farm, the blind man, the greater perspective—but he felt mentally choked off, constrained by an unseen force that held his thoughts and voice tightly in its clenched fist. He tried moving down the tunnel with his hands out in front of him as he struggled to breathe, reaching out for something to anchor him in the darkness.

"What do you want to know?"

Thrashing around for clarity, he finally remembered the strange incident on the road the previous morning and searched for the words to ask to understand it, but he couldn't form them or even utter a sound. If he could only speak! Whatever was happening, he knew—he *felt*—from the center of his being that if he were able to ask, he would receive an honest answer. This was his chance to get to the bottom of the feeling he had had the night before and had set his intention to understand, the same feeling that the morning event had forcefully thrust into his awareness.

Slowly, a question began forming in his head, one he hadn't thought of before or even knew what it meant for him. It didn't convey what he thought he wanted to understand but rather carried a quality not grounded in the reality around him that could help him with his present difficulties.

Who am I?

With the words ready, he fought for control of his voice while barely able to breathe, finally forcing his vocal cords to untwist just enough to squeeze out an incomprehensible squawk.

Christopher bolted up in bed and gasped for air. He had been holding his breath in the dream, and his heart and lungs raced to get oxygen to his body.

What on earth was that? he thought as his breathing gradually slowed to a normal pattern. He searched his scattered mind for what he was going to ask as his recall of the dream quickly diminished. He couldn't remember much—only the voice's question stood out—but he knew it was yet another bizarre episode to cap off a day full of surprising events.

The light feeling in his chest continued for a few minutes, contrasted by the tightness in his throat that slowly released as he coughed and sputtered to clear it. Even though it was just a dream, there was a lucidity about it that made it feel real. His physical reactions were a testament to that.

He rose to go to the kitchen and poured a glass of water from the pitcher he had filled from the well pump earlier. Taking a drink, his throat felt better, but a slight tickle remained as he went back to bed to try to sleep again before morning. He laid down and took a deep breath, let it out, and closed his eyes. Exhausted from the day, he tried to melt into the comfort of his straw mattress. As he did, the last thing he thought before drifting off was that there was more, so much more.

Anna

More? More than what? Anna thought, blinking and looking up at the ceiling to stretch her neck. *More strange incidents? More troubles? More revelations?*

As was typical for her when reading stories, she was connecting easily with the setting and characters as they became more defined, which helped paint a three-dimensional picture in her mind that brought her into the story like she was actually *in* the world rendered in the pages, which she was. Because the tale was set in the Territories, she already knew about the Grand Wall, the marketplace, and the government's laws, making her wonder if she might see Christopher, Martel, Ariana, and the blind beggar sitting on the cobblestones if she went to the market and looked for them. But the owner of the antique store had said he had gotten the manuscript decades ago, so the characters would be much older and likely not there anymore, if any of it were true in the first place.

Beyond the familiar setting, she could feel Christopher's stresses and could identify with his desire to escape them for a time to have a chance to figure things out. As the beginning of his journey unfolded, she shared his yearning to be free from the confining circumstances that limited his options, but she couldn't understand why he wouldn't share his feelings with Ariana and enter into a full-blown courtship with her. With their past interactions, it seemed they had both the family connection and a familiarity with each other that would make that decision easy. But, like the boys she knew, Christopher seemed insecure and clueless, like when Ariana gave him the opportunity to see what was right in front of him and he didn't recognize it. Nevertheless, she hoped they would get together as the story progressed.

There was something about the tale that was different from the fiction in the books on her shelves. It had more self-reflection than those stories, which often moved forward with breathless action that kept her reading deep into the night. This tale, on the other hand, engaged her in a way that helped her *feel* Christopher's plight, more so than anything she had read before, and she wondered if that was typical of writings, and perhaps symbols too, that were forbidden within the Territories.

Not wanting to take a break, she looked down at the last page she read and repeated to herself, . . . *more, so much more*, and turned to the next chapter.

First

The one light gives life to the shadows, rendering their creation equal from the source. Masculine and feminine dance in desire to go forth and multiply, and their expression in the shadowlands grounds upon the stage their belonging to the light.

~

Standing behind his cart in the marketplace the next morning, Christopher stared across the street at the blind beggar, who showed only his typical, cloudy-eyed, unassuming countenance as if nothing different had occurred yesterday afternoon. Christopher was puzzled and a little annoyed, almost feeling like he was the object of a joke, and he was bothered that he hadn't learned anything about the blind man since his father said he would so many years ago. In addition, he was feeling the struggles of the farm more acutely today and was frustrated, and he wanted to direct his emotions toward someone, to place blame for his own discomfort outside himself.

He contemplated not giving anything to the beggar today, but his father's instructions were so etched into his behavior that not doing it would be like not rising in the morning. That didn't mean he had to do it nicely, though. He grabbed an apple from his cart and marched quickly over to the beggar, dropped it brusquely in his lap, and turned to walk back to his cart.

"Wait."

The word shot through his ears like an arrow. He spun around in surprise and scowled at the man, who showed no signs of movement, the apple resting in his lap. His continued serene demeanor almost made Christopher think that the word wasn't spoken but in his head. He had never heard the man speak before.

He took a step forward. "Did you say something?" he asked irritably, nervously.

The blind man slowly opened his milky, off-white eyes and looked up at Christopher, who felt like he wanted to take a step back but didn't, although his energy retreated.

"Come with me," the man said, slowly rising to his feet, apple in hand.

Christopher took a step back. "Uh, no, I can't. I'm . . . I'm working," he stammered. *What's going on? Why is he speaking to me? Where does he want to go?* His mind was racing, trying to understand what was happening.

"It's time," the blind man said.

"What do you mean, 'It's time?'" replied Christopher.

"It's time you learn how to see."

Christopher noted the irony of the blind man's statement. "Um, I can see fine, thank you."

"If you can see fine, then tell me . . . what do you want to know?"

Christopher froze upon hearing the question the voice asked in his dream. He stared at the beggar, not understanding how seeing and knowing were related but feeling it was more than just a coincidence that the language was the same he had heard in his head last night. He tried to think of what he had tried to say in response in the dream, but the words wouldn't come.

"I'll show you the city," the man continued, "if you desire to see it."

"I've seen the city," replied Christopher, hesitant.

"You think you have, but you don't know it like I do," the blind man said. "I'll wait." And he half-closed his eyes and stood there, motionless.

Seriously? Christopher thought. *You realize you're blind.*

It reminded him of some of his father's directives on the farm when he was younger, commands that he resisted but knew he was going to have to do anyway despite his protests. They infuriated him because, well, teenagers always know better, and he often wound up completing them while thoroughly annoyed that they even had to be done in the first place, although he now understood why because of having to do everything himself. The difference was that back then, with the dynamic with his father, he really had no choice. This time, however, he did.

But despite not being either a request or a demand, Christopher somehow knew he would go with the man. He silently objected but could feel that the battle of wills was over before it had even begun, and both of them knew it. It was just a matter of time before he gave in to his burgeoning curiosity.

He breathed out heavily and stormed back to his cart, unsettled and defiant but willing, the buried inquisitiveness of his childhood peeking out from its hiding place. He could have Martel or Ariana watch his goods for a while, something they did for each other at times. *How long will this take? Perhaps an hour? Then I'll be back by midday when it gets busier.* He was thankful that at least right now it was one of the market's slower times.

Martel was busy with a customer, so Christopher stopped in front of Ariana and her flowers. "Hi" he said.

"Hi," she replied, mimicking his clipped tone.

"Um . . . can you watch my cart for a bit?" he asked. "I have to go do something."

"Sure. Where are you going?" she asked as a woman approached and picked up a bouquet of assorted flowers and inspected them while digging in her pocket for payment.

Christopher tried to hide the reason. "Uh, I have to talk with a few people around the city today. I'm not sure how long it'll take." He didn't want to take the time to explain what was going on, even though he thought she might understand.

"No problem," Ariana said, collecting coins from her customer and thanking her. "I'll take care of you . . . uh, I mean your cart!" she spluttered, blushing.

Christopher couldn't suppress a small smile, pleased at hearing her slip of the tongue. "Thank you."

"I was . . . you know . . . distracted by my customer . . . making change for my customer," Ariana mumbled, attempting to cover her embarrassment.

Christopher smiled more broadly and leaned in close to her, his right cheek almost touching her beautiful, brushed-back, golden hair, and whispered, "She gave you exact change."

Now both of them were blushing. Christopher hadn't flirted so openly with her since his father's passing, and it was exhilarating, as if the oxygen that had just rushed in to reignite the smoking embers of their past connection had enabled him to breathe again. It had mercifully taken his mind off what had transpired with the blind man just moments before. His smile faded as he remembered what he was doing, and he thanked her again and went to check his cart to make sure it was organized.

Notwithstanding being relieved at having an excuse to escape the enchanting awkwardness of the interaction with Ariana, he could feel his connection with her strengthening with a freshly-stoked desire. He didn't like how they had parted yesterday but certainly enjoyed what had just transpired, a heightening of their increasingly playful and flirtatious relationship. He thought of the possibilities as he walked over to the blind man.

The beggar stood patiently waiting for him, expressionless. Christopher's demeanor shifted as he approached, quickly changing back to the same irritation he remembered when hearing his father's directives. It contrasted starkly with the delightful hiatus with Ariana, and it made him a bit apprehensive at what this excursion with the blind man might reveal. He had been around the city countless times and had seen most of it, save for the few areas his father had warned him to avoid, shadowy places that held stories of disreputable figures and occupations.

"Okay, you've made me curious," he said, coming up to the beggar. "Where are we going?"

The blind man expressed a barely perceptible smile and said, "Follow me and you'll see," and he turned and began walking down the side of the square.

Christopher stood still and watched him for a moment, still silently objecting to the request but knowing that he couldn't ignore the urge deep within to comply. *This should be interesting,* he thought as he took a deep breath, let it out slowly, and took his first step forward to follow the mysterious figure down the street.

~

Despite the appearance of being homeless, the daily begging for food and spare change—if one could even call it begging—and, of course, being blind, the man moved with a grace, confidence, and simplicity of someone who lacked for nothing. There was a lightness in his step that reminded him of Ariana, but also a surety and precision that anchored him to the earth, something she did not seem to have, at least not to the level of the man he followed. The beggar's lack of sight seemed to have no effect on his navigation; he walked like someone who could see everything, which made Christopher wonder if his blindness was just an act.

As the two men walked out of the square, Christopher saw an older woman emerge from the door of the antique shop on the corner. She was fairly tall and had wild, messy, black hair that framed her dark, penetrating eyes. She moved somewhat disjointedly, as if she were a stranger in her own body, and Christopher's initial impression was that she was a bit challenged, like some of the homeless vagrants that wandered about the city with no purpose or ability to contribute to the Territories. He might have mistaken her for one of them if not for her simple and clean white kaftan that reached to her ankles.

As the door of the shop closed behind her, she stared at Christopher with an intensity he had never encountered before, and her gaze didn't waver as he and the blind man approached. Her concentrated focus on him seemed to exclude everything around her, like nothing else even existed in her world, the wild potency of her eyes making him think of a predator that had zeroed in on its prey. He felt strange and unsettled as he advanced towards her, almost wanting to turn back to avoid any interaction. He hadn't seen her before in the square, and he did his best to avoid eye contact as he approached.

As the beggar led him past the antique shop, the woman reached out with both her arms in a pleading manner, and the blind man, without looking, accurately placed Christopher's apple into her hands as if to answer Christopher's thoughts about his blindness being an act. Christopher didn't have time to silently register an objection—after all, the apple was his gift to the beggar to do with how he pleased—because the woman spoke to him when he came abreast of her a moment later.

"When the darkness comes, will you be ready?" she said in a heavy, uneasy voice tinged with the anxious shadow of fear that sounded like the gravel he walked upon outside the blacksmiths' shops.

Christopher ignored her—clearly, she was somewhat disturbed—and kept to the pace of the blind man, who hadn't slowed.

After they had passed her and turned the corner, she shouted after him, "You need to be ready!"

Christopher ignored her, as he had done with other similar interactions with unstable people over the years, but something about her was different. Her demeanor, movements, outfit, and what she said just didn't make sense when taken all together, even with his experience seeing and engaging with the vastly different personalities that came to the market. Perhaps it was because she didn't fit cleanly into the defined and judgmental categories he had about people, like merchant, panhandler, baker, teacher, customer, churchgoer, constable, and farmer. Regardless, the interaction unnerved him as he continued following the blind man.

The two men headed away from the busier marketplace where they made a left onto a small street, a one-lane road that connected to an area with residential buildings. Christopher stayed several paces behind the beggar, suspiciously observing him despite not having a reason to do so. As they continued through the narrow, mostly-empty streets, Christopher gradually caught up to the man and matched his easy walking pace, staying to his side and a half step behind him.

"What's your name?" Christopher asked.

The man seemed to reflect on the question, as though he was evaluating his options and searching for a suitable answer.

"Lucas," he replied after a few paces.

"Are you really blind?"

As soon as the words left Christopher's lips, he felt ashamed that he had asked so bluntly, but it was already verbalized, so he followed up. "I mean, you seem to know your way around . . . everything."

Lucas stopped and looked directly at Christopher with eyes so pale they looked like the high, white clouds that preceded the fall rainstorms. These were certainly not the deep, black eyes he had seen after his father had died, nor the ones he had seen yesterday as he left the market. Observing them so closely, he took a step back.

"It is true I cannot see with these eyes, but sight is not relegated to the eyes of form," Lucas said. He turned and continued walking.

Christopher dutifully stepped behind him again, trying to control his surprise and process what he had said at the same time. Many questions ran through his head. *Can this man actually see without functioning eyes? How does it work? Is he one of the monks or the Ancients with otherworldly abilities? If he is one of the mystics from the tales, where are the others and why isn't he with them? What does he want with me?* One question he verbalized.

"Why did you ask me what I want to know?"

"Because I can see you are struggling with the question. Where we are going will help you begin to learn the answer," Lucas responded.

Christopher didn't ask anything further. He didn't understand how the blind beggar could know anything about him, let alone what he was struggling with, what the voice said in the dream, or what he might learn. Nevertheless, he felt a strange, inherent trust in Lucas and his apparent mystical powers of perception.

He was reminded again of the monks in the parables he had read when he was younger who contrasted considerably with the priests from the city who operated the churches, performed religious ceremonies, and who often seemed more concerned with opulence than with the duties they were supposed to carry out. These monks from the tales were described as simple and peaceful stewards of truth who deeply appreciated living in harmony with the world, which allowed them the gift of being able to bend the laws of nature. But since they hadn't been around in ages and any sightings were suspect, he wondered about the veracity of the stories. Christopher stared at the blind man as he followed him. *Could they be true?* he thought.

As if hearing his thoughts, Lucas said, "It doesn't matter, if you believe them to be true."

Things were getting strange fast.

~

After a few minutes and several turns down progressively narrower city streets, Christopher recognized the district they were going to, or at least he thought he did. They were entering an area known for the pleasures of the flesh, where prostitutes plied their bodies for money. Sure enough, he and Lucas began seeing scantily-dressed women half hidden in the doorways they passed. Their seductive movements distracted him, and he fell a few steps behind the blind man before realizing it and quickly closed the gap.

As they walked further into the depths of the quarter, Christopher saw the occasional man scurry forth from a shadowy doorway with head hanging low and eyes darting back and forth, apparently trying to avoid being seen. It seemed only

Christopher and Lucas walked assuredly, especially Lucas, confident in his direction and purpose.

Christopher had never been to this section of the city but had certainly heard about it. People would go here to enjoy the pleasures of being with a woman, or a man, and he understood that they could indulge every fantasy, for a price.

A few times in the marketplace he had overheard men talking about some of their adventures here. What they had shared was unfamiliar, but it also aroused something in him that he had felt occasionally but hadn't known what to do with due to his limited experience with women. He also had heard rumors that government officials were sometimes seen here, which was probably why such places were tolerated and the constable presence was minimal compared to other areas of the city with more consistent law enforcement patrols.

Lucas seemed to have a particular place in mind. They made one more turn and came upon an old, three-story building with pillars on either side of an ornate doorway. Lucas paused in front of it, and Christopher did the same, looking up at the balconies attached to the stone façade.

Leaning over the railing on one of the second-floor terraces was a dark-haired woman observing the two men dispassionately, her languid figure draped over the brass railing like a melted candle overflowing its container. Gorgeous, serene, and with one of the most open and approachable bearings he had ever seen, she locked eyes with Christopher, who unexpectedly found himself losing his sense of place as he fell, trapped, into the whirlpool of her gaze. Without moving a muscle, she casually held her drowning captive hostage for a few moments before turning to go inside, mercifully allowing him to surface to regain his breath. Gathering his wits about him, Christopher found himself alone in the street watching the door in front of him close behind Lucas, who had entered the establishment. He hurried to catch up.

Inside, a reddish glow pervaded the space, the candles on the tables scattered about the room illuminating the dark, crimson-colored walls. Several men and women sat at a bar on the right having drinks and engaging in light banter as a general atmosphere of people out enjoying their time together infused the room. Most of the women were dressed provocatively.

Since Christopher had never been to a place like this, his senses were ablaze, taking in everything—the varying, vibrant colors of the women's revealing outfits, the scents of whiskey, incense, and fragrance, the soft chatter of anticipation, the beguiling movements and looks of seduction, the energy of inebriation and desire, the inexpressible feelings in his own body—and all the sensations heightened his awareness to a level he hadn't felt before. Everything about the place seemed designed to stir the physical senses to an awakening, and the overt temptations made the experience of simply being in the room physically intoxicating.

He watched as one woman took the hand of a young man and led him to the stairs at the back of the large room. As they climbed out of sight, the woman he had seen on the balcony outside slowly descended the steps, surveying the space.

Meanwhile, Lucas was conversing with an attractive older woman near the bar. Christopher stepped over to him and heard, "Treat him as my brother." Her eyes darted to Christopher and looked him up and down.

"Of course," she replied. "Always a pleasure, Lucas." She kissed him on the cheek, and he walked over to a chair by the entrance to sit down as the woman came up to Christopher, lightly touching his arm and playing with his collar.

"You haven't been here before, have you?"

"Uh, no," replied Christopher.

"Well, don't you worry about a thing. We're going to take very good care of you."

He swallowed heavily.

She motioned to the woman who had just come down the stairs, the woman from the balcony, who drifted over to them while keeping her eyes on Christopher.

"Shae, this is Christopher," the older woman said. "Would you like to show him around?"

Shae reached out her hand. Christopher was taken by her relaxed, feminine beauty. It seemed like her every motion was like a dancer's movement, flowing so naturally as to be moving artistic expression. He extended his hand and looked at her, immediately falling into her eyes again, just as he had done outside.

"Of course," Shae said to the woman while still looking at Christopher. "I'd be happy to."

"He's a friend of Lucas's," said the older woman, gesturing behind her to where the blind man was sitting by the entrance.

A look of disappointment ran across her face. "Oh, that's too bad, but I figured. I saw them come in together." Her voice was like nectar to his ears.

With that, she hooked arms with Christopher. "Shall we proceed?" she said and guided him toward the tables.

Christopher didn't know what to think. His mind and body were buzzing, and he wondered if the air was tainted with opium, something his father had cautioned him about. It was one of those pieces of advice from his father that he obediently followed because he had no prior experience with it, and it also happened to align with the Church's view on the subject, that compromising one's awareness was frowned upon, as was visiting brothels. Still, he obediently followed Shae, who had a firm grip on him through their interlocked arms. He glanced back at Lucas, who sat maddeningly motionless by the entrance.

"Please, sit," said Shae, gesturing to a chair. Christopher obeyed and looked around but kept getting drawn back to her focus on him. "Would you like a drink?"

"Um, no thank you." He didn't want to diminish his senses. For some reason, he felt slightly on guard. Shae waived off a skimpily-dressed waitress who had approached.

"So, Christopher, why are you here?" Her large brown eyes examined him with clarity as her perfect, full lips formed the words.

Christopher's muddled head attempted to answer. "Um, I don't know. Lucas led me here, but I don't know why. He apparently wants me to learn something."

Shae gave a hearty laugh. "Oh, this is certainly a place you can learn something!"

Christopher stared at her, self-conscious and embarrassed by her laughter. She reached out and touched his arm. "Oh, no, honey. I'm sorry. Don't you worry. I know you're not here for that."

Electrified by her touch, he didn't know how to respond.

Seeing his hesitation, Shae said, "Lucas is unlike anyone I've ever met, so I suspect you're a bit different too, and you're not here for what we typically do."

"What am I here for then?" Christopher asked, regaining his composure.

Shae just looked at him. "Why do you think you're here? What are you supposed to learn?"

Christopher had no answer. He didn't know why he was there, why Lucas took him to a place he would never consider going. Still, he felt there *was* a reason, but one that he couldn't quite fully grasp at the moment.

"Come with me." Shae stood up and took Christopher's hand, gently tugging him toward her. He stood and she guided him past the other tables toward the stairs at the back of the room. Noticing where they were heading, Christopher pulled his hand back when they neared the bottom step.

"I don't need to go upstairs," he said.

Shae paused, looked at him, and said, "It's not what you think."

Christopher didn't move.

"Aren't you curious?" she asked.

He was, and he believed her for some reason, believed *in* her. Like Lucas, she exuded a kind of trustworthiness he rarely encountered. He relaxed, nodded, and allowed her to lead the way.

Halfway up the stairway, Christopher looked down upon the men and women at the tables below reveling in the overloaded sensuality of the establishment. Yes, he was curious, but not curious enough to *do* anything. His mind was spinning again, bewildered and distracted by the sights, sounds, and smells of the place. He felt anxious and bothered that he had allowed himself to follow Lucas here to a place he really didn't understand, yet he felt as if something undefined inside him knew that whatever he was to experience would be a part of what he was to learn. And he also recognized that spending time with Lucas, wherever it led, would help him understand what his father meant when he had told him to give something daily to the blind man and that *You will understand why . . . someday.*

Shae led him up two flights of stairs to the third floor, which was much quieter than the first and second floors. They entered a room painted a bright, lively red, which had a table and three chairs, a bed, a dresser, and a closet on the side wall. Patio doors opened to a small balcony, surely one of the ones Christopher saw on the way in. Shae gestured for him to sit at one of the chairs at the table. She sat in another one and stared at him.

Christopher looked around the room. The décor was plain, simple, unlike the fancier furnishings of the first floor. What he at first thought was an abstract painting hanging above the bed was instead upon closer inspection a pair of intertwined bodies in an erotic embrace, their torsos and limbs almost blending together to become one body. He looked back at Shae, who was watching him, then realized that his knee was bouncing up and down, so he put his hands down to stop its movement.

"So, why am I here?" he asked.

Shae smiled slightly, leaned over, and touched his arm, and said, "Besides that, do you have any other questions for me?"

"Um, uh," Christopher stammered, unsure of what to ask. He had a lot of thoughts, but they were all jumbled in his head. Besides, he had a nagging feeling that he had to sort them out himself. He searched for a line of questioning that might clarify his reasons for being there. He decided to get personal.

"Why do you work here?" he asked.

"Because I choose to," Shae replied. "Do you think less of us who work here? Or who come here?"

Defensively, Christopher blurted out, "Oh, no!" But even as he said it, he recognized that his response was not wholly honest and that the presumption in her question had some truth to it. His preconceived notion was that both the courtesans and their clients didn't have the good, moral character of others, that they were slaves to their base desires. In particular, he saw the prostitutes as not contributing substantially to the functioning of society; rather, he thought they were an unhealthy distraction to those who succumbed to their enticements. Noticing this view in himself—something he now saw he had adopted from beliefs that came from his family, the Church, and society at large—now in the presence of one of those workers, he felt ashamed.

Christopher looked down, "Well, I suppose I do. I'm sorry. That's not for me to judge." For some reason, he couldn't help but tell her the truth. "This . . . profession is not one I'm familiar with."

Shae half smiled. "Many aren't. But are we not the same as you, as everyone? Call it circumstance or desire, are we not fulfilling a role just as you are and trying to live our lives with purpose?"

The question lingered in the silence as Christopher contemplated it, as if together they were waiting for the echo of what she had spoken into a canyon to return.

"Most people think we're just here for physical pleasure," she continued, "but the truth is greater than that. We offer connection, in whatever form is desired . . . or needed."

"What if someone isn't desiring connection?" Christopher asked.

Shae laughed. "Everybody desires connection. They just might not know it, or what it looks like to them. That's why they come here."

Switching the focus to him, she asked, "So, what do you do?"

"I'm a farmer and I sell fruits and vegetables in the marketplace," he replied, relieved to have a simple question.

"Why?" she asked.

The question surprised him. His family had done it for generations, so of course he was a farmer. He really hadn't given any consideration to the reasons behind it, but he knew he played an important, albeit recently diminished, role in the complex system within which they all lived. *That's just what you do*, he thought, *follow the family trade.*

Filling the silence that followed, she added, "Have you ever thought about doing something different?"

"I don't know. Um, no," Christopher confessed, but as he said it, he felt the curiosity of his childhood once again peek out from its hiding place within.

"Think about it," said Shae as she rose from her chair and floated over to the closet. Opening it, she pulled out an old, thin, woven rug with different-colored, dried paint drips all over it and a bucket of brushes and paints and put them in the room. She reached back into the closet and removed a folded easel and a blank canvas about two feet by three feet in size. Methodically, she laid out the rug and set up the easel with the canvas on it. Grabbing an empty cup from the bucket and moving to the washroom that he could see had a basin and a pitcher of water, she proceeded to fill the cup, which she placed on the table near the easel. Taking some small jars of paints from the bucket, she uncorked the tops and dropped a few drips of the different colors onto a palette she had also removed. Brushes came next, which she laid out on the table, using one to mix a few of the colors together before rinsing off the brush in the cup of water.

Christopher watched the scene unfold, entranced by how she moved—gracefully, lightly, purposefully. Her movements were simple yet sophisticated, elegant yet grounded. There was a beauty in her being that made him think that if an angelic presence came to earth, this is what it would look like. In some way she was a physical representation of where his feelings for Ariana seemed to be headed, and although Ariana wasn't there, Shae reminded him of that special connection with her.

She snapped him out of his reverie. "Well, go ahead."

Christopher looked anxiously at her. "What?"

"This is for you. Paint."

"What do you mean, 'Paint'?"

"It's easy. Just paint."

"What am I going to paint? I don't paint," Christopher said, crossing his arms.

"Ha-ha! That's because you never really have. Surely, you have something creative to express. Don't think, just paint."

Christopher sat in his chair looking at the blank canvas. He felt uneasy, even queasy. He had never painted before and didn't consider himself artistic, so this was certainly testing him.

Observing his discomfort, Shae slowly slinked her way toward him. She put a hand on his lower arm as she passed, slowly dragging her delicate fingers up his arm to his neck as she snaked around him and came to rest standing behind him with both hands on his shoulders.

Christopher was woozy. Her movements and commands were doing something to him, but he didn't know what, only that his head was buzzing like a beehive. He couldn't think straight.

She leaned over seductively, her hair brushing the side of his head, and whispered in his ear, *"Paint."*

Her proximity, presence, and sultry whisper put him over the edge, and he bolted out of the chair exclaiming, "Okay! Okay. I'll paint." He turned around to look at her, and she nodded slightly and slipped into the chair he had just risen from.

Refocusing himself, Christopher stood looking at the blank canvas. *What to paint . . .*, he thought.

As if reading his mind, Shae softly and gently repeated what she had said before, "Don't think, just paint."

She rose from the chair, took a brush from the table, and dabbed it in a dollop of red from the palette. Approaching him from behind, her body touching his, she slid her hand with the brush along his right forearm and placed it in his hand, allowing the body contact to remain longer than necessary.

Christopher accepted the brush, and the physical contact, without objection. His focus was shifting to the fabric in front of him, which began to pull him into its vacant depths, calling out for the extraction of some hidden treasure. Shae withdrew from him and sat down again, and Christopher took a deep breath, raised the brush, and placed it on the canvas.

~

"Wow," Shae said.

Christopher stepped back and looked at his creation, a completed abstract painting of different colors, lines, shapes, and inspired movement. He glanced at her and thought he saw her eyes begin to well up. "It's beautiful," she said.

He moved back next to her chair to see his handiwork at a distance, trying to be objective. *Interesting*, he thought. *Who knew I had it in me?*

The dark lower third of the painting spun upwards toward a lighter top third, with the middle encompassing a transition of mixed, swirling colors. As he continued to view it, he felt drawn into its center, and emotions of an unknown origin began to rise. He felt out of place, more present inside the painting than in the room, as though a hole had opened in the canvas and had sucked him into another world to hold him forever.

He couldn't identify the multitude of emotions he was experiencing, which culminated in an overpowering sadness that burst forth as tears began to stream down his face. Something was opening, releasing, and although he didn't know exactly what it was, he knew it was unlocking something old, deep, and sacred.

He could feel the numbing prisons of his past—a tangled web of inhibitions, limitations, and timeworn ways of thinking—fall away. The path that lay before him now was unfamiliar but unquestionably brighter, unadulterated by the stress, guilt, and frustrations he struggled with most days. He wanted to be at the end of that path, in that future, facing it with nothing but the clarity of this natural state. The feeling was so deep as to consume his physical form right there in the room, bridging his perceived wrongdoings of long ago with the promise of a sunnier future and annihilating what stood in between.

As Christopher stood there and wept, lost in the vortex of the painting and feeling a freedom he had never felt before, Shae rose from her chair and held him, silently, lovingly. With their arms around each other, they rocked back and forth as one.

After what felt like an eternity, Christopher released his hold and gazed into her eyes. He was raw, naked, and newly born, laid bare before her. In her eyes he saw the stars spiraling, and he wanted to dive in to experience their weightlessness and freedom beyond the limitations of the physical world.

And they kissed.

~

The rest of his time there was a blur, and Christopher didn't regret any of it. Eventually, he walked downstairs and made his way through the tables to the entrance. Lucas stood up and led the way out of the building.

Neither voiced anything on the way back to the market, for there was nothing to say. Everything had happened exactly the way it needed to, and Christopher walked with a previously unknown confidence, almost matching Lucas in his self-assured striding.

When they got back to the square, Lucas sat down cross-legged in his usual spot while Christopher continued to his cart, somehow knowing that this wasn't the last of his interactions with the blind man. He didn't know how much time had passed, but it was at least a few hours, as the sun appeared to be past its peak in the sky. He hoped Ariana was okay with watching his goods for so long, and Martel, too, if he helped.

There weren't many customers along the row of vendors as he approached his space down from his friends, who both gave him a friendly but mildly annoyed look upon his return.

"Have a nice adventure, did we?" Martel asked.

"Yes, something like that," Christopher said. He felt that the internal shifting he experienced would have transforming and long-lasting effects, something he needed time to understand.

"Making us take care of your stuff during the midday crowd, huh?" Ariana asked with a half-joking, shaming glint in her eye.

"I know. Sorry about that," Christopher said. "I lost track of time."

"Well, lucky for you, you have good friends who will take care of things when you shirk your responsibilities," she said playfully.

"And my gratitude exceeds any aggravation I may have caused you," he said with a bow, first to Ariana and then to Martel.

"She did all the work," Martel said. "I was just here making sure she didn't skim from you."

Ariana picked up a pebble and threw it at Martel, who laughed as it bounced off his arm. Christopher smiled, happy to know that he was supported by friends who knew how to take things lightly.

"So, where did you go?" Ariana asked.

It wasn't something he wanted to discuss with her or with anyone at this time. It was an experience he needed to contemplate without the opinions of others interfering with his own thoughts and feelings about it. He also wanted to be truthful with her, but now in her presence he was feeling guilty about his kiss with Shae. He quickly wiped his mouth on his sleeve, hoping that any color that might have transferred from Shae's lips to his hadn't been noticed.

He tried to look Ariana squarely in the eyes, but his gaze faltered as he said, "Um, just deeper into the city center on a personal errand. That's all."

"I saw you leave with the blind beggar. Did it have something to do with him?" she said.

Christopher hesitated, then spoke carefully. "In one sense, yes, but it's . . . I can't talk about it right now."

Ariana paused, then smiled and nodded. "Okay. I'm here if you want to talk about it . . . about anything," and she walked back to her baskets of flowers on the other side of Martel. He could tell she was a little taken aback at his dismissal of her simple question, but he hoped she appreciated his honesty. He certainly valued and respected her offer of support.

He looked down to assess his remaining goods, then looked up and saw her glancing sideways at him past Martel, as if trying to figure out why he was acting a little differently. He caught Martel's eye, who seemed to be observing him similarly.

"So," Christopher said, wanting to take the focus off himself, "looks like business was decent. Maybe you two should take over more often."

"If you mean that your friends worked hard for—" Martel began ribbing him, but he was cut off by the loudspeaker on the corner crackling to life. He, Christopher, and Ariana exchanged puzzled glances and then looked up at the speaker in front of the antique shop on the corner, joining everyone but Lucas in their attention to it. Three rising tones in succession blared out, and after a few squeals and sounds of static, a voice blanketed the land inside the Wall.

This is a Level 1 Warning by the Council of Governors. We have discovered an enemy force assembling outside the Grand Wall. Do not panic.

Currently, it is many days away, and we are doing what we can to prevent any attack, but we are preparing the Grand Army as a precaution. Please see your zone's manual for the necessary steps you must take for your designated area. This is a Level 1 Warning.

The message repeated two more times, followed by the three tones again. Level 1 was a cautionary condition, a notification that a threat *could* be coming. Christopher knew that at this level, the manuals for all the zones were identical, requiring increased vigilance and reporting of anything suspicious, but the first warning was also a signal that the danger could intensify, necessitating higher level notifications.

When the warning finished, Christopher looked over at Ariana, and she returned his glance with a slightly worried look. The marketplace immediately erupted in chatter about what it could mean, if more messages might be forthcoming, and what to do if foreign invaders attacked. Christopher had a pang of worry as well, but the practical side of him knew it was better to wait and see what might happen next as the announcement indicated. He didn't want to succumb to the fears that so easily spread among the citizens if it wasn't warranted. Plus, he was perhaps more confident than others about the unbreachability of the Grand Wall.

"Interesting," Christopher said, looking at Martel, who simply nodded thoughtfully. Ariana also was quiet, listening to the talk in the square.

Martel and Christopher immediately became busier as concerned customers lined up to buy from them. It seemed people wanted to make sure they had enough food and supplies for their families if the level of the threat escalated. Ariana's flowers didn't sell quite as fast, but it seemed that once customers had enough provisions, some stopped by to purchase a bouquet before they left the market. Over the next hour, Christopher was able to sell the rest of what he had brought to the city that day.

While interacting with his buyers, he thought about the two times he had heard warnings from the speakers before. The first time was after the Wall had shockingly made its first movement when he was seven, the day after the grief from his mother's death seemed to have left him, at least temporarily. It was early in the morning, and he had been closely observing a grasshopper in the field by his house with an intense, curious focus, losing himself in the minute details of its legs, eyes, and antennae as it chewed on the dewy blade of grass it clung to. He hadn't noticed that the Wall had expanded overnight.

Despite being in a rural area, the sound from the many speakers in the Territories reached all households within the Wall, and they had sizzled uncomfortably to life before a voice floated across the field to his young ears. It said to remain inside because of a danger that could be coming to the Territories. He ran back to the house where his father all but dismissed the warning, but he wouldn't let Christopher outside again until an announcement later cancelled the first one and thanked the citizens for their cooperation and for being vigilant.

The second time occurred when he was a teenager after a morning of good, hard, satisfying work on the farm. Interestingly, the Wall had expanded the previous night. His father was in the market in the city, so Christopher was laboring in the gardens and fields on his own, occasionally glancing up at the Wall, wondering about its magical properties. Despite the distraction, he had fallen into being very present with the work he was doing, feeling that his actions were their own reward. It was a continuation of what he had felt the previous day: a clear mind and effortless exertions that made him appreciate and find joy in his place in the world.

There were two warnings that time, the first while he was outside tending the orchard and the second an hour later after he had gone into the house to wait for his father. When he heard the third and final announcement soon afterwards stating that everything was safe and that it was acceptable to get back to normal activities, he went back outside to resume his work.

At the time, he tried to think of reasons why the Wall might have moved, but he couldn't find any connection between the two expansions and anything happening in the Territories. The only association he could make was that the government warnings followed its movement both times.

Since then, the government had issued specific manuals for each zone in the Territories, which people had to keep ready to refer to in case warnings were issued. He had looked at his zone's manual briefly out of curiosity once, and it was simply a list of instructions based on seven levels of notifications on what steps to take if the Territories were ever threatened again. Citizens were required to follow the protocols within it, and the rules dictated that those not following their given procedures could be arrested for crimes against the Territories. This was not something Christopher ever wanted to experience. Since the warnings had been so infrequent, the manual had found a corner of a shelf in the house and had remained there collecting dust for years.

After the initial reactions to the announcement had settled down in the market and the lines for goods had thinned, Ariana asked Christopher and Martel, "What do you make of it?" She seemed a little unsettled after hearing some of what people discussed. Christopher had heard some of the talk as well, and he viewed much of it as overly fearful.

"Hmm," Martel mumbled. "Well, there's no invasion yet, and we can trust that the government is watching out for us. But think about it, maybe we can make customers of the foreigners when they come!"

Ariana shot him a stern look, then glanced past him at Christopher.

"What he said," Christopher said, smiling, then dropped to a more serious tone. "It's just Level 1. We'll be okay."

That seemed to help Ariana relax, and she nodded slowly in agreement. "Yes, we'll be okay."

Christopher looked out over the people in the square. It appeared that most of their initial fearful reactions had lessened and they were once again going about their day without too much distraction. He was glad to see that, as he always felt more comfortable when his views matched the crowd's. From experience, the first warning wasn't something to really worry about. Nevertheless, many had a new topic of conversation and a certain level of concern not previously present.

Having sold out, he packed up his empty crates, said goodbye to his friends—Ariana was staying as she had several bouquets left to sell—and left the market to head home, wondering if the Wall had moved last night and if additional warnings would be coming.

~

That evening, after filling his crates with freshly-picked produce and preparing the cart for the morning, Christopher sat on the porch and reflected on the day. His father's words were present as he watched the Wall's shadow extend toward him in the fading light. *Someday.* Perhaps that was what was driving him to learn more about the blind beggar. But there was something else there, something within that he needed to understand with more than just the reasoning in his head.

He got up and went to the kitchen to pour himself a small glass of whiskey, something his father used to do occasionally in the evenings before settling in on the porch to watch the sun set over the fields. Christopher copied him, returning to the porch to kick back in the old rocking chair that had seen better days, sipping his drink and trying to put the day's events into perspective. The cool air wafted over him, as refreshing as both the nip and the view, and he tried to find the peace he usually experienced during porch time.

Reflecting on his excursion with Lucas, he recognized that Shae had helped him bring forth a creativity he didn't know he possessed. There was something about being in that establishment and connecting with her that allowed what was buried deep inside to come out onto the canvas in its swirling presentation of emotional release. As much as the visit seemed to be all about him, he couldn't have done it without her taking him by the hand to a place he didn't know he needed to go.

And when he and Shae embraced afterwards, Christopher understood why her profession was not solely about sex. It was, as she had said, about connection in its various forms. He faced a raw, primal desire when in her presence physically, but she somehow knew how to bring forth a deeper, more profound, and more transforming experience from within him. He was, for the first time, able to connect and create without conditions, which he could tell opened up a new way of seeing, or rather *feeling* things.

But even though he felt a new kind of openness, he could feel his old, heavy emotions still simmering in the background, waiting patiently for a time and place to manifest. Time would tell if today's experience had changed their expression at all.

After his kiss with Shae—that was as far as their physical intimacy went—they sat and talked about his hopes and fears,

118 A TALE OF AWAKENING

and he shared the issues he was having with the farm, his growing need to figure out the numerous questions tumbling around his head, and his desire for a partner. Even though he realized she might have been performing, just listening and doing her job as a courtesan, it was a wonderful and fitting end to his time there, a closure to the emotional experience.

The way it had unfolded all seemed part of some grand design, and he was struck by the idea that his family and everyone he had ever interacted with in his entire life all may have done exactly what they had needed to do at just the right time to get him to precisely this point. In recognizing this, his gratitude to everyone who was now or who had ever been in his life—to the whole that they represented—brought him to tears.

A layer of fear had left him, which mercifully reduced some of his underlying anxiety about the farm. It was as if he now had permission to let go of the self-imposed pressure he so expertly submitted himself to. The facts were still there—he hadn't paid his taxes and the property could be confiscated—but he could tell that his worries about it had lessened. Consequently, his physical body was able to relax more than it had in months. He even noted on his walk home with his empty cart that he was moving differently, more freely, feeling he had finally been unwound after having been twisted for most of his life.

Christopher was sure Lucas knew exactly what would take place today and so had taken him to the brothel intentionally to have that experience. Whatever the purpose, he was beginning to wonder if the blind man just might be able to help him in other ways. *Could this be why my father wanted me to bring something to him every day?* he thought. *Maybe he holds the solutions to my problems.*

The novel experience and its lingering effects seemed to portend something greater, and the longer he thought about it, the more his prior feeling of emotional heaviness returned, once again agitating his attempts to find the peaceful evenings he used to enjoy on the porch.

Lately, these active twilight reflections, which had increased in number and intensity, had disrupted his precious, evening idle time, and they were doing so again now. Although they often helped him make sense of the day's activities, they also frequently caused his mind to run unchecked, which made it more difficult to allow the stresses of the day to be carried away by the cool, gentle breeze.

At this point, the sun's long, red-orange streaks were still illuminating the tops of the trees across from the fields. Soon, the light would be below the West Wall and all the Territories would be in shadow, including the tallest of the trees and the spire of the cathedral.

Christopher put his head back against the chair and tried to relax, allowing the happenings of the day to drip from his memory. He felt weary, beat up, wiped out. His eyes closed as the evening's dusk subsumed the rest of the landscape, all he had ever known.

~

He was dreaming, or so he thought. He was standing on his porch, looking out at the waning glow from the sun in the distance, feeling what could only be described as a lightness of being. He wondered if the whiskey had gone to his head because thought was absent; everything was a feeling, a sense, an impression, a *comprehension*. He simply *knew*.

All he looked at seemed brighter, enhanced. Even though it was getting darker, he could see and *feel* the *life* of the apples in the orchard, the grand stoicism of the large trees that marked the property, and the vitality and diverse energies of the different vegetables in the gardens, the ones in the ground vibrating differently than those that grew above it. He felt an intimacy with whatever he placed his eyes on, a connection of understanding and the purpose of the object of attention.

As he blissfully surveyed his surroundings with this newfound perception, he turned around and felt a shock as he saw himself dozing in his chair on the porch. Startled but for a moment, he stared, seeing himself as he saw the elements of nature just before, connecting with himself in a manner beyond possibility.

He broke focus with his seated form and looked up at the sky. Immediately, he began rising, which heightened the already light feeling he was experiencing. It wasn't strange, as he didn't seem to have the ability to understand why it would be.

As he continued to rise, he was able to look down upon all the life-giving collections of fruits and vegetables around his house, the beautiful flowers and bushes lining the path to the porch, the stream that ran beside the dirt road along the lane, and the far-off trees that sheltered the fields from the winds. Even the untended and overgrown parts of the farm blended beautifully with everything around him into a magnificent tapestry of color and light, all holding their precise place in the earth's livingness.

With the sun setting behind it, the Wall in the distance drew his attention, and even though he was leagues away, he could see farther than ever before as he continued to rise and approach its height.

As he rose, the light beyond it began getting brighter, and not because he could see more of the sunset. Whatever was beyond the Wall was somehow becoming more illuminated, which at first seemed odd, but he didn't have the mental processing capability to try to understand why. Continuing upward, the increasing brightness became so brilliant and intense that it obscured what his eyes could take in. Now higher than the distant Wall, he was almost able to see the land—or whatever it was—that was on the other side of it, and the radiance coming from beyond blinded him with a snap and he found himself jolting forward awake in his chair on the porch.

Blinking, Christopher looked out over the darkened gardens and fields. His mind was back—the analytical tool that helped him navigate the world—and the feeling of the deep connection to the various living aspects of nature had diminished. He could sense it though, there under the surface, as his mind rushed to try to make sense of the dream. Despite the reduced awareness of what he had experienced, he looked out from his porch with fresh eyes, as if a thin layer of fog had been cleared from his vision.

He didn't notice in the darkness, but the Grand Wall had moved outward.

Anna

Anna looked up from the open manuscript in her lap. *What's going on with the Wall?* she thought. *Is it being triggered by Lucas or Christopher somehow?* She liked how the story was getting into more magical elements.

She wasn't sure how much time had passed, maybe an hour since she had started, but it felt like much less. Adjusting her position, she brought up her legs to sit cross-legged and leaned back against her pillow.

She wished she had someone like Lucas in her life to guide her in the way he seemed to be guiding Christopher, someone who could really *see* her beyond how others saw her. But the adults in her life—her parents and teachers—didn't seem to want to get to know her, let alone guide her; they just wanted her to fulfill their expectations and have her paint within the lines they had already drawn. It was a good thing she was smart enough to manage their demands successfully—like doing well in school and complying with household rules—because with the lines defined, she knew how to avoid scrutiny when carefully pushing the boundaries, like when acquiring the book from the antique shop.

Seeing the flirting between Ariana and Christopher reminded her of one of her classmates. Her mother sometimes asked if there were any boys she liked, or if any liked her, but she avoided answering because it wasn't really boys she wanted to get to know better. With the limited social time she was able to spend with Melissa and Laura, even though she liked Melissa as more than a friend, she knew from their conversations about boys that Melissa wasn't interested in other girls. In addition, her family's, the Church's, and society's overall view of the different kind of relationship she desired left her unable to share her feelings with anyone. So, she was left with finding romance in the stories she read, and she hoped Ariana and Christopher would give her what she wanted and become a loving couple as the story progressed.

There was a knock on the door and Anna's mother opened it and poked her head into the room. Anna quickly and awkwardly covered the manuscript in her lap with her blanket, even though it was open with the cover facing down. "Can I get you anything?" her mother asked.

"No, thanks. I'm still full from breakfast," Anna replied.

"How's the story?"

"*Really* good. It takes place in the Territories, so a lot of it is familiar."

"Very nice. Don't forget you have that birthday party at Melissa's later," her mother said.

Right, the birthday thing, Anna remembered. "Yes, mother. I know."

As much as Anna had been looking forward to getting out of the apartment and away from her parents, she was now so engrossed in the engaging tale before her that she wanted to finish it before the party. There was time, though, and looking at the number of pages remaining and judging from how fast she had read the first few chapters, she figured she might be able to get to the end before she left for Melissa's.

The connection she had had to the manuscript when in the antique shop had not disappointed, a connection that was only increasing in feeling as she continued reading. She knew somehow there was no accident in her finding it, and at this time in her life too. The story was bringing up ideas that matched the limitations she currently felt, ones she hadn't necessarily created or defined herself but which had placed her life within uncomfortable boundaries, and she wanted to break free from them. *Maybe this story will help me do that,* she thought, thinking of what she knew of Christopher's progress so far and how he seemed to be learning and growing.

She flipped the edge of the blanket off the manuscript and looked down at the loose sheets nestled in the leather covering. Shifting to sit up a little straighter, she took a deep breath before continuing her journey through the handwritten pages.

Second

The one light produces the performance as the shadows identify their roles and choose how each is played, the more dramatic positions attracting the heavier shades. Inspired are those who perform with comprehension, for they find the beauty to be who they are.

~

"Good morning, Martel." Christopher pulled his cart toward his friend just after Martel had arrived at his usual place in the market and was setting up. "Do you mind if we switch spots? I may need some coverage while I do something later, and I think it's easier to be next to Ariana . . . I mean between you two if you're able to help out again."

With all that had happened yesterday, Christopher wanted to be ready for the unexpected, and he had a feeling he might be engaging with Lucas again today. He probably shouldn't have been thinking about leaving his cart at all given that Saturdays were generally more consistently busy, but he was distracted from his normal routine due to what he had experienced yesterday.

"Good morning," Martel replied. "For you, my friend? Yes, not a problem, but are you sure the reason is for coverage?" He raised an eyebrow and gave a roguish smile.

Christopher grinned back. "Perhaps there are multiple reasons." He didn't care at this point that Martel recognized his and Ariana's flirting.

Martel laughed and began moving his cart. "Ha-ha! I will not be known on this street as someone who stands in the way of true love!"

"Um, we're just friends."

"Hm mmm," Martel said. "For now."

Christopher chuckled, knowing that he and Ariana were more than friends, something as yet undefined but with promise. Still, he was glad she wasn't there to witness the exchange.

"Did you see that the Wall moved last night?" Christopher said quietly. They were alone, but he had a habit of lowering his voice when talking about the Wall, like most people in the Territories. He had noticed the barrier was further away on his trip into the city.

"Yes, strange days we're having," Martel said, also in a lower voice. "It's been what, over a decade since the last time, right?"

"Yes. There's something going on . . . first the warning, then the Wall. They must be related."

"Maybe the outsiders are the ones moving it, somehow weakening it for an attack."

Christopher shook his head, "Mmm, I don't think so. It was still solid and impenetrable after its last expansion, so why wouldn't it be this time?"

Martel shrugged. "Good point. I saw a few people get arrested this morning near the new land. They were demanding an allocation of it from the government, but the constables were having none of it. I kept my head down and came straight here." Martel lived close to the East Wall.

The Territory Governors had previously reviewed and allocated the newly-acquired land from the Wall's expansions according to need, or so they proclaimed. But it was clear they instead gave it to their associates and those who already controlled more land than most, hiding its ownership behind relatives and agreeable friends.

"Good reason not to talk about it. I guess we'll have to wait and see if there are any additional warnings," Christopher said, suspecting there might be another one today because of the Wall's movement, or because the foreigners might still be planning to attack.

Martel nodded, and they both adjusted their carts in their new spaces and began setting up as Ariana came around the corner with her flowers. Martel shot Christopher a mischievous glance, but Christopher barely noticed because he was staring at the flowers in her baskets. They seemed to be vibrating, almost singing to him like in his dream last evening.

Yesterday's events had put him in a strange state, almost as if he had partially regressed to a time of childlike wonder. He had slept well, more deeply than usual and with vivid dreams he couldn't now recall, and he had gone about his morning in a semi-detached trance, having breakfast and completing his preparations quickly without much thought. His grounding walk to the city brought him mostly back to normal, but he couldn't shake the feeling of connecting more deeply to his surroundings, which he welcomed because it distracted him from worries about the state of the farm and its finances. He didn't mind the feeling; it was just different, a remembering of a time past when he was more present with the world.

"Need my help again while you go wandering off on another adventure?" Ariana asked brightly as she approached, snapping him out of his focus on the flowers.

"Um, perhaps, yes. Good morning!" He put on a big smile.

"Good morning." She smiled back, placing her baskets on the cobblestones. In a quiet voice, she added, "Just tell me you're not going to go check out the Wall. You know it moved last night, right?"

Christopher nodded. "I saw it on the way in. No, I don't think I'll be going to the Wall, but yes, I might leave for a short time. Would you mind helping out with the cart again?"

"Maybe," she said, "if you tell me where you're going."

"Yes!" Martel said behind Christopher. "We want to know all about your secret rendezvous, especially now that we've had a Level 1 warning. Are you a spy?" he jested.

"Um, no," Christopher said in a hushed tone. "And you know you can't be overheard saying that."

"Yeah, sorry," Martel said, making a face as he turned and looked around, but no one was within earshot.

"What I did yesterday was something personal I'm still trying to figure out," Christopher said.

"And what about today?" Ariana asked. "What special trip is making us do your work today?"

Christopher took a moment to think about how to answer. He didn't want to get into a big discussion about the blind man when he was still trying to wrap his head around his experience with him, but he couldn't come up with anything that he felt would end the line of questioning, so he just told them the simple truth.

"I'm not sure yet, but it has something to do with him," and he pointed across the square at Lucas.

Ariana and Martel both looked at the blind man sitting peacefully on the cobblestones.

"The blind panhandler?" Martel said. "The one you're always giving something to?"

Christopher nodded.

"Yeah, he's a strange one. Definitely different than the others."

"Yes, he is," Christopher said, looking at Lucas.

"Why do you do that?" Ariana asked. "Give him something? Why him?"

"It's a long story," Christopher said.

"Is there a short version?" she asked.

"Uh, my father said I should, and that someday I would understand why."

"Interesting," Martel said.

"And mysterious," Ariana added.

"Yes on both counts. So you see, I may need to go do something with him to try to figure out the mystery."

Martel puffed out his chest and loudly proclaimed, "I will help you on your quest, brave adventurer!"

Christopher and Ariana both burst out laughing.

"Me too," Ariana said when she recovered. "Just try not to be gone too long."

Back in his normal voice, Martel slapped Christopher on his back and said, "Don't worry, we've got you covered, brother. Do what you need to do."

"Thanks, I appreciate it."

In his grand voice again, Martel added, "But the payment for such assistance is that you must share in the treasure you discover on your quest."

Christopher looked at him blankly for a moment before Ariana clarified, "We also would like to know what you learn."

"Yes, of course," Christopher said, chuckling. "I'll share when I can."

With Christopher in Martel's usual spot next to her, Ariana looked him and his cart up and down. "Nice to have you closer," she said.

"Nice to be closer," he replied with a smile.

"Hm mmm. Every quest needs a fair maiden," Martel murmured under his breath.

Christopher heard it and shot Martel a stern look. Ariana must not have caught the comment because she said, "What's that?"

"Oh, nothing," Martel said. "Just nice to have something different going on to spice up the day."

"Maybe that's a new selling tactic for you," Christopher said. "'Don't forget to spice up your day with Martel's famous spices!' or 'Are your days and meals boring? Add some spice to both!'"

Martel and Ariana laughed, and Martel said, "I'm actually going to try that." Christopher chuckled along with them.

All three went about setting up their goods for the day as Christopher glanced across the street at Lucas sitting silently, patiently. *What will this day have in store for me?* he thought.

~

Yesterday's warning and the movement of the Grand Wall had shifted the energy in the market. Besides the intermittent, anxious conversations about predicting what might be coming next, Christopher found that many people were looking to purchase extra food to have on hand in case the Territories went into lockdown, which hadn't happened in his lifetime. He hadn't anticipated this but made a mental note to be sure to bring some of his canned and jarred goods from the cellar tomorrow if the warnings continued. They would sell well.

He wasn't too troubled about the first announcement. He had heard the warnings before and trusted there would soon be another one saying that all was okay and there was nothing to worry about. Besides, the Wall was secure, or at least he believed it was. Between it and the standing Grand Army, he felt protected and didn't need to engage as deeply in the concerns of others about the declared threat.

He believed that because when he was a young boy, his parents told a story from his grandparents' time about how the Wall and the Grand Army had protected the Territories. It was during a period of great accomplishment and realization in the land; the economy was booming, resources were plentiful, and it seemed everyone was prosperous and joyful.

One day, the Territory Governors received word of an impending attack by foreign invaders from outside the Wall, and the newly-installed loudspeakers that covered the landscape began their public warnings. Government workers ran about the city cautioning everyone to stay inside, and they called in all families from the rural areas to the center of the city for protection. The Governors declared martial law. A sense of fear pervaded the land as the Grand Army—a dedicated, rarely seen force that trained exclusively for combat—marshaled by the South Wall and waited.

Christopher's grandfather was about thirty at the time, with a wife and two small children, Christopher's father and aunt. They were required to move from their farm to a sheltering facility just south of the city center to wait out the attack with the other farming families from their zone. The facility was an old, government building, and they joined their neighbors, friends, and fellow citizens in a large, gloomy, dirt-floored cellar, hiding in the dark like creatures afraid of the light.

Everyone huddled together as the loudspeakers escalated their warnings of the impending attack. The government official assigned to the building kept repeating words of caution and fear, and he explained that they were being attacked because society had grown complacent and ignorant of the dangers out in the world beyond the Wall.

Many tense and frightful hours later, an announcement was made that the army at the Wall had successfully repelled the invaders, leaving all citizens within the Territories unharmed. Some land inside the Wall had been burned and was still smoking when his grandparents emerged from their shelter and began their walk back to the farm. They could see the heavy, dark smoke in the distance as it swirled upwards past the great height of the Wall, finding definition against the lighter sky before it dissipated in the winds.

The Governors said that the Grand Army's courage and heroism were unparalleled in its history and that it was invaluable to remember the importance of having such extraordinary protection, along with the magnificence that was the Grand Wall. They also said that being steadily fearful, even during peaceful times, was important as it was a continuous alert system to unknown and unseen threats. With such a heightened awareness across the population, the government would be able to hear about and respond more quickly to dangers.

Afterwards, Christopher's grandparents said that a few hushed rumors buzzed about the land doubting the veracity of the official government account of the engagement, but the quick arrests of those who spread the suspicions rapidly quelled any further talk of it. And since the soldiers in the army were isolated from the rest of the population for non-stop training dedicated to the protection of the Territories, no one could confirm anything but the government's position. His parents would say no more about his grandparents' story, and Christopher could tell, even as a boy, that they didn't want to jeopardize themselves, the family, or the farm.

So, even though the government had issued a warning yesterday, Christopher felt safe within the Wall and simply went about his day like any other, the stresses of the farm's finances mercifully absent after talking with his friends.

It was a little after midday when he looked up to see Lucas in front of his cart, the blind man's milky, half-opened eyes staring straight ahead.

Christopher waited for words to come forth, but the man expressed nothing. After a few moments, Christopher said, "Um, it's kind of a busy time."

"Come with me," Lucas said, and he turned and began walking away.

"Wait! Hold on!" Christopher said, but Lucas didn't stop. Christopher took a quick, deep breath and let out an aggravated exhale while helping his next customer.

"Ariana, Martel, can you guys watch my cart?" He hated to ask at this particular time but felt he had no choice. The previous day's events and reflections had piqued his curiosity with Lucas. And besides, he was now on a brave quest, and nothing should stand in the way of it.

"What? Now?" Ariana exclaimed.

"Yeah, I know. Please? I'll owe you," he said with a smile.

"Oh, really. I'm going to hold you to it!" she said, remarkably exhibiting a brightness under her irritation.

Martel added, "We got it. We'll figure it out. Do what you need to do." He positioned himself between his cart and Christopher's fruits and vegetables.

"Thanks Martel," said Christopher, and turning to Ariana, "Thank you."

Christopher shuffled between his cart and Ariana's baskets while Ariana silently mouthed, *You owe me,* to him. He half-smiled and nodded, and then focused on catching up with the blind man, who hadn't slowed his pace and was far down the street.

Christopher caught up and, saying nothing, slid in step beside and slightly behind him, matching his stride. As they neared the corner of the marketplace, Christopher once again saw the tall, odd woman who had accosted him yesterday emerge from the antique store. She was staring at him again. It appeared as if she and the shop owner had been waiting together, as the owner was standing just inside the doorway, also eyeing him. Even after the door closed behind the woman, the shopkeeper continued watching Christopher and Lucas approach through the door's unique, six-sided window.

Christopher hadn't seen her at all after yesterday morning, nor today until just now. It was almost as though she were hiding in the antique store and miraculously appearing only when he was to walk by. As he examined her craggy face and erratic movements, she appeared even more agitated than yesterday. Having difficulty suppressing his newfound ability to connect with the people and objects around him—the feeling from the dream experience last night—he could sense that beneath the intensity on the surface of her physical form there was a clarity to an anguish in her core, one he could just barely discern below the charged, chaotic energy she expressed. He had the impression that it was holding back a worry about the future, like knowing that an inevitable suffering was approaching and she wanted to prevent its torment.

As Christopher passed, she again spoke, this time her gruff voice containing the shrieking undertone of a cry for help.

"The darkness is coming! You need to be ready!" she said with a breathless intensity. "Tell me you'll be ready!"

Christopher held her abrasive gaze for a moment in an attempt to understand before breaking it off with a half-smile and nod and continuing after Lucas around the corner. It bothered him, not only because the constables usually removed from the square those who disturbed the marketplace merchants and customers, but also because all her attention and message seemed directed solely *at him*. He couldn't help but feel that there was something more to her than what he perceived, especially after spending some time with Lucas and his unnatural ability to *see*.

Lucas again walked like a sighted man, confident and strong. They marched for a few minutes, taking a different turn than they had yesterday, up a slight incline toward another area of the city, passing a school, some residential structures, and a number of drab, nondescript offices and shops. As they progressed, the number of people on the streets began to thin out, and Christopher noticed they were heading toward another one of the sections of the city his father had cautioned him about, and he was beginning to get a little nervous. It was one of the areas of gang-related activity, where criminals and thugs had carved out their territories. From what his customers had told him, the groups did not take kindly to strangers trespassing on their turfs.

He had heard that the activities in these districts—primarily gambling, theft, drugs, and prostitution—had slowly proliferated over the years with the implementation of more strict policing and the Church's more vocal admonitions for pious living. Although he agreed with the government's and the Church's moral precepts that opposed the gangs' activities, he also had heard rumors of high officials defying their own regulations and gambling or going to the brothels, which was a favorite forbidden topic of chatter in the square and made him question why these rules were in place if they were being violated by the very people who made them. The brothels in particular seemed to have thrived despite the stricter policing and had spread into other, less threatening areas of the city, like the place he and Lucas had visited yesterday.

What stood out in his mind now, though, was an incident that his father had told him about just before he had passed away.

Before gangs had fully taken over these neighborhoods, crime was less frequent and consolidated to a few small sections deep within the city, but the lawbreakers kept testing the constabulary by attempting to expand their turfs. One of the gangs had come to the popular marketplace, and the thugs had begun harassing the customers and intimidating the merchants, bullying them into giving their goods away and forcefully suggesting that the gang get paid for protection. At that time, constables were not as numerous as they were now and so did not have a regular presence in the market, as none of the gangs had yet boldly extended their reach so far from their tightly-controlled areas.

Christopher's father said that he had done what he had needed to do to get through the situation in the market safely, giving the brutes free food and even paying something for protection, but he emphasized to Christopher that these types of people should be avoided at all costs. They were dangerous and unscrupulous and would take advantage at any opportunity.

Christopher hadn't encountered a situation or people quite like that before. The closest thing he had experienced was when one of his customers had begun yelling at him, arguing that he shouldn't have to pay the given price because the produce was bad, and then the man just walked away with the goods. Christopher at first challenged and followed the man, but after their argument in the middle of the square, Christopher finally said, "Consider it my donation to your family," and walked back to his cart. He was still angry, but he had remembered his father's story. Fortunately, the man hadn't returned, and others who had witnessed the scene seemed to more frequently patronize

Christopher's cart, so the outcome wound up being positive for him anyway.

When the government tripled the constabulary soon after the gang incident in the market following pressure from the Church and an outcry from the residents of the city, the gangs primarily retreated to their home neighborhoods and flourished there, and it was these places that Christopher had never felt a need to venture into and so had kept his distance, until now.

With last evening's dream still present in his mind, his alertness was primed, and the connected feeling he had experienced during his nap on the porch now gave him the distressing, crawling sensation of being unwelcome in a foreign land.

Every movement and out-of-place sound received the full attention of his awareness—the brash swagger of a short, wiry man carrying an overstuffed sack, the muffled crash from behind a doorway, the cold, detached look from a woman leaning against the wall, the echo of the rattle of stones or dice being thrown in a darkened alley. An impending sense of dread dripped down his spine, as if he had stepped outside the Wall and into the dangerous, foreboding environment where survival was questionable. He found it interesting that the same feeling could come from inside the Wall as well.

Becoming more open and perceptive wasn't just relegated to good things; it seemed the connection had opened him up to feel *all* things more strongly than before. He undoubtedly preferred the lighter, more refined feeling of being connected with nature, like in his dream, than what he was feeling now in this neighborhood.

Lucas and Christopher strode more deeply into the area, watched carefully by a few shady-looking characters. As they continued, Christopher noticed that those who saw them walking together looked at him differently from how they looked at Lucas. They appeared angry and suspicious of Christopher but generally accepting of Lucas, which didn't make sense to Christopher, but then again, not a lot did.

"Hey!"

A gruff voice called out from a doorway they had just passed, spoken by a large man sitting in the shadows. Christopher hadn't noticed him, even in his heightened sensory state.

"This isn't a great neighborhood for a country mouse," the man said, looking at Christopher's apparently obvious rural appearance. Even though this wasn't one of the nicer neighborhoods in the city, the man sported a shirt with a collar and puffy sleeves, a mark of urban living compared to Christopher's old vest and collarless shirt, which was more common outside the city and in the fields.

Christopher didn't know how to respond, so he kept walking. *Yes, I know*, came to mind, but he didn't verbalize it. Lucas stopped a few steps ahead and looked back at the man, then turned forward and waited. Christopher had no choice but to stop as well. He needed to stay close to his guide.

The man stood up and Christopher turned to him as a young girl came out of the doorway behind the man, half hiding behind one of his massive legs. He reached around and picked her up, then stepped down the few steps to the street, towering over the farmer. Christopher's head was level with the girl's head in the man's arms. She had dark hair, and her clothes were dirty, likely from playing in the street. Her blue eyes held Christopher's gaze until the man spoke again.

"You'll be safer if you're more confident," he said.

Easy for you to say, Christopher thought. He was much smaller than the well-built man, although quite strong for his size from working the farm.

"Okay," Christopher said, "thanks." He tried to stand up a little straighter while glancing at Lucas, who hadn't moved.

The man's eyes followed his, and the man angled his head like he was trying to get a better look at the blind man. Christopher thought he saw a flash of recognition cross the man's face.

"Even if you have to fake it," the man said before turning and carrying the girl up the steps. Without looking back, he added, "Good luck," and he crossed the threshold and closed the door.

What a strange and random encounter, Christopher thought, but he heeded the man's advice nonetheless. As he and Lucas began walking again, he tried to feel more confident as the man suggested, and it indeed seemed to lessen some of the apprehension he was experiencing, even knowing that he was faking it. But he also recognized that some of that was likely due to being close to Lucas, whose strong, self-assured pace hadn't faltered since they left the marketplace. Christopher took a few quick steps to close the gap between them.

They turned down a narrow lane guarded by two large men who shot daggers from their eyes at Christopher as he passed. Halfway down the alley, Lucas stopped at the second nondescript doorway on the right, part of a low, ordinary, wooden building guarded by another large man. He had several sharp-edged tattoos that appeared to crawl from his forearms past his sleeves all the way up to his neck. His eyes were cold and detached, and they widened slightly when he saw Lucas.

"What do you want?" the man said gruffly.

"We're here to see him," Lucas said.

A heavy voice barked from behind the door. "Who is it?"

The man half turned and said through the door, "Looks like the blind guy with someone."

"Let 'em in," said the hidden voice.

The man stepped forward and stood directly in front of Lucas. "So, you're the Untouchable," he said. "You don't look so tough to me."

Untouchable? Christopher thought. He assumed the man didn't mean a lower-class status as a beggar but rather that he was not to be accosted. *How could he possibly know Lucas?*

The blind man stared forward and remained unmoving, as if he could see through the man's chest.

The man moved out of the way and let them pass, and Lucas led the way, opening the door and entering the structure. Christopher quickly followed.

It was dark and dirty inside what looked like an apartment, the gloomy atmosphere enhanced by the dingy, orange walls. Christopher could see an older, muscular man and a thin woman sitting at a table at the far end of the room, partially illuminated by the light from a nearby window. The man had heavy features, dark hair with veins of silver through it, a full beard that was also peppered with gray, and some of the same tattoos as the man outside. The light from the window traced the curved shadow of a deep scar around his left eye, and the knuckles on his right hand looked battered. Christopher immediately felt that this man had power, physical and otherwise, and was someone he would have wanted to avoid.

The woman, on the other hand, was very different, *felt* very different. She was leaning over the table on her elbows when Lucas and Christopher entered. It was difficult to tell in the dim light, but Christopher thought he could see the faded discolorations of healing bruises just above her wrists, and the long, dark hair that fell in front of her face may have been trying to hide the remnants of a black eye. She glanced up at the two visitors, and Christopher wasn't sure how he could tell, but the blank look on her face belied a sense of fear underneath. He wondered if she was a willing participant in whatever discussion was occurring.

"So, who are you?" the bearded, tattooed man said slowly at his visitors, his smooth, deep voice resonating off the walls. There was something about how he said it, the measured pacing of the words, that totally controlled the room. He was clearly someone who was used to being in charge.

Christopher could feel his face redden as fear trickled up his body. He couldn't tell who the man at the table was looking at, but he assumed it was himself, because if Lucas was known as the Untouchable, then somehow the people here knew something about him.

Christopher tried to resurrect some confidence, but it was elusive in the man's commanding presence. He glanced at the blind man, who stood motionless and silent.

"I'm a friend of his," Christopher said, trying to answer confidently, hoping that being associated with Lucas would generate some goodwill.

"Yeah, he's everybody's friend," the man said sarcastically. "Try again."

Christopher wasn't sure what kind of answer the man was looking for. "Uh, I'm a farmer, and I sell my goods in the market." His voice came out thin and cracked, not the level of confidence he wanted to express.

The man shook his head. "Try again."

Christopher furrowed his brow in puzzlement. "Um, I'm a citizen of the Territories?"

The man scoffed and the woman at the table next to him glanced downward. "Let me guess . . . a 'law-abiding citizen of the Territories,'" he said mockingly, marking the air with his fingers as he said it. "No." He paused. "Like the rest of them, you're a sheep."

Christopher shuffled in place, swallowed, and didn't say anything more.

The man stood up slowly. "Let me tell you something, *farmer*. I've seen what so-called upstanding and law-abiding people have done." He took a step around the side of the table towards Christopher as his deep voice rolled across the room. "I grew up here. This neighborhood used to be like all the others—clean, safe, flourishing." He opened his arms wide with the last word as he took another step. "But then the Territory Governors decided to dump all the lawbreakers here once they had served their sentences." He took another step. "Because they wanted to keep the delinquents out of the neighborhoods *they* chose." Another step. "So, over time, what do you think happened?" He paused and stood in place.

Christopher said nothing, hearing about this for the first time and mesmerized by the man's dominance of the scene. He felt the hollowness of fear low in his stomach.

"You see, criminals will be criminals," the man said, resuming his slow walk. "That is their nature. They don't know how to do anything else." He took another step. "So, as this district deteriorated with crime and wasn't given any help from the government," another step, "I decided that the best thing for this neighborhood was to control the criminals." Another step. "Because the government was only contributing to the problem." Another. "That man," he looked at Lucas, and Christopher followed his glance, "helped me see what I needed to do." Another step. "Now *I* run everything around here, and crime is down and everyone is better off."

He was now standing directly in front of Christopher, just inches from his face.

"I know who I am," the man said, drilling into Christopher with his dark, piercing eyes. "So, who are you, *farmer*?" The word dripped with condescending judgment.

Christopher swallowed and again glanced at Lucas, looking for help. He couldn't express anything with the man's proximity and dominating presence sucking out any remaining will that he had. He hoped the shaking he felt inside wasn't visible.

The man possessed Christopher's gaze for another minute before breaking off and walking back to the table. Once again seated, he waited another minute for an answer, but none came. Christopher was speechless. A part of his mind was struggling to integrate what the man had said about the Territory Governors into his own knowledge, experience, and beliefs about them, but that quickly gave way to full attention to his current, precarious situation.

The man leaned back in his chair. "You're nothing," he said, answering his own question. "You're going about your days clueless about what's really going on, and that makes you a sheep." He leaned forward over the table and growled, "And sheep shouldn't just walk into a wolf's lair."

The man glared at Christopher, saying nothing more. Christopher felt there was nothing he could say that would calm the man's intensity, so he just stood there as the feeling of dread crawled over him. He glanced again at Lucas, frustrated that he wasn't helping, and then at the woman at the table, who was still looking at him with an uneasy, distressed expression. He didn't know what to do.

After making him suffer in silence for what felt like an eternity but was probably just a few seconds, the man slowly snarled, "Who are you and why are you here?"

Christopher still said nothing. Even if he could find the words, he probably couldn't utter them. Fear had rendered him mute. His mind raced for answers that would pacify the man, but it came up empty. Lucas was of no help as he continued to stand there silently, letting Christopher take the full force of the man's ire.

Breaking the apparent standoff, the man stood up quickly, kicking his chair back. This surprised the woman next to him, who went from leaning lazily on her elbows to sitting upright in her chair, looking directly at Christopher with her anxious eyes half hidden behind her cascading hair. *Do something*, she seemed to say with both her expression and her energy.

Christopher was frozen with fear. He had encountered irritated and even angry people before, but he couldn't recall ever being confronted with this level of hostility. Even if he could, he knew that getting angry in return would be exceedingly dangerous. He searched for something to say.

After a long pause on the receiving end of the tattooed man's animosity, he remembered the past situation with the customer who hadn't paid, as well as his father doing what he had needed to in order to escape the gang in the marketplace safely. So, Christopher said with as much confidence he could muster, "I don't know why I'm here."

The man took a deep breath and stared at him, slowly nodding. "An honest answer," he said. "Something rare around here."

Christopher again looked at Lucas, who could very well have been a statue. But after a moment, the blind man turned purposefully to look at him with deep, black eyes that Christopher could barely make out in the dark room, but they were certainly not their usual milky, off-white color because their blackness reflected the light from the window at the far end of the space.

And Christopher understood.

The thoughts came fast and furiously. He remembered his father coaching him on how to handle tough customers, teaching by example as he deftly took the negativity out of tense situations, treating customers like royalty but also standing firm to the principles Christopher grew up with, even if it meant sacrificing some goods, money, or pride. "When you know who you are, the rest becomes easy," his father had said.

He recalled his mother standing up for a quiet woman from a poor and rough part of the city—like where he was now—who was being harassed by a constable, which caused her to be written up, threatening the family's permit to sell in the city.

And he remembered his father telling him to give something to the blind man every day, no matter what.

Christopher felt a surge of understanding rush into his mind. He could tell that the people in this place, this section of the city, viewed themselves as different from others, and they reveled in it. At the same time, he saw that much of the rest of the populace, people like himself not from this area, considered those from here different as well. Each side held fast to its prejudices of the other, however they were defined. The barrier to seeing what they had in common was identical; each group simply perceived their own side of it, thereby remaining stuck in their thinking and sustaining the wall between them.

By example, Christopher's parents had instilled in him a sense of acceptance of others that he was just now realizing the depths of. They were willing to sacrifice to help those unlike themselves, whoever they were and wherever they came from. And he realized that it stemmed from something deep within, but not from thoughts or fearful emotions. It was, as his father had said, knowing who he was, which came from recognizing the common thread of connectedness he had experienced the previous evening. Although everyone was different, on a deeper level they were all connected whether they wanted to be or not, and to focus on the differences that the world presented to the eyes would be to overlook what made them all the same.

With these thoughts, Christopher's rigid, fearful demeanor melted as he looked into the blind man's eyes. Newly and genuinely confident and self-empowered, he turned his attention back to the couple at the table and gazed not at the bearded man, who fell outside his sight. He was looking at the woman as he heard himself say, "Ma'am, are you okay?"

The bearded man exploded in a rage, shouting obscenities and telling him to get out or suffer the consequences, but Christopher barely heard him. His eyes were locked onto the woman's eyes, *feeling* her somehow. It was as if he had tunnel vision with his whole being, not just through his eyes, with the focus on who she really was underneath her appearance.

The woman nodded imperceptibly as her worried bearing eased, despite the outburst occurring next to her. Christopher got the sense that indeed she was okay, or was going to be okay, even though she seemed to have a tense and traumatic dynamic with the gang leader. He somehow felt that simply asking the question had taken her briefly out of the bearded man's domineering prison of control.

With Christopher still staring at the woman and the tattooed man bellowing threats, Lucas said, "It's time to go," and turned toward the door. Christopher broke his gaze with the woman, looked at the dark man dispassionately, and followed Lucas out the door and onto the street. Once outside and walking back the way they came, Christopher snapped out of his concentrated focus and a rush of delayed fear arose. He nervously looked over his shoulder to see if the bearded man or those outside the door were coming after them.

What was I thinking? he thought. *Why did I say that?* But even while asking himself those questions, a deeper part of him really wasn't afraid. He knew that what he had asked the woman was exactly what he had needed to say and exactly what she had needed to hear.

Lucas and Christopher zigzagged their way back down the alleys and streets toward the marketplace. They moved swiftly, not in an anxious manner, but one that had purpose and didn't leave room for conversation. At one point, they found themselves walking down a busy thoroughfare lined with shops and lodging houses.

"Not in my house!" a man shouted from above and ahead of them. There were many terraces and open windows from where the outcry could have come. A moment later, a visibly irate man stepped out onto a balcony in front of them and threw a collection of papers over the railing. They rained down on the pedestrians in the street like large pieces of confetti, with most pages instantly being stepped on and mangled in the mud and dirt under their feet.

Christopher stopped and picked up one of the sheets that had landed in front of him. It was yellowed with age and appeared more worn than the other pages that had fallen. Reading the only two words on the page, he paused in thought, then decided to fold it along its existing creases and tuck it in his pocket.

Turning and looking up to where the papers were thrown from, the angry man had been replaced by a girl with red hair who was standing at the railing watching him. When their eyes met, Christopher felt a connection of some sort, something profound that resonated with him that he couldn't explain. She seemed upset and on the verge of tears, but underneath her evident suffering Christopher could feel a sense of wonder and curiosity—similar to himself as a child—albeit seemingly confined, unexpressed, and fearful. He felt the urge to tell her that it was all going to be okay.

A muffled shout came from behind her, and she quickly withdrew from the balcony, went inside, and closed the terrace doors. Christopher stood staring up at where she had been, then looked down at the scattered pages along the street, wondering what the commotion was about. As he leaned over to pick up another sheet, he realized he had fallen way behind Lucas, who had not slowed his pace, so he hurried to catch up with him.

~

Upon returning to their common street with the merchants selling foods and wares, Lucas simply sat down cross-legged in his regular spot without saying a word, leaving Christopher to stand there awkwardly for a moment before speaking.

"Uh, why . . . what was that about? Why did you need to take me there?" he asked, even though he suspected he wasn't going to receive an answer.

"We'll have another outing tomorrow," Lucas said.

"We'll see," said Christopher defiantly after a pause, not happy with the lack of communication. If he was going to be ordered around and taken to dangerous areas, he wanted a good reason for it.

He was about to turn to go back to his cart when he remembered a question he wanted to ask. "Why did they call you 'Untouchable'?"

Lucas paused before answering. "I helped him see at one point, and what he is now he attributes partially to me, but he didn't use what he learned wisely."

Christopher nodded. That made sense, the gang leader feeling some kind of indebtedness to Lucas and so renders him untouchable by his gang.

"What did you help him see?" Christopher asked.

"The same thing as you," the blind man said.

Christopher stared at Lucas as the surprising answer swept over him. He still couldn't fully articulate what he had experienced recently with the unusual events, dreams, and feelings, but now he began to worry that he could wind up like the gang leader, living dangerously with an angry and bitter outlook at the world. *Is that my fate?* he thought.

"You'll see," Lucas said, and Christopher wondered once again if the words were spoken aloud or just in his head.

His brain was already muddled with various questions about the blind man—*Why did he want to take me there? What's his angle? What's with the eye changes? Is he really blind? Is there magic going on?*—none of which really had an answer at this time, and this last exchange just added to Christopher's confusion. He also knew that although these were questions relating to his quest to find the answers to his father's puzzling *someday* comment, he had today's powerful and profound experience to think about now as well, which added yet another stony weight to his mind.

He headed back toward Ariana and Martel, lost in thought, almost walking into a few people as he struggled to make sense of the outing. He approached Martel's cart and started to move behind it before coming face to face with his grinning friend.

Ariana and Martel burst out laughing as Christopher confusingly took a step back before remembering that they had switched places that morning.

"Ha-ha. Very funny," he said, forcing a smile as he maneuvered to get behind his own goods.

"Sometimes it's just fun to watch you," Ariana said.

She and Martel laughed again, and Christopher joined in half-heartedly.

"Thanks for taking care of things again. I owe you."

"Yes, you do," Ariana said with a glint in her eye.

"It was all her," Martel said.

Nodding and looking at her, Christopher said, "Really, thanks Ariana." He realized he didn't say her name that often.

"You're welcome, Christopher," she said, returning the courtesy. Hearing her say his name brought a smile to his face. "So, where'd you go? You weren't gone that long."

He took a deep breath to buy time before responding. He still didn't know what it was all about and didn't want to complicate things by sharing too much of the experience before he had some answers. She would likely have the same questions he was grappling with. What happened on the surface, however, he could talk about.

"The blind man took me to meet one of the gang leaders, and it was . . . intense," he said.

"Really? Why would he do that?" she asked. "Wait. First of all, how could he *take* you? He's blind." It was not an unreasonable question, and it warranted her confused look.

Christopher chuckled. "Yes, he is, but he has some sort of second sight or something. He can get around pretty well."

"Wow."

She disengaged for a moment to accept payment from a customer who had been browsing her flowers.

"Apparently, he's trying to help me learn something," Christopher said when she turned back to him.

"Like why your father told you to give him something every day?" Martel asked. Martel seemed to be focused on Christopher's quest as much as Christopher was himself.

"Perhaps in some way. It's not that obvious right now. It's . . . subtle, like there are layers to the answer and it'll take some time to figure out."

"As I said before, it sounds mysterious," Ariana said.

"Yes, it is a little bit," Christopher said.

"Ah, the journey to discover the truth is encountering difficulties!" Martel said. "How fitting. We trust our intrepid adventurer will find the fortitude to prevail!"

Ariana laughed and Christopher shook his head and looked at him. "Do you ever stop?"

Martel gave him a huge smile. "If I stopped, I wouldn't be me."

Christopher chuckled and nodded. "That's for sure."

"So, what happened with the gang leader?" Ariana asked.

Christopher didn't know how to fully convey what had occurred, but he attempted to anyway. "Lucas—that's the blind man's name—took me to meet him, and he said that the government had essentially made his neighborhood worse by relocating criminals there. That's why crime thrives there more than in other places."

"I haven't heard that before," Ariana said.

"Me neither," said Martel.

"Neither had I," Christopher said. "Then something strange happened, and we had to get out of there quickly."

"Strange, like what?" Ariana asked.

"Just . . . strange. Still trying to figure it out myself. I'll let you know when it's clearer."

"Okay, no problem, whenever," Ariana said, clearly picking up on his hesitancy. "I'm here. Anytime you want to talk." She turned back to her flowers, then spun around and looked him in the eyes. "So, nothing enlightening yet with the blind man?"

Christopher looked across the street at Lucas through the people milling about the square. Keeping his eyes on him and with his father's words echoing in his head, Christopher said, "Not enough to answer anything yet, but I'm going to figure it out." He looked at her. "I'll let you know."

"You better," Martel said. "As your trusty companions on this quest, we have a right to share in the glory of your achievement."

Christopher smiled and nodded. "You'll know when I know."

Martel turned to attend to a customer lingering in front of his cart. Christopher heard him describing different spices in his enthusiastic yet smooth and persuasive manner that always seemed to convince shoppers to buy more than they probably needed. With business still to be had, Christopher focused on a woman who had paused briefly in front of his cart to look at his produce.

He remained partially lost in thought over the next hour despite selling and exchanging pleasantries with his buyers. He felt that everything around him was more serious, almost sad, which was discordant to his normally amiable demeanor. He hoped others didn't notice, especially Ariana.

Without warning and jarring everyone in the square, a piercing shriek emanated from the loudspeaker on the corner as it came to life. A low hum followed, and three rising tones once again spread across the marketplace toward the many upturned faces.

This is a Level 2 Warning by the Council of Governors. We have evidence that the enemy force has now fully assembled and may be preparing to march toward the Territories. Level 2 protocols are now in place. Please see your zone's manual for the necessary steps you must take for your designated area. This is a Level 2 Warning.

As before, the message repeated two more times followed by three rising tones. Christopher looked at Ariana and Martel, and their knitted brows reflected the same surprise and concern as others in the marketplace, and probably the same that Christopher himself showed. It had been years since there had been a second warning, so the surprise that it wasn't an announcement cancelling the first one apparently unnerved many folks. Nervous chatter exploded throughout the square again.

"Do you guys know what the Level 2 protocols are?" Ariana asked, looking over at Christopher and Martel. Martel shrugged and looked at Christopher for an answer.

"I think it's similar to Level 1," Christopher said. "Keep an eye out for anything abnormal." He chuckled uneasily to himself. What he had experienced the past few days certainly wasn't ordinary.

"Well, the warnings aren't normal, so I'm noticing them," Martel said, apparently trying to lighten the mood. It worked, and all three were able to laugh away some of the tension the announcement had brought.

"I guess we'll have to wait and see what happens next," Christopher said, wondering if anything else could surprise and challenge him more than what he had already experienced the past few days.

Ariana nodded, and the three turned to focus on their trades.

~

The market buzzed with activity and gossip as the day waned, and Christopher left the city early after selling out again. The warnings had been good for business, and he thought that maybe, just maybe, if it continued, he'd be able to pull himself out of his financial hole and pay his overdue taxes.

He was reflective all afternoon as he worked on the farm, and the introspection carried into the evening. It was more ruminating than he was used to, and the questions spinning in his head took their toll and mentally exhausted him.

Besides the ones about Lucas, the experience with the bearded gang leader and the quiet, submissive woman unsettled him, and he thought about his verbalized question to her, *Ma'am, are you okay?* Other questions arose from this: *Why did I ask her that? Why did I ignore the dangerous man? Why did I feel calm when I asked it, despite the threat? Why did it seem that she felt more at ease just by hearing my question? How did I know she was really okay?*

The answers to the questions all seemed to point to the blind man and what he had somehow conveyed to Christopher when his eyes changed color. It was magical, or mystical, and it had brought him to a place where he could stand confidently and say what he did in the face of the difficult circumstances.

The beggar was an enigma, but he appeared to be helping Christopher realize things about himself that he might have never seen without the assistance. Whatever it was, Lucas was bringing a new perspective to Christopher's practical and commonsense way of seeing the world.

The gang leader had painted him as a sheep, and Christopher wondered if there was some truth to that because of his belief in the integrity of the government and his willful and perhaps blind following of its rules. He knew nothing about what the gang leader said the government did to that neighborhood, but if true, it was contrary to his understanding and experience of what he thought was the government's good and moral protections of the citizens of the Territories.

He also felt a new, more receptive perspective about people vastly different from himself, seeing now how they were shaped by their circumstances as much as he was. Although their lives and paths may be different than his, he could feel himself becoming more accepting of them, in part due to having remembered his parents' actions that treated all people the same regardless of their race, status, or occupation.

Twice now he had followed Lucas, at first reluctantly but knowing it was something he had to do. And both outings had been exceptionally eye-opening; he felt greatly changed by the experiences. Something in him had shifted, was still shifting, and he felt a greater clarity with how he looked at the world, even as his challenges continued. He hoped any additional time with the blind man would increase that clarity but also help him find a way out of his difficulties.

The past days had brought some of his fears and anxieties to the surface—frustration, nervousness, dread, helplessness—which had reflected concretely in his experiences, but he was able to find a path through them, no doubt because of what Lucas had added to the encounters. He had been able to face his emotions directly, whether by freely choosing to or being encouraged to like with Shae, and he was finding that they were simply fragile facades, empty threats with no real foundation of strength. Their structures had begun moving and crumbling around and within him. However, he knew he still had a long way to go if he was to be rid of them all, but at least some kind of transformation had started. He took comfort in the fact that perhaps there really was a way out of his predicament with the farmstead, not to mention what he could accomplish if his fears and inhibitions could miraculously vanish.

But as he felt like he was overcoming some of his fears, they were being replaced by the government warnings that now sat uncomfortably in the forefront of his mind. Yes, Level 2 still wasn't an imminent threat, but it was very rare to even have a second warning, so it bothered him and got him reflecting on what might be coming next.

After a few minutes, finally having had enough of thinking about it all, he closed his eyes and shook his head, trying to get rid of his thoughts like a wet dog shaking off water. He sat quietly on the porch and looked out over the fields as dusk encased the landscape, feeling a deep, incoming sense of peace, something he hadn't felt since well before his father had died. It was more than simply calming his thoughts; he was beginning to feel comfortable, more present, and accepting in his own skin. Although irritated with Lucas earlier, he now could see that the result of the two days of events with the blind man had left him feeling fundamentally more like the Christopher he had always seen himself as but never really was. He smiled to himself, happy with the unfamiliar path he was now traveling, even relishing for the first time the possibility of the unknown before him.

As he stood up to go inside some time later, he remembered the folded piece of paper in his pocket. Taking it out, he unfolded it and read the two words again. He wasn't entirely sure what to make of them but felt they were important for some reason. Proceeding inside, he put the paper in a drawer in his desk and got ready for bed.

He lay down and closed his eyes, anticipating falling asleep quickly in this pleasant, relaxed, and contented state, but questions began to creep back into his mind, and he couldn't ignore them. Tossing and turning, the swirling thoughts in his head obscured a faint rumbling that rolled over the landscape.

The Grand Wall was moving again.

Anna

That was intense, Anna thought, thinking of Christopher's experience with the gang leader in the rough part of town. She only had offhand knowledge of the different sections of the city and certainly hadn't ever been to a district like that. Her parents would never allow it, and now she wouldn't even dream of willingly going to such a dangerous area. She began to think that maybe the rules she lived under were in place not simply to control her but to keep her safe; they just came from her parents' perspective, which was different from how she viewed the world.

She could see this differing viewpoint in the stories told by her constable father about following people he thought were suspicious because of what they looked like or how they dressed. That bothered her because she tried to treat everyone the same regardless of who they were, where they came from, or how they appeared. She was encouraged that Christopher had a lesson that validated a similar perspective rather than her father's.

And thinking about it now, she realized that what Christopher had described was like what she experienced at school, with differing groups of classmates sometimes clashing with each other, usually over silly, judgmental things like what they liked to study, what area of the city they were from, or what they wore. Each group seemed stuck in their views, sometimes tormenting others until a teacher stepped in to stop it. She liked to think adults grew out of that kind of behavior, but perhaps they didn't.

She flipped to the last page in the leather covering and ran her fingers over the wrinkled, weathered paper with the two words of old, blurry ink on it, wondering if it could be the sheet Christopher brought home. If it was, it would mean that the story was true, or at least some of it was. The possibility tingled her with excitement, and she couldn't wait to find out.

Turning back to where she had left off, she whispered the title of the next chapter, *Third*, and continued reading.

Third

The shadows feel their way about the theater as awareness expands beyond the stage. Sensing the light's work in their performances, they bring forth their role's purpose while masquerading through the shadowlands.

~

Christopher awoke feeling mentally exhausted, his questions and concerns having interrupted his sleep, and they continued to tumble incessantly in his mind. He kept to his regular morning routine, however, but struggled to do it with any sense of efficiency. After looking over the produce he had packed in the crates last night, he remembered that the government's warnings had initiated demand for nonperishable goods, so he went to the cellar and brought up what canned and jarred items he could fit in the leftover space in the cart. Fortunately, he was consistent in keeping a good inventory of those goods and had plenty for himself and for several days of selling in the market. Once he had filled his cart, he began his trek to the city, pulling the weighty load solemnly behind him.

He walked with his head down, the ruminating in his mind bearing down on his neck and shoulders like an oxen's yoke. Although his thoughts started off muddled and abstract, they became more defined as he continued to the city, and he began to reflect on his life in the family business.

He had come of age with it all around him, with his parents busy keeping the home, farm, and business in the market healthy and successful. An only child, he helped his mother around the house and often tagged along as his father tended the fields and sold the harvest in the city. He learned everything he could from them as he aged and matured into taking on more and more responsibilities, especially after his mother passed away.

With limited exposure to other vocations growing up, he naturally accepted his role as the son of farmers, as did others whose working family stations were fixed like his. He also recognized his value to the land, the community, and the Territories as a whole, as not everyone knew how to do what he and his family did. That gave him a certain level of satisfaction that he was fulfilling his duty, both as a son and a citizen.

Automatically assuming his family's line of work was expected, but it didn't always feel right to him. Now, he began to wonder why he and everyone he knew felt the need to follow in the work-related footsteps of their families without question.

And with that thought, a thin, fiery, long-buried tongue of resentment flickered in his stomach, a part of him that felt angry with his parents for forcing him into the family trade. The work wasn't forced as much as it was expected, but to a young man growing up, anything limiting his choices felt forced. Not that he had much choice; he wasn't trained in anything else, and besides, it was the family's position in society. Still, he wished he had had the opportunity to experience other kinds of work, especially occupations associated with new ideas, as his curious mind always enjoyed trying to figure things out. But at the same time, he also really *liked* working with the land and being in nature much of the time, so even as his internalized anger rose, he felt conflicted about being constrained to his role as a farmer.

He knew that everything his parents had done they had done for him and for the benefit of the Territories as best they knew how given the circumstances. With their premature deaths, he felt the pressing obligation to continue the farm and the family's role, especially after a serious, hard-faced government official visited and strongly encouraged it after his father died, "for the sake of the Territories," he said. Nevertheless, despite taking on the grand responsibility of running the farm, there lingered a resentment that things could have been different.

As he walked, the heated emotion continued to build, toward his father especially, manifesting as remembrances of the frustrations from the sometimes-abrasive nature of his father's directives as they worked together. The irritations came up easily, lining up like obedient schoolchildren in his mind as if order would reduce their influence. But the fact that the anger was there in the first place meant it was already comfortably housed within him and was simply displaying its unsightly face from the windows of its shadowy dwelling place. How could Christopher be mad at his father, who had prepared him so well for his current existence but had died all too early?

There were times in the intervening years after his father had passed when these fiery emotions had decided they needed oxygen, as if remaining quietly in the background for too long would snuff them out permanently and leave an even greater hole in his center. He tried to isolate himself when he felt them smoldering in order to save others from the potential eruption, and the resulting silent screams, tears, beaten walls, and the occasional broken item indicated that this had been the right choice. In one sense, he felt better after its expression, as it seemed there needed to be a physical manifestation of the destruction he was feeling within before it overflowed its limited holding tank and its toxic contents further seeped into his body.

But witnessing it come forth also fed the lingering frustration of never quite being free from it, even though the outbursts temporarily released some of the internal pressure.

What he was feeling now, once again, was that *he* was to blame for his father's accident, and the anger at himself—the hot flame licking at his heart and mind with its forked tongue—made his heavy walk to the marketplace even more difficult. But he submitted himself to the penance, for on some level he still felt he deserved it.

After some time wallowing in this self-created furnace of dark emotions, he thought about what he had learned the past few days: things were not always what they seemed. With enormous effort, he turned down the heat on which his anger and self-blame simmered and tried to think his way past them.

He considered his transcendent experience on the road a few days before a reminder of the many times his mind went to ideas greater than his current reality. He knew there was more to who he was—the last two days had certainly showed him that—but still he was stuck doing what he had always done in this world. Except for the events the past few days, his routine was as deep as the grooves in which his cart traveled on the dirt road. *Is this my plight?* he thought as he trudged forward.

As if the heavens were answering the question with a prank, one of the wheels of his cart ran into a deep rut at the side of the road, turning the heavy load so that it leaned over almost to tipping. His stacked goods teetered precariously but remained contained within the wood slats that made up the sides of the cart. Christopher sighed deeply—it's not like this hadn't happened before—and he proceeded to unload a few of the heavier crates to reduce the weight before trying to release the wheel and level the cart.

As he lifted and pushed, his mind went to Shae and then to Ariana. He and Shae had shared a beautiful, intimate connection, but he knew it was fleeting, as it didn't have any history or the potential of his relationship with Ariana. He had known Ariana for far longer, and even though he had opened up and shared deeply with Shae, no single-day bond with her could erase or even compare to how he felt about Ariana. So, he felt some semblance of guilt about his time and experience with Shae, like he had been a part of a betrayal.

"Come on. Let's give it a go."

Christopher turned around to see Vincent, a tradesman who was occasionally in the marketplace, leave his own cart to come to Christopher's aid, leaning his large, muscular frame against the edge of the tilted, wooden platform. Together, they gave one big heave, and the cart was free and back on the road.

"Thank you, Vincent," Christopher said, breathing heavily from the effort.

"No problem," said Vincent, breathing normally, a testament to his strength and stamina. "Gives me a chance to return the favor."

Vincent wasn't married, and he was known to catch the eye of the ladies. Christopher had looked after his goods a few weeks ago when he had snuck away from the square for what Christopher assumed was a midday dalliance.

"I think your situation was a bit more fun than this," Christopher said, chuckling.

Vincent laughed.

"Will we see you today in the market?" Christopher added.

"Not today. I'm laying a new floor at one of the Governor's places. That's why I have the good stuff today." He pointed back at his laden cart filled with finely engraved and colored tile. He was an expert stone and tile craftsman.

"Looks nice. Hope it goes smoothly," Christopher said. "Thanks for the lift."

Vincent slapped him vigorously on the shoulder, picked up his cart, and went on his way. Christopher reloaded and balanced the crates he had removed and followed.

~

When Christopher arrived at the market, Martel was speaking with a nearby vendor but had placed his cart where it was yesterday, leaving the space next to Ariana's usual spot open. Christopher slid his cart into the space and set up his goods robotically, still feeling mentally and emotionally scrambled. When Ariana arrived next to him, her cheery disposition snapped him out of his inner unrest.

"Good morning!" she exclaimed.

How could he *not* be affected by her? Always in the mornings she came bearing an outlook of that which she sold, untainted by the happenings of the night before or previous day, nurturing an ever-present and joyful attitude and living life as if the dawn brought her new eyes every day.

"Good morning," he replied with as much enthusiasm he could muster in an attempt to equal her energy. His morning reflections and physical heaviness, however, dampened any excitement.

"Did you see that the Wall moved again?" she said.

"Really?" He hadn't noticed on his way into the city as he was looking down for most of the journey. Indeed, seeing it now far off in the distance, he could just barely tell that it was further away. "Hmm."

"That's it? 'Hmm?' Aren't you curious why?"

"Oh, I am. I guess right now I just have a lot on my mind and . . ." He trailed off.

"And?" Her look begged for him to continue.

"And, well, for some reason, I think the more I find out about my *quest*, the more I might find out about the Wall."

Ariana looked over at Lucas, then turned back to Christopher. "You think they're related?"

"Well, they're both pretty mysterious, aren't they?"

"I suppose so. Anyway, how are you doing today? You seemed a bit off yesterday afternoon after what you went through."

With his foggy brain affecting his ability to come up with a suitable response that wouldn't get into the details again, he demurred with a question. "Oh? How so?" But he liked that she had noticed.

"You seemed . . . well, you seemed detached from reality, like you lost your head," she said. "Not 'lost your head' like going crazy, but like you actually accidentally left your head at home."

Christopher chuckled. "Yeah, I was feeling a bit like that but wound up feeling good later after some reflection. Today, though, I'm just not feeling that great."

"Oh? What's wrong?"

"I don't know. I just feel heavy everywhere, like I've had the wind knocked out of me."

Ariana pouted, and it reminded Christopher of his mother when she had tried to sympathize with him when he had hurt himself or was sick. "Well, after what you told us and with the second warning, I'm not surprised. The experience with the gang leader sounded like it was a lot to go through. If there's anything I can do . . .," she said, smiling, then turned back to her flowers.

Christopher liked that she was trying to understand what he was going through, which helped his mood. He knew he was presenting a gloomier disposition today, and as someone who he knew liked to take care of those who were hurting, he assumed she would be feeling as though she wasn't doing enough.

He also had the feeling that his heaviness might be due to letting go of aspects of the old Christopher on his path to a newly-becoming Christopher, like a snake shedding its skin to allow for a fresh one to take its place. Unfortunately, as with a snake, it was an uncomfortable and stress-inducing process that would leave him raw for a while. Not knowing where in the process he now was, he hoped he could emerge as the new Christopher on the other side of it soon. His strengthening connection with her was resonating on a deeper level, and he could easily see himself safely and securely enveloped in her supporting arms and uplifting energy. Then again, maybe that's exactly what he needed right now to help him get through the feeling of molting.

~

There was much chatter again in the marketplace about the warnings and the Grand Wall moving, with customers engaging with the merchants and each other to express their fears and anxieties, as if talking about them would make them disappear. It helped Christopher sell much of his nonperishable inventory early as people stocked up on goods to prepare for whatever might come next.

Mid-morning, during a lull in the crowd, he felt a bit better and strolled over to Lucas to give him an apple. Lucas accepted it, stood up, and said, "Come with me." Again, it was inevitable that Christopher would follow.

Because the blind man had said yesterday that he would take Christopher on another adventure, Christopher had already spoken with Ariana and Martel about covering for him again. They reiterated their desire to know more about what was going on with Lucas, and Christopher promised he would share more when he returned. He could sense they were hiding a little annoyance at being asked to help again.

"Where are we going today?" asked Christopher as he and Lucas started walking.

"To the cathedral," replied the blind man.

"Why?"

Lucas didn't answer. As with their previous outings, he was reserving his words for when they were most essential. Christopher knew at this point that any lack of response meant that he probably needed to figure it out for himself, but he found it frustrating.

As they approached the corner of the square, once again Christopher saw the unstable, messy-haired woman emerge from the antique store, and she looked even more agitated than before. She was shaking and breathing intensely as Christopher and Lucas approached. Christopher tried to give her a wider berth this time, but she lunged at him and grabbed his arm with both hands and held him. He noticed a strange symbol tattooed on the back of each hand.

"The darkness is coming! What are you going to do? You need to be ready! You need to see! We need you! The world needs you! You can't let the shadows win! The darkness is coming, and *you* are our only hope!"

Startled at her aggressiveness, he pulled away as two constables who had heard her outburst came running over. They forcefully grabbed her as one said, "We'll take care of this."

As they started to haul her away, she reached out and grabbed Christopher again, pulling him in and holding on more tightly, and she said in a hushed tone, *"Before the ring you'll kneel. Whether you live or die is up to you. You need to be ready."*

She held Christopher's gaze for as long as she could until the constables managed to wrestle her away, leaving him staring at her as they marched her down a side street and away from the people in the square.

He was rattled, not so much because of being grabbed—it had happened on occasion and he was able to easily extricate himself from the situations—but because what she had said, as senseless as it sounded, had somehow found some foothold in his mind. He didn't know what she was talking about, but her words echoed anxiously in his core.

Christopher caught up to Lucas and asked him, "What's going on with her? She seems really unbalanced."

"She has trouble here," he said. "She's better off in another world."

"Another world?"

"Yes."

"What do you mean, another world?" Christopher asked.

"There's more to this world than what you perceive."

"Like what?"

"You'll see," said the blind man.

Upon hearing those words, Christopher felt a presentiment of what was to come. It was elusive, but it was as though a distant realm was opening that would put his life into perspective. It was the same feeling he had had a few days ago but with an additional tingling of excitement in anticipation of what it could bring.

"And what about what she said, that I need to be ready for the darkness? What does she mean?"

"You don't need to understand that right now."

"Okay," Christopher said hesitantly. "And what about the ring, that I'll kneel before the ring as if my life depends on it? What is that?"

"You'll figure it out . . . or you won't," Lucas said.

"Uh, that sounds ominous."

Lucas didn't say anything in response, and they kept to their pace.

Christopher continued. "I want to understand. I want to find the ring, if it exists. I want to be ready." They took a few more steps as the blind man said nothing. "Am I ready?"

"No."

Lucas's solitary word hit Christopher harder than he would have anticipated. With everything else that was going on, he didn't need one more thing to add to his distress. He couldn't deny that the unstable woman had introduced something into his awareness that he knew he was going to have trouble ignoring. His curiosity was too great and, of course, was he going to die if he wasn't ready? He asked directly.

"Am I going to die if I'm not ready?"

"In this world, it is the nature of the living to die. You are going to die whether you are ready or not."

Annoyed that the blind man wasn't giving him any helpful information, Christopher nudged the subject toward the Wall and asked, "Like those who go beyond the Wall?"

"How do you know they die when they go beyond the Wall?" Lucas asked in return, which left Christopher feeling that there was more to the rumors than what he had heard.

"They're never seen again, and it's dangerous outside the Wall, so that's the likely outcome. At least that's what everyone thinks," Christopher said.

"And what do *you feel?*" the beggar asked, emphasizing the last two words. Christopher noted that with the first stressed word, Lucas probably meant for him to not listen to others but rather to himself. And with the second, Christopher noted that Lucas switched the word from his question from *thinking* to *feeling*.

"I *feel* there's a great mystery about the Wall that I want to understand," Christopher said.

"Good."

"Like why it moves. It did again last night, you know."

"Yes."

"Why?"

"You'll see."

That was the third or fourth time the blind man had used those exact two words over the past few days, and Christopher was tired of the phrase already. It was annoyingly evasive.

He asked nothing further. Clearly, Lucas didn't want to give him any useful answers, instead leaving him with responses that only allowed his questions to persist.

They walked down the main streets, the sound of their footsteps eventually synchronizing with each other's. Christopher noticed that his stomach relaxed, and he could breathe more calmly and deeply as they continued.

Slowly making their way up the sloping hill to the city center, past the turns they had taken the previous two days to the other sections of the city, the streets became cleaner and the architecture older and grander.

Close to their destination, they passed by the city's detainment center, an oddly insubstantial building considering it was where people were taken for questioning and confinement after being arrested. A large sign with block letters spelling "Department of Enforcement of Government Operations" hung above the large, wooden door that served as the main entrance. The door seemed solid, but Christopher could see that the structure itself was not built to the same standards as many of the surrounding buildings. The sign, made of glass, also seemed tragically fragile given what the operations of the building represented: the strength, security, and enforcement of the laws of the Territories.

His only encounters with the constables of the city had been out in the streets, and they had generally been positive, although he knew they could be stern and rough when necessary as he had just witnessed. What little he had heard about the workings inside this building, however, made him certain he never wanted to experience detainment, which probably contributed to his typical rule-following behavior.

He and Lucas continued, passing by others on the street, and Christopher could already see and feel the occasional judgmental looks pointed in their direction. Neither he nor Lucas was dressed as most others, with Lucas in his plain, somewhat old and simple trousers and tunic and Christopher in his modest marketplace outfit, which, with his best pants and old vest, was essentially just a step above his normal farming clothes. This compared to the more formal, Sunday attire of others on the street and commonly in this part of the city—fine suits on the men, some with tails that indicated wealth, and extravagant dresses and bonnets on the women. Even the shopkeepers had newer and more polished clothes than what Christopher was wearing, although not to the richness of their customers.

They arrived at last at the vast center of the city, a large cobblestone square with the cathedral on one side opposite the government's primary executive building. Christopher remembered the first time he had been to the cathedral as a child with his father and recalled being astounded at the size and openness of the plaza and the impressiveness of the church. His visits, however, had become rather infrequent, and this was his first time back in close to a year.

The blind man slowed down and allowed Christopher to dictate their pace, and they strolled around the outside of the square, which was lined with high-end shops. They stopped when they got to the cathedral steps.

Christopher looked up, marveling at the elaborate architecture. He had always been fascinated by what human beings could build, and to him the towering structure reaching to the heavens reflected a faith in something so grand and magnificent that its source must be beyond this world.

The cathedral was built centuries ago—he didn't know exactly when—and the architecture reflected its age. It was certainly one of the oldest buildings in the city, said to be erected before the Wall was built, a time prior to external threats when peace reigned in the land. It must have taken many, many years to construct, as it was a colossal structure made of massive stone blocks standing as tall as a man, with intricate engravings rising as high as he could see.

Inside, enormous columns of carved stone supported the great, lofty ceiling, with the long arms of the arches coming together in the center directly above the pews. It looked as though a gargantuan, off-white spider had taken up residence and the stonemasons had built the cathedral around it to prevent it from leaving and rampaging the city. What was likely bright white when it was built had yellowed with age from the years of candle and incense smoke. Light streamed in through stained-glass images on all sides to illuminate the vast space, giving it an otherworldly feel from the varied colors that changed depending on the time of day and angle of the sun.

Side chambers held paintings depicting tales of the early years of the spread of religion, bucolic images of men and women receiving teachings and healings from the Perceiver, or Grand One, the individual who didn't start the Church but was its impetus. In them, the Perceiver was portrayed as larger than life, granting his divine touch to the faithful citizens of the land.

Christopher remembered enjoying the stories that accompanied the paintings when he was younger and attended services more frequently with his family, but as he aged he found them less compelling and eventually put them behind him. The themes most often emphasized the believers of the religion and the services the Church and its adherents provided, as if the scaffolding they had created around the Church's tenets were the only way to build faith, something Christopher's ongoing curiosity and penchant for discovery saw as limiting. And after his mother and then his father passed away and he took over all the responsibilities on the farm, he found himself unwilling to devote the effort to something he seemed to believe in less and less as time progressed, despite the societal pressures he faced to continue to attend.

The Church had been created by some of the Perceiver's followers to provide a way to access his grand perception, but Christopher felt the resulting dogma confining. As he had reflected on religious devotion over the years as his attendance dwindled, he found he rather liked sitting quietly and alone before a sculpture of the Perceiver instead of following a scheduled set of services that spent more time in reverence of the Grand One and the Church than encouraging living like the Perceiver had.

Perhaps that was why he didn't come here much anymore. Attending the services never resonated with him because they were prescribed by the organization that had been built *around* the source, the Perceiver, and didn't foster connecting with the source directly. He preferred his personal, non-religious connection to the Grand One. The doctrine the Church provided might be a method to get to a personal bond with and understanding of him, but it couldn't be the only path or a replacement for how each person demonstrated their unique beliefs.

Christopher also found that the government and societal pressure to conform to the Church's accepted practices added yet another layer of pressure to his life that he didn't need. So, his faith, where he devoted his energy in this realm of his life, bypassed any prescribed Church dogma and went into nurturing his individual connection with the Perceiver. But at this point, with his struggles with the farm and after what he had experienced so far this week, he didn't even know what he believed anymore.

The apse was the most decorative in the cathedral, with elaborate, silver-framed paintings on either side of a golden disk, which had sun-like rays emanating from its center. The polished disk served as a dazzling backdrop to an aged, wooden carving of the Perceiver, which hung in its center tilted downwards to face the pews, its feet shoulder width apart, arms outstretched to the sides, and head held high. There was something about the statue that spoke to Christopher.

The Perceiver, it was said, was the individual who had created the great city. He had transformed the nothingness of the desert into an oasis of community and endowed it with life. The legend was that his vision knew no bounds, that he could see everything that was, is, and would come to be.

The carving was very old and weathered—it had once been outside but was now more protected—which gave it a certain melancholic feeling. The face's features had smoothed over time, endowing it with a calm yet generic countenance exhibiting a perceptible sadness in its expression. The Perceiver looked like it could be anyone, or everyone, and Christopher wondered if that was part of the original carver's intent or whether it was due to being worn by the ravages of time. And wherever Christopher sat, it appeared as if the Perceiver was always looking directly at him due to the angle at which it was hung. He would have preferred to see it upright as it originally stood because he felt it would convey even more power.

The carving was both welcoming and unattainable, a combination that invited him in yet stood in a place he could only dream about. It was this dichotomy that he found fascinating, and it drew him back many times to the pews.

There were other ornate and opulent objects and sculptures in the apse, but they never grabbed Christopher's attention, as he was always focused on the Perceiver. He thought that the grandiose visual display around the carving was surely an attempt to recreate what those who designed the cathedral thought the Church's patrons wanted to see—a showcase of their wealth and presumed faith—but it seemed like a waste to him. Still, it was impressive in its demonstration.

Thinking about the interior, Christopher followed Lucas up the wide, stone steps. They passed through the open, oversized door and into the cavernous, hallowed space.

A flickering, yellow glow pervaded the expansive room, light from the hundreds of candles lining the perimeter. Looking around, Christopher once again marveled at the magnificence of the structure and display before him, but something within caused disparate questions and thoughts to tumble through his mind.

This is man's physical manifestation of something beyond comprehension. What are people really worshipping? It is extraordinary what faith can accomplish. Do people really find the wisdom of the Perceiver here through the Church's services? The questions had an abstract quality, not begging for examination but rather sitting uncomfortably just out of reach of his analytical mind. He allowed them to drift from his awareness once they entered, but they left an imprint, like the reverberation of a bell that had been rung, echoing in his core.

Lucas had moved to the side by the entrance and was standing there silently. Christopher took it as a blessing to spend whatever time he needed, so he slowly made his way up the center aisle.

It appeared to be a time between services and so was not very crowded, with only about a dozen worshippers scattered about the pews. He passed by a kneeling woman mumbling a prayer about keeping the city's residents safe and pleading for no more warnings, and he realized many would be coming here to do what they could to enhance the Territories' intangible protection through pleas to the Perceiver.

Christopher proceeded up to the third pew and sat.

Seeing some people kneeling in worship brought to mind the unstable woman's words outside the antique shop. The riches displayed before him presented nothing ring-like, but then he wondered if the woman had meant the ring on the finger of the patriarch of the cathedral, but even as he thought it, he could feel that that wasn't right. Still, if he was to kneel before a ring, praying before one on his knees in a church made the most sense to him.

Looking up at the simple, beautiful carving of the Perceiver transported Christopher back to the feelings he always had when sitting before it: reverence, connection, and awe. As he gazed at the wooden face looking down on the great hall, familiar questions arose in his mind: *Who are you? What did you perceive? Why do I feel connected to you?*

And the answer to the last question suddenly burst forth from his center, a gut-level feeling that somehow came attached with a phrase spoken in his head: *Because we are the same.*

Christopher glanced around because the words sounded like the voice from his dream the other night, but no one in the church was close enough to him to have said it. An understanding began to rise like the dawn as a knowingness infused his being. He felt an out-of-body merging of his thoughts and emotions and a physical buzzing like when stunned on the road a few days ago. The increasing realization overcoming him as he finally fully grasped the meaning behind the words blasted away any previous misunderstanding or rejection of the concept, and he felt the clean, pure lightness of the truth. He knew that this moment was the beginning of his being able to accept the fact that *he* could do what the Perceiver did.

He believed it, intuitively *knew* this was possible, and not just for him but for everyone. The Perceiver wasn't just a gifted individual who had reached the highest states of awareness. He was someone who was showing—still, through the artistic depiction and placement of him in the cathedral to foster this connection—that others could do the same, as he was no different from everyone else. He *represented* an awakening, but it was not exclusive *to* him.

Struck by this realization and staring into the wooden eyes that gazed back at him, Christopher could now see that the Perceiver was recognized because of what he had accomplished, but he was accomplished because of what he had recognized.

And Christopher wept.

With his tears were carried all his past misconceptions of the Church, the cathedral, the religious stories, the Perceiver, the tales of the Ancients, the parables of the monks, as well as any other misinterpretation he had learned and believed from his unenlightened perspectives growing up. What he had understood previously had been tied up in the structure and dogma of the Church, the rules that promoted the belief that adhering to the Church's doctrine was the only way to live piously, the only way to receive divine favor. And the government's entanglement with the Church led to Territory laws that reflected similar regulations on behavior, like banning talk of the Ancients, the monks, and the old, pagan faith. He now could see those rules as man-made attempts to bring followers under the Church's spell and the government's control, but in reality, it was so much less complicated than what the Church encouraged and the government commanded. What he was feeling now reduced all of it to the simple truth of who the Perceiver was, how he had lived, and how everyone could connect to and accomplish what the Perceiver had accomplished.

As these misperceptions fell away, Christopher felt a new appreciation for the parables he had found under the floorboards of his room and a clarity to the role he had played, was playing, as a farmer on his ancestral land within the social and economic systems of the Territories. He was following the rules—written and unwritten, personal and societal—as most everyone around him was doing as well, which kept him corralled within boundaries that the Perceiver must have seen in his time and yet demolished to find the personal freedom that in truth was available to everyone. Even the so-called sacrilegious talk Christopher had occasionally heard in the square and the guilty thoughts he had when thinking about the mystery of the Wall now shifted in their impressions. With this new way of seeing these issues, he wiped the slate clean so that what remained in him was a fresh, uncontaminated landscape for the truth to take root and grow. He felt overwhelmingly inspired and energized by the possibilities for himself and his fellow citizens, as another world had just opened to him, a world within.

He now understood why the cathedral was ornamented as it was. How could it convey the majesty of this man in the physical world except by placing him in the center of this great church and surrounding him with riches? But it was not the materiality around the symbol that gave it its power, nor was it the symbol itself. No, its power lay in the observer's connection to the source, to the Perceiver himself.

Christopher breathed a sense of relief and wiped away his last tears. His awareness made the happenings over the past few days begin to make sense. Changes were occurring within him that could not be taught except through direct experience and reflection. And even though he could now consciously grasp this new truth, he knew—absolutely *knew* in his gut—that there was more to this modest, cognitive understanding. It was as though an intangible comprehension had been awakened in him, the stirrings of the beginning of the rest of his path forward.

After a few additional minutes sitting in the pew and communing with the wooden figure in front of the golden disk, Christopher felt he had received what he had been brought there for. Standing to go, he looked once more at the Perceiver bathed in buttery candlelight and gave a silent, *Thank you.*

And his mind must have been playing tricks on him because he thought he heard a soft, clear, and kindly voice, the one from his dream, say back to him, *No, thank* you.

~

Stepping outside the cathedral, Christopher and Lucas began to walk back to the marketplace but were immediately approached by a simply-dressed, middle-aged woman carrying a thick satchel. Christopher noticed a few strange, tattooed symbols just above her wrists and below her sleeves that looked like they were some kind of writing in an unknown language. She had a sparkle in her eyes that made Christopher think she was either very wise or somewhat disturbed, which reminded him of the woman outside the antique store who had grabbed him, whose marks on the back of her hands looked like this woman's tattoos. Other than that and her simple dress, she looked like any other person in the plaza.

"Excuse me," she said. "Would you like to buy something?" She opened her bag and began to pull out some leather goods.

This type of peddling wasn't permitted in the plaza, but people did it anyway, only leaving when the constables came around. Christopher had been confronted by peddlers many times there and on the streets and had never bought anything, let alone engaged beyond a "No, thank you." This time, however, he felt he wanted to see what she was selling.

He stopped, and Lucas stopped with him, and they watched as she pulled from her bag seven folded pieces of leather that looked like finished book covers, and she placed them on the cobblestones in front of them. Each had a different design embossed on the cover and a different kind of clasp or tie to secure it closed. A few looked new, a few old, and none appeared to have any papers inside.

She looked up at the two men and with a smile said, "How many would you like?"

Christopher was surprised he was considering purchasing one, especially given his financial condition. He didn't need something to store papers in, but he was drawn to examine them anyway. As he did, one stood out, almost magnetically pulling his attention to it.

It was one of the older ones, well-worn and clearly used, with the cover having three faintly embossed spirals coming together in the center. Thin leather ties held it together. Without picking it up, it drew him forward and seemed to collapse the space in between them. For some reason, he felt he had to have it.

"How much for that one?" he said, pointing to the faded spirals.

The woman gave him a knowing look, picked it up, and handed it to him. Leaning in, she whispered, "Good choice," and began stuffing her bag with the remaining covers.

Just then, one of the constables came around the corner and the woman quickly pulled her sleeves down over her tattoos and finished packing. Christopher dug into his pocket for change and handed her a few coins. Not even looking at them, she smiled at Lucas, patted Christopher on the shoulder, and scurried off.

Christopher found the whole encounter strange, and the fact that he had actually bought something like what he now held added to the peculiarity of the moment. He turned the leather covering over in his hands, drawing his fingers over the raised spirals on its face.

The Church didn't look kindly upon spiral designs, nor did the government, which had made them illegal to possess or talk about. They were old, pagan symbols from before the Church was founded and as such threatened the origin story of both the Perceiver and the Church. Perhaps this was why Christopher chose this particular cover, because it came from a time before the mischievous minds of lesser men had a chance to exert their influence on what was already pure and mold it into something it was not. He felt the design was closer to the unadulterated source, closer to the Perceiver, closer to what he had just experienced in the cathedral. Time would tell what his attraction to it meant.

~

The two men were quiet on their walk back to the marketplace. Something new was awakening in Christopher from his experience at the cathedral, and he knew it was going to change his life. As much as he thought he understood it with his head, he could feel that its power came from more of a gut-level feeling, an intuition that subsumed his mind.

Given his practical streak from operating the farm, he craved actionable steps to take, something tangible and physical he could do to move forward with whatever this was. But he also had a sense that it was not to be rushed, that it was more about resting with the understanding and allowing the next steps to unfold naturally without being forced. Although frustrating, he resigned himself to begin to try to follow what he felt within rather than what his active mind generated. And with that decision, he had a strange, distant sense of feeling more empowered and ready for whatever would come next.

Upon re-entering the marketplace, Christopher walked with Lucas back to the blind man's usual spot and said, to his own surprise, "See you tomorrow," before heading back to his cart. He felt good, uplifted after the experience with the Perceiver, and was flowing with the confidence of having received a perfect gift. Something was shifting in him again, framing the inauspicious beginnings of the day with a context that begged further reflection.

After he strode back to his cart and slipped the leather covering out of sight between his crates, Martel said, "So, what's going on? I hope you learned something new today." There was a hint of irritation in his voice, something Christopher rarely heard from him.

Christopher looked at his friend. "I really appreciate your help. It's giving me the time to get to the bottom of some things."

"Like the quest, I hope."

"Yes, and more. I didn't learn that much more about the beggar today, but I'm learning more about myself, which I think is helping the quest."

Martel stared at Christopher. "Like . . . how?"

"I don't know for sure yet, but I believe the two are related."

"Mmm," Martel said, handing over the proceeds from selling Christopher's goods. "Well, I hope you get to the bottom of it soon," and he turned to a customer before him.

Ariana had been watching, and she picked up a bouquet from one of her baskets, stepped over, and reached out to hand it to Christopher.

"I think it's good you're learning more about yourself," she said. "I hope you feel better."

Christopher paused for a moment before accepting the flowers, looking first at the bouquet and then into her eyes.

All the times he had interacted with her came rushing forward in his mind: the boyhood memory of her bounding through the fields with the sun streaming through her hair; the time as an anxious teenager he had seen her with her aunt when he was out walking with his friends, his friends egging him on to go talk to her and him blushing in response; the instance a few weeks after that when they exchanged nervous pleasantries as their families talked in the square; the day he saw her at the fairgrounds with another family with a young man, her smiling at Christopher from a distance and confiding with her rolling eyes that she wasn't enjoying the interaction; the first time they touched, when he brought her a freshly-picked apple and their hands accidentally brushed each other's with a feeling he savored the rest of the week; the beautiful day when he had asked her to accompany him to the fair, which she had enthusiastically agreed to.

That last rendezvous, however, had not been fated to happen, as his father had unexpectedly passed away before it could take place, and Christopher could not fathom to rekindle the possibility of seeing her in the grieving state he carried forward. He was going through too much with the house, farm, and business, not to mention the internal swirling of emotions from losing his family. She had reached out, as was her inclination to help others, and had offered to help him with any and all of his responsibilities, but in the angry and guilt-ridden state he had assumed, he couldn't accept anyone's help. Such was his perverse need to punish himself. Consequently, he had shut himself off from feeling and had devoted himself to the robotic work of taking care of the property.

Thankfully, as time passed and he had buried most of the negative, self-destructive feelings, he and Ariana's engagements once again took on a flirty tone. Now, though, he could tell he was feeling things very differently, and the old, stuffed down emotions didn't have the danger of erupting chaotically as they had done occasionally in the past. With his experiences the past few days, he could feel a fundamental shift in his core, a transformation of what previously had limited him. This allowed him to feel once again what he had felt when he and Ariana had interacted years ago.

Feeling this rediscovered sense of connection with her, he spontaneously reached out and grasped not the flowers she held out but the hand that was holding them, and he pulled her in for a kiss.

Ariana stumbled forward, clearly not expecting the embrace, but didn't resist it. Their lips lingered together for a few seconds before Christopher gently released her, taking the flowers from her hand.

"Thank you," he said, their faces just inches apart.

"About time," mumbled Martel from the side as Ariana blushed.

Christopher smiled and stepped back, looking deeply into her eyes. He was surprisingly unfazed by his action. It felt so natural, and their connection in that moment simply demanded it. Her reaction, leaning in to reciprocate, confirmed it.

But as Christopher held Ariana's gaze, his joyful bearing quickly evaporated as a wave of anxiety washed over him, and he didn't know why. He looked around, feeling that something was about to happen.

Ariana saw his concern and stepped back. "What? What is it?"

"I don't know. Something's about to happen. People are about to get—," and he was cut off as the loudspeaker on the corner crackled to life with three rising tones. He looked up at the speaker and somehow knew that the forthcoming announcement wasn't going to be a recall of the previous warnings but rather another warning that the danger had escalated. He stepped forward and pulled Ariana into his arms.

This is a Level 3 Warning by the Council of Governors. The enemy force has begun its march to the Territories. Our Grand Army is ready to defend and counterattack the foreign invaders if they reach the Grand Wall. Please see your zone's manual for the necessary steps you must take for your designated area. This is a Level 3 Warning.

After its third delivery and subsequent tones, Ariana released her grip on him and looked him worriedly in the eyes. "Have you ever heard us get to Level 3?" she asked.

"No," Christopher said, shaking his head. "I don't think we've ever gotten to it since they implemented the seven levels."

He could see and *feel* the agitation of people in the square, but something about the warning left him sensing some kind of disharmony in what was announced, an underlying feeling that there was more to the story that wasn't being communicated.

"What are we going to do?" Ariana asked.

"What else is there to do besides what we're doing?" Christopher responded.

Ariana slowly nodded in agreement. He gave her a quick kiss, squeezed her hand, and slid back behind his cart to attend to the concerned citizens lining up to buy food.

~

It was a busy afternoon, and whatever anxious talk there was in the square earlier had increased in intensity. People were worried, and Christopher easily sold the rest of his nonperishable goods and most of his produce before getting ready to leave. He checked in with Ariana to see if she would walk back with him, but she said her aunt was meeting her shortly, so she had to stay. He feigned being hurt but understood, so he gave her a kiss and a hug and bid her goodbye. She was noticeably a little embarrassed by the display of affection in front of others, as she said nothing but "See you tomorrow" to him when they parted, still smiling and blushing. Martel simply gave him a wink and hearty slap on the back.

At home after depositing the leather book covering into the bottom drawer in his desk and Ariana's flowers into a glass jar with some water, Christopher went to work in the orchard and gardens, preparing for the following day. Afterwards, feeling good, he had enough energy to spend some time canning selected vegetables to replenish the inventory he had sold and to have more ready to peddle if needed. With a few good days of selling, thanks to the warnings, he was pleasantly surprised when he counted his proceeds, which indicated that he might very well be able to pay his taxes if the higher demand persisted and he was able to continue to work hard in the afternoons to fill his cart. Thankfully, his gardens were producing well, despite some overgrowth and lack of maintenance.

When finished with his chores, he grabbed an empty pitcher from inside and went out to fill it from the well. Returning to the kitchen, he poured himself a glass and went outside to sit on the porch to let the physicality of the day drain off him in the diminishing light. There, he sipped his drink and mentally reviewed the events of the day.

From starting out feeling down and overly serious to now feeling terrific, whatever self-confidence he lacked earlier was more than made up for as he sat viewing the trees in the distance. His revelations at the cathedral and actions with Ariana, although somewhat out of character, had been clear and purposeful, and he had no regrets. The government announcement somehow really didn't bother him that much, but he got up to check his zone's manual to make sure he wasn't missing anything.

The primary change besides increased vigilance was that the constables now had more discretion in applying the laws. Since Christopher always obeyed them anyway, he wasn't too troubled by what the manual stated.

He did think about the potential invasion, though, because it was an unknown. His only reference to something similar was the story his parents had told about his grandparents' experience being in lockdown during the previous attack, which was the last time those outside the Wall had tried to enter the Territories. He was hopeful, bordering on confident, that the barrier and the Grand Army would keep the land safe this time as well.

He looked at the Wall in the distance. He couldn't *not* think about it and its mystical properties now, as his curiosity was too great and was becoming greater by the day. And it wasn't just thinking about it, he was *feeling* that this pulling of his attention toward it would result in *something*, although he knew not what. The happenings with Lucas seemed to have intensified his desire to know more about it, yet the Wall remained a mystery detached from that feeling of connection he was having with so many other things—the natural world around him, the Perceiver, and now Ariana.

The fact that the Wall could move and change was against all that he knew about the physical properties of the world. It didn't make sense, but there was some comfort in knowing that others had also questioned it, and some of them had believed in their path and purpose strongly enough to risk their lives to attempt to transcend it.

He remembered going to the closest section of the Wall with his father as a child, the massive, rough-hewn boulders towering above him to an impossible height. As a teenager, he went with some friends and followed a portion of the Wall for hours, convinced they would find a way through before they all eventually got bored and returned home. He recalled running his hands over the enormous blocks, pondering their origin and qualities, wondering if anyone would ever figure out its mysteries, or if the one parable from his adolescence was true and he could somehow move through it like the monks in the tale. A few other times he had traveled to the Wall and had run his hands over the heavy, stone structure, but it was always the same: cold, damp, and impenetrable.

He thought about its significance in his life. Besides containing everything he had ever known, it was also a grand limitation of his world. He sometimes fantasized about going beyond it to learn what was out there, to explore something truly unknown, but his mind couldn't picture what wasn't in his experience, so his imaginings died at the stone border that defined the Territories.

Now, however, the travels in his mind had given him glimpses of what felt like new ground, and it prodded the boyhood curiosity that hadn't had a chance to fully develop and flourish to come out from hiding. Newly revealed, it now screamed out for attention like an ignored, wounded child, which was exactly what it was. The events the last few days had flushed it from the shadows and into the light where it found Christopher's awareness ready and willing to listen to its pleas.

He knew he had to *do* something, and he knew intuitively that he had to take a step immediately to satisfy the urge. So, he grabbed an apple and a flask of water and began to walk to the closest section of the Wall, about an hour away.

It was already dusk when he departed, but Christopher knew the way and wasn't worried about coming home in the dark, especially since he knew he could count on at least some light from the crescent moon once it rose. Most of the route was on the main road past several familiar farms, but then there was a pathway, half hidden by the brush at the side of the road, that was the most direct course to the West Wall. He had been on it a few times before.

From the road, he ducked through the bushes and onto the narrow, well-worn, path, moving swiftly through the trees. Before long, he emerged from the woods and stood at a clearing where the immense obstruction used to be, but he knew it had recently moved by that unseen force that few, if any, knew anything about.

The earth beneath him was scarred with dirt where the Wall had been, but strangely he could already see shoots of grass beginning to come up that looked like they would soon be indistinguishable from the surrounding field. Peering ahead, he could see the great obstacle a few hundred yards in the distance, and he realized he had been walking with his head down and not looking up at his intended destination. He continued forward, creating a fresh path as he went.

When he arrived at the Wall, it was as he had seen it before, a colossal creation with a solemn weight, reaching upward to an inconceivable height to support the sky as if the heavens might fall upon him if not for the reinforcement. He touched the massive, stone blocks and ran his fingers across the gritty surface, feeling its substance.

What are you? he intoned in his head.

As if to answer, the Wall groaned deeply and trembled, causing small stones and dust to fall from above, shocking Christopher and sending him scurrying backward to a safe distance. Incredulous, he waited for something else to happen, but the tremors quickly stopped, and he stood in silence.

Coming to his senses and recognizing that he didn't want to be in a new area next to something that could crumble upon him at any moment, he turned his back to the Wall, found his way to the old path, and followed it to the road that would take him home.

On his way, thinking about what had transpired, he wondered if the Wall would be in the same place tomorrow.

~

Lying in bed that night and ruminating on the day's events, Christopher thought about the escalated warnings and the potential invasion that the Territories hadn't experienced in ages. The government must have received some good information to know about the foreign army's buildup outside the Wall, but he couldn't grasp how they had received it because no one could get outside the barrier. Since he still trusted the Territory Governors, despite the questionable story he had heard from the gang leader, he figured they must have some way of monitoring activities outside the Wall. Perhaps they had access to other secret scientific and mechanical arts like the loudspeakers but kept the discoveries to themselves. Regardless, he had full confidence in the strength of the Wall and of the Grand Army to keep the citizens of the Territories safe.

His mind drifted to his sweet kiss with Ariana, something he now realized he had wanted to do for ages. With her holding out the flowers, eyes and smile lighting up the street, and their history of connecting and flirting, the impulse had, rightfully, overcome him. Despite people milling around, there was no other time it could have been. He knew it, *felt* it, and so committed to the kiss without thought, consummating their mutual yearning.

He smiled to himself, the stresses of his daily responsibilities having faded in his awareness like the mist in the fields under the morning sun. *So, this is what happiness feels like,* he thought. He looked over at Ariana's flowers, which he had placed next to his bed, and felt love begin to expand in his chest.

Anna

Anna sat on her bed and looked up from the open manuscript in her hands. She had been so engrossed in the story that she had hardly moved. It was as if her portal to another world had once again opened to give her the escape she so desperately desired and she had become lost in it.

She wanted to be Ariana. Or Christopher. Or Lucas. Or any of the other characters that populated the all-too-real yet magical world described in the tale. Well, maybe not the government people; they sounded a bit like her father.

Marking her place in the book with a slip of paper, she flipped the leather covering closed to look at the spiral design on the front and drew her fingers across the raised lines. *It can't be*, she thought. *Could this really be Christopher's?* Touching the symbol made the skin on her arms tingle and her face flush with the possibility.

She heard a distant thud somewhere in the lodging house and looked up quickly at the door, listening intently to make sure her parents weren't approaching her room. The expanded silence that followed revealed nothing further, and she let out the breath she was holding. The thump sounded like it came from downstairs anyway, but she couldn't be too careful, especially with the potentially true story in her hands that she was sure her parents would find sacrilegious if they knew what it contained, not to mention if they even just saw the cover.

She turned to the first page and looked at the title: *A Tale of Awakening by Erich Evepret.* Perhaps that was Christopher's pen name, or maybe the author just knew Christopher really, really well, like Ariana or Martel, or even Lucas.

She closed the book, moved it off her lap, and stood up. Feeling stiff from sitting for so long, she stretched her arms out to her sides and took a deep breath. That wasn't enough—her body called for more movement—so she swung her arms around like a windmill and crouched down and stood up a few times.

Physically refreshed, she deliberated for a moment before moving her chair to the corner of the room. Grabbing a piece of charcoal from a drawer in her desk, she stood on the chair and, as she had done years before, drew a circle high up on the wall and wrote beneath it, "to another world." She stared at it, contemplating her next action, then took a deep breath and filled in the circle so it was dark and had depth, a secret tunnel from this world that could lead her to the light of another. It was bigger and bolder than when she had drawn it previously. She swallowed nervously in anticipation of what her father might think, if or when he saw it.

Something was bubbling into her awareness as she followed Christopher's journey. It was unfamiliar yet empowering, abstract yet influential. She already felt changed by the story— her drawing on the wall proved that—and she was only halfway through it. She couldn't wait to finish it to see what other challenges and revelations Christopher, and she, might have. And, of course, she wanted to see where things went between Ariana and Christopher.

Leaping back into bed and settling in against her pillow, she picked up the manuscript and found her placeholder for the next chapter. But before continuing the tale, she glanced up at the new portal to another world she was about to travel through, closed her eyes, and felt the deep connection to the book she experienced earlier in the antique shop. Only then did she open her eyes and began reading.

Fourth

Frolicking in the light, the shadows play as they craft the drama and dance across the stage. Having created new worlds, they struggle to perceive the one world that contains all others, the one that animates the masquerade. For the few who risk this journey of remembrance, the excitement of the shadowlands yields to the inexplicable.

Trusting the light that has given them life, the shadows see beyond the masquerade and forgive their brethren for their tragic roles. Knowing that the truth of the theater calls them forth, they discover their love for the perfect stage and the flawless performances in which their own reflection shines.

~

Opening his eyes, Christopher sat up in bed feeling *gooood*, much better than yesterday morning. It was as much his mind as it was his body, feeling physically refreshed from sleeping deeply but also having a head clear of the tumbling reflections of the previous days. He hopped out of bed eager to meet the dawn.

He engaged in his morning routine feeling unflinchingly positive, with a newfound focus and raised awareness. His tax problem seemed far away, as his confidence in being able to earn enough this week to take care of it overcame any related worries.

He thought about Ariana and their kiss. It was something a long time coming, and he was relieved to have finally gotten past it, which he hoped would lead toward a union like what his loving parents had enjoyed. The years of history he had known her, the fun and flirty conversations, and the feeling he had when around her, all combined to prompt him to lean in for the embrace. It was so simple and natural for him, as he hoped it was for her, and he thought about what it might be like if she were beside him on mornings such as this.

He began his walk to the city, pulling his cart behind him. Still thinking about Ariana, he realized that his usual quickened pulse when he was with her had been absent yesterday. Generally, their flirting led to sense of exhilaration, and sometimes embarrassment, which elevated his heart rate and flushed his cheeks, but there was nothing like that when he had kissed her. It was either too spontaneous or because he was in a more self-empowered space, or perhaps it was something deeper. *Is this love?* he mused.

He let go of his ponderings as he moved forward, deciding instead to be present with the sound of the crunch of his boots on the dirt and the tensing of his muscles pushing the handle of the cart. He looked up to see the line of workers and goods in front of him winding its way into the city and felt a sense of joyful contentment at his place in the landscape.

Seeing Vincent's cart ahead of his, moving slowly as it was laden with brick, Christopher picked up his pace and pulled alongside him when the road widened.

"Good morning, Vincent!" Christopher said. "How did the job go yesterday?"

"Good morning, Christopher," Vincent replied, huffing a little as they were going uphill. "It went well, at least the flooring did."

"Oh? Sounds like something else happened."

Vincent looked like he was struggling with something, and it wasn't from the load he was hauling. "Well, I'm not really sure. I was working on tiling the floor in the front hall of this grand property near the city center, and a bunch of other government officials arrived. They had a meeting, and I overheard through the door some talk about the warnings we've been hearing."

"That makes sense," Christopher said. "Did they discuss the information they've been getting? I've been wondering how they obtain it. And anything about the Wall moving? Are they related?" He suddenly realized he was speaking at a normal volume and looked around to see if anyone had heard him. Vincent did the same, but others were too far away.

"Well, no," Vincent said in a lower voice, "but they talked about how they felt they were losing control and needed to be ready to increase the warning levels."

Christopher also dropped his voice. "Like losing control because the people are scared or losing control because they can't handle what's coming? Are the Territories in real danger from the Wall moving, which could let in the foreigners?" The second thought gave him a shiver.

"Um, no, nothing about what might be going on outside the Wall or about the Wall moving. It was more like . . ."—he paused, taking a breath and looking confused—"like they were discussing what would trigger the next announcements, and it wasn't from out there but from something in here, from inside the Territories. And then it sounded like they wanted to use language that would *increase* fear and uncertainty, using the foreigners as the excuse. It didn't make sense."

"So, what do you mean? Is the threat even real? Are they manufacturing the invasion?" Christopher said it more loudly than intended.

Vincent hushed him and looked around. "I could only hear snippets of the conversation, but it was more like they were manufacturing the *fear* of an invasion."

"Whoa. That's . . ." Christopher couldn't finish the sentence. His mind didn't want to put what he was hearing up against his beliefs about the government. He took a few steps, thinking. "That doesn't make any sense. Why would they do that?" But even as he asked, he felt a warm, expansive openness in his body, an intuitive feeling that seemed to confirm what Vincent had heard and accurately understood. The deception was going to happen, or rather continue to happen.

"I don't know," said Vincent.

Christopher continued his questioning despite what was arising within him, his mind not fully trusting what the feelings in his body were telling him. "So, is there a real threat coming from outside the Wall?"

Vincent shook his head. "It didn't sound like it."

Christopher's mind was spinning, trying to make sense of the difference between his logical thinking and the knowingness coming from his center. The contrast was bringing him down from his early morning positivity. He believed Vincent, who was known for his hard work and forthrightness, but perhaps the big man had missed some crucial part of the discussion. Christopher wanted to believe the government wouldn't do something like this, but his doubts were prominent and were becoming louder by the minute.

"Taken all together, it just didn't make sense," Vincent added. "And when they left, they looked at me suspiciously, like with a combination of guilt and shame that they might have been overheard, as well as anger at me just for being there."

"That *is* strange."

After walking together in silence for a few minutes trying to wrap his head around it, Christopher said, "Thanks for sharing, Vincent. I know you didn't have to."

"Sure. I'll let you know if I hear anything else. I'm building an outside wall there today so maybe I'll hear more about it. Probably best not to share this with anyone. I'm sure they wouldn't want me talking about it, and you never know who might be listening."

"Yes, of course."

Christopher knew the constables were often eavesdropping for violations, and although this wasn't necessarily illegal to talk about that he knew of, it certainly had the feeling of being dangerous to do so, especially during these times of elevated warnings.

"Be careful," Christopher added. His mind didn't know why he said that, but his heart did.

Vincent looked over at him, grinning, and said, "I'm always careful," but a shadow of apprehension flashed under the smile, and Christopher worried for his friend.

~

Arriving at the market before Ariana again, Christopher set up his cart and made idle conversation with Martel and the other vendors. His good mood had returned despite the unnerving conversation with Vincent, which continued to occupy a portion of his mind like a distracting and unwelcome melody repeating in his head. He made sure to mentally compartmentalize it so that he didn't accidentally let anything slip out.

Martel was a good sport to not bring up what he had witnessed the day before between Christopher and Ariana, but even if he did, Christopher didn't feel that the friendly ribbing would bother him. He had no regrets.

Martel suddenly interrupted their conversation. "Well, I guess we'll see you later."

Christopher turned around and there stood Lucas, who said, "Come with me," before walking away.

Christopher froze for a second before glancing back at Martel with a look of surprise. "Yeah, yeah," Martel sighed. "I got your stuff. Go ahead. Go on your quest." He didn't use his grand voice.

"Thank you," Christopher said. He knew he wanted to accompany Lucas again, or rather already knew he was going to. His only misgivings were burdening his friends once more with watching his cart.

"Just make sure you give us an update later," Martel added.

"Of course," Christopher replied. At this point, he couldn't turn away, even if he had to leave his cart unattended. Doing that would speak volumes to him, as it would indicate that his selfish chasing of time with the blind man was more important than the farm, his family's lineage, and his contribution to the Territories. Thankfully, he didn't need to do that because of the generous support of his friends.

As he turned to follow Lucas, he saw Ariana come around the corner carrying her flowers. He paused, mesmerized by her smile, and smiled himself. She looked like when he first saw her as a child, so innocent and full of beauty, and he became trapped for a moment in the collapse of time. Blinking himself back to awareness, before he could think, he waved, turned, and continued after the blind man, leaving Ariana's radiant face lingering in his vision.

What was that? Christopher thought, immediately second-guessing his priorities. He could feel her disappointment as he walked away but inherently knew that it was necessary that he accompany Lucas again. She would understand . . . he hoped.

He didn't look back even though part of him wanted to. He stayed focused on the blind man, who set a leisurely pace as if he were slowly strolling through the woods listening to birdsong.

They passed the corner with the antique store where the unstable woman had been the past few days before being taken away by the constables. Christopher noted her absence and thought about what she had said about the darkness, the ring, his life, and what it all meant, if anything. There was something there that he couldn't quite dismiss, so he tucked it away and out of his thoughts for the time being.

He caught up with Lucas and walked a few minutes next to him, enjoying the slower pace. It was nice to move through the streets in an unhurried manner, having the time to look around and take in the bustling city as an observer rather than as an active participant. With the blind man silent and no conversation to attend to, Christopher's mind relaxed and he let go of any questions in his head.

His demeanor softened as his mental body calmed, and he realized that he usually went about his days on a mission to *do* something. If there was a task to accomplish, he got it done with his head heavy with focus and his body going through the motions to make it happen.

In comparison, what he was currently experiencing was new to him. Instead of being in his head, he was *feeling* his surroundings, like in his dream the other evening when he connected with the abundance in nature around him. As open a person he thought he was, he realized that his typical behavior had been to shut out the world, that most of the time he was either overthinking or coming *from* himself, getting things done without *taking in* what was around him. What he was feeling now was a different experience, and he loved it. He just didn't know if it was going to be compatible with the practicalities of keeping up with his typical daily concerns, like working the farm and selling in the marketplace. So far, though, things had worked out with his friends helping while he went on excursions like this with the blind man.

Christopher and Lucas continued sauntering through the streets, wandering with no apparent destination in mind. Christopher took note of the colorful characters that passed—in both directions, as they were moving more slowly than most— and found himself marveling at the abundance of differences encompassed within the city limits.

There was the smartly-dressed man carrying a case and walking with a haughty determination, his fine suit, tails, and bowler likely signifying his success at some business. A baker with a white apron pushed his cart of fresh breads and pastries on his delivery route, the sweet-smelling goods making Christopher's stomach rumble and mouth water as he caught a whiff of the delicious treats. They passed an older, female artist with tremendously long, gray hair who had set up an easel on the side of the road and was painting the streetscape in the morning light, trying to capture the robust shadows created by the Grand Wall and surrounding buildings. A mother holding the hand of her son rushed past, seemingly late for something, although it seemed too early for school. Two constables strolled by, their eyes darting about evaluating the passersby, no doubt on a higher alert because of the warnings. Behind them, he saw the flash of a girl's red hair emerge from cellar stairs after the constables had passed, and she darted in the opposite direction carrying a sack over her shoulder, her ponytail swinging back and forth in her haste. She was the only one who seemed somewhat out of place in the parade he was in the midst of.

Already starting the day in a good mood, he experienced an openness and lightness in his chest that spread throughout his body and saturated his energy in a sacred embrace. Whatever expansive and wonderful feeling he had before seemed to be multiplying itself, and he almost couldn't take it. It was as if he were blind and deaf and someone had opened his eyes and ears for the first time and he didn't know how to process all the stimuli. It was overwhelming.

He touched Lucas's arm and they both stopped. "What's happening?" he asked.

Lucas looked at him with his cloudy eyes without saying anything, and beneath his demeanor, Christopher understood that it was not for the blind man to answer.

They had stopped in front of a long, nondescript building that blended in with the other structures on the block. Signs hung above the doors indicating storefronts, and Christopher's eyes looked past Lucas to one sign displaying "Jacquie's Artisans" with a partially open door below it painted a soft, light green. Christopher felt a desire to enter and, seeing that the blind man wasn't pressing him into continuing their walk, he stepped toward the entrance. As he did, he wondered if it was a coincidence that he had stopped Lucas at just this spot. Chuckling to himself, he thought, *No, of course not.*

Christopher stepped through the arched doorway and into the shop, which was filled with the most magical pieces of art he had ever seen. From the magnificent paintings on the walls, to the small wooden and stone sculptures on the tables, to the blended tile, glass, and fabric figurines, they all exuded the authenticity of pure, creative expression.

Most items appeared to reflect pairs of people in different forms of embrace—hugging, kissing, making love, holding hands, gazing into each other's eyes. Some depicted non-traditional or multiple couplings, portraying different genders and sexes. Regardless of any individual's representation within a piece, the power of connection between and among the persons in the renderings was extraordinary.

The walls of the shop were of the same green color as the door, although brighter and more vibrant, with pink trim along the ceiling and bookcases. The air was light, as was the greeting of the older woman at the counter who welcomed them.

"Good morning!" she said joyfully, her warmth projecting across the store. She wore a beautiful robe dyed with all the colors of a rainbow.

"Good morning!" Christopher said, trying to match her enthusiasm.

Lucas had followed him in and now stood by the entrance as Christopher walked further into the aisles, glancing around at the merchandise.

"I love your store," he said, and he sincerely meant it. Being there made him feel wonderful, like the feeling he was experiencing within had been made manifest.

"Thank you," said the old woman. "Have you been here before?"

"No, but I'm glad I stopped by."

"Me too! If there's anything I can help you find, please let me know," she said before disappearing through a curtain of beads into a room behind the counter.

Christopher looked about. The skill and artisanship of the creations surrounding him impressed his not-so-discerning eye, and in the elevated state he was experiencing, it was as though he could *feel* each piece and the artist's intent just by observation, and the feeling was of love.

Out of the corner of his eye in the next aisle he saw a wooden carving of a man and woman in embrace and was instantly drawn to it. He walked over and gently picked it up.

The craftsmanship was exquisite. The couple had their heads bowed toward each other with foreheads touching, their artistically lean bodies pulled together at the center. The man's hands were on the woman's waist, her hands on his shoulders. At the bottom, the flare of her dress beautifully curved away from him, elegantly balancing the piece on a small round base. It was about three hands tall and made of a light-colored wood. The figures conveyed a reverence—to each other and to the observer—bordering on the celestial.

The piece captivated him. He had never seen anything like it, *felt* anything like it. It spoke deeply to an emerging part of him that had been only partially awake, and as that part surged to life right there and then in the shop, he knew he had to have the creation, no matter the cost. He carried it to the counter as the old woman emerged from behind the beads.

"I'd like this, please," he said.

"Oh, that's a good one," she said. "For a special someone, I presume?"

"Yes," replied Christopher. She was like everyone's favorite grandmother, with kindness flowing off her multicolored robe.

"Would you like it wrapped?"

"Yes, please."

As the woman took the carving to wrap it, Christopher noticed something etched into the bottom of the circular base.

"Hold on. What does that say?" he asked, pointing to the base.

She turned it over and put on her glasses.

"Oh, that's in the language of the Ancients," she said.

A warm chill ran across Christopher's skin, and for a moment he thought it was because talking about the Ancients was forbidden, let alone having something actually written in their language, and it worried him if they were going to have a conversation about it. But the shudder he experienced was from something different, something that went beyond his mind to a long-forgotten resonance within.

The Ancients' mysterious language had supposedly passed down through a sacred lineage of believers and was alive today, or so he had heard from a strange man spouting nonsense in the marketplace years ago. But perhaps what he had heard then hadn't been the ravings of a disturbed vagrant but rather a truth that the man just happened to know, even though it was expressed eccentrically. Within minutes, constables had apprehended the man, and Christopher, besides having taken a moment back then to think about how it might relate to the parables of the monks he had read as an adolescent, hadn't given the incident a second thought . . . until now.

The carving on the base struck him as familiar, and he realized it looked like the tattoos on the arms of the woman he had bought the leather book cover from, as well as the tattoos on the back of the hands of the unstable woman outside the antique store. Excitement surged up his spine.

"Can you read it?" he asked, expecting a negative answer.

The old woman raised her glasses and smiled at him, and he couldn't help but feel as if she was appraising whether he was worthy of hearing the translation. She glanced over at Lucas, who stood unmoving at the entrance, then lowered her glasses and peered at the small, carved lines.

"It says, 'for the love that you are.'" She took off her glasses and looked at him.

The words struck Christopher as a gentle blow to the chest that was not as much an external impact as it was a soft unlocking and releasing from within. The feeling expanded like a bubble, enveloping first his torso, then his whole body, and then what must have been out to ten feet around him, enclosing the old woman within it. He felt alive and connected in a manner he hadn't dreamed possible.

The shopkeeper looked at him, joined in his uplifted, loving energy, and spoke slowly. "I've had that piece for a very long time. I'm glad you finally found it."

Christopher was speechless, reveling in the tenderness of the experience. His mind jumped to a time in his childhood when he had run back to his room after being yelled at by his parents. He had done something—he couldn't remember what—that had caused both his parents to come down on him harshly. At the time, he had taken it as a criticism of *who he was*, not of what he had done, and had since retained some old, perverse, negative view of himself because of it.

But his perception of the criticism had been flawed. He was now beginning to recognize the unbounded being he was and always had been, and that was distinguished from his actions, both from back then and continuing to the present moment. The idea of simply being something that was so much more than what he did was becoming real, in addition to feeling that he was more than who he was in the physical world.

That past occurrence, along with others that had accumulated similar heavy emotions, dissolved in forgiveness as they fell into the spiraling, loving energy emanating from his chest. He knew that discovering the words on the base was no accident. They fit perfectly with the statuette, the shop, the shopkeeper, and the love he was experiencing.

He gathered his thoughts and attempted to bring himself back to some sense of normalcy in the conversation.

"How do you know the old tongue?"

"Oh, honey," she replied, "if you've been around for as long as I have, you pick up a few things." She smiled warmly, embracing him with her eyes. He smiled back from within his heightened space, sensing her feelings through their connection and reflecting her loving demeanor.

A pendant hanging from her necklace drew his attention, as it appeared to be in the shape of one of the carved symbols she had just read. "I can see that it's familiar to you," he said.

She touched the symbol on the chain and gave a slight nod. "You could say that."

"Who's the artist?" he asked, gesturing to the piece she had begun to wrap in burlap. His expanded feeling was shifting, slowly withdrawing back into him, and his mind was coming back. His curious child needed to understand.

She shook her head. "I don't know."

"But it's your shop and you somehow can read the ancient tongue. You don't know who it is?" He felt more grounded in his body but with a retained sense of connection to his surroundings. His mind was back, and he desperately wanted to know more.

"No, my dear. I don't."

He believed her but was disappointed she didn't know where the wooden carving came from. Apparently, there were limits to the wonderful day he was having.

She finished wrapping the gift, and he paid, an amount far less than its invaluable worth to him—he would've paid anything. Handing him the package, she looked at him deeply and said, "One more thing. Whatever you hear, whatever you think, whatever appearances try to tell you, trust this," and she placed her palm on his chest.

"What do you mean?" he asked reflexively, even though he knew what she meant on some level.

"You'll know," she said. "At the right time, you'll understand." And with that, she smiled and glanced over at Lucas, nodded, and turned to disappear again behind the beaded curtain.

Christopher stood unmoving for a moment, wanting to figure out what she meant besides the obvious, but his logical, rational mind couldn't process it. He had a feeling though, and that would have to be good enough for now.

He turned and headed out the door. Lucas followed, and they both began heading back to the marketplace, back to the familiar.

Their pace was again unhurried, and Christopher basked in the heightened, loving awareness that still infused him. When they finally turned the corner and arrived at their common street, Lucas went to sit in his usual spot as Christopher strolled to his cart. From a distance, he observed Ariana speaking with some potential customers who were appraising her flowers. Her bright smile was infectious, and they were laughing with her.

He could see her, really see her now. The opening he had experienced, was still experiencing, took him to a depth of love he didn't know existed—love of Ariana, love of self, love of everything around him being in perfect order. He connected with her beyond their history and physicality of their lives in the market, past time, to a shared wellspring of divine existence. And from that common source, Christopher saw that they had always been as one.

He watched as she closed the transaction and her customers walked away with a beautiful bouquet. She turned to him with a cheery, "Welcome back!"

He stared at her with his whole self focused through his eyes and heart, no words coming forth from his lips.

"Um, are you okay?" she asked, stepping over and putting her hand on his arm.

Gathering himself, Christopher smiled tenderly and held up the gift. "I got you something."

"Oh, you didn't have to!" She gracefully took it from his outstretched hand. "Thank you!"

"It was . . . it is something you need to have," he said, still gazing at her.

Ariana unwrapped the present, and when it came into view, she put her hand on her chest and caught her breath.

"Oh, it's beautiful!" she exclaimed, turning it over in her hands. "Why . . .? What . . .?" The questions didn't come. Her eyes teared up and she jumped into Christopher's arms, hugging him tightly.

He embraced her back and, in his sensitive and aware state, saw the two of them together in the light, recognizing that they had been inseparable since before time began.

"I love you," he said to her, pulling back enough to gaze into her eyes. "I hadn't known that before now, couldn't have known it before today." His voice had a strength of conviction in it, the authority of truth about love that he could now understand. Martel, despite all his joking, had been right after all.

She responded in kind. "I love you, too," the power of their shared connection expressing through how they looked at each other.

After a moment, she playfully slapped him on his shoulder. "What took you so long?"

They both laughed, and Christopher said, "I wasn't ready, but I am now."

As he said that, he had the faint thought that maybe the unstable woman with the supposedly prophetic words meant kneeling before Ariana with a ring. *Before the ring you'll kneel,* he remembered. But the rest of what she had said didn't fit the feeling he was immersed in. *Whether you live or die is up to you. You need to be ready.* It seemed extreme to apply it to his relationship with Ariana, even though he could indeed see himself kneeling before her with a ring or putting his life on the line for her after what he had experienced in the artisan shop and what he now felt with her in his arms. Still, something felt discordant about applying the woman's words in any way to Ariana. He dismissed the thought and they kissed again.

Martel watched it all unfold and muttered, "Mm hmm," and went about his business.

~

About an hour later when the number of people in the square subsided, Martel came over to Christopher and said, "Okay, so what have you been learning from the blind beggar? Did you find any reasons for your daily offerings?" Ariana overheard and took a step closer to listen better.

"Well," Christopher began, "he's been taking me to different places in the city, which have brought interesting experiences to say the least. They've been challenging in different ways, but they've given me a new way of looking at things."

"How so?" Martel asked.

"I feel more connected to everything around me, like I was just going through the motions before but am now more aware of the bigger picture and how everything works together. I'm also *feeling* more."

"And I'm happy for that!" Ariana said, sidling up to him and giving him a hug.

"Me too," he said, embracing her back.

"So, it's like you're figuring out that thing about perspective you had the other day on the way into the city," Martel said.

"Yes," Christopher said. "Exactly. It's at least a start."

"But does it solve the quest-tion?" Martel said, chuckling at his play on words.

Christopher smiled. "Um, I'm not sure. In some ways, yes, because I feel I've grown from the experiences, but I sense there's still something more to uncover about Lucas that relates to it."

"Well," Ariana said, "if it brings more of how you've already changed, then I'm all for it."

Christopher nodded and squeezed her hand in agreement.

The rest of the day was uneventful yet relatively busy, with talk of the warnings and the movement of the Wall generating robust sales for most merchants, that is until mid-afternoon when the loudspeakers hissed awake and again emitted three rising tones. Everyone in the market froze and looked to the nearest speaker, except Ariana, who stepped over to hold onto Christopher, and Lucas, who remained seated facing forward. Christopher couldn't help but think about his conversation with Vincent that morning before the announcement began.

This is a Level 4 Warning by the Council of Governors. The enemy force continues its march toward the Territories and should be at the Grand Wall in a few days. The Grand Army is ready to repel any attack. As stated in your zone's manual, you must take this time to prepare for lockdown and potential sheltering in the secure, government facilities. Please see your zone's manual for the necessary steps you must take for your designated area. This is a Level 4 Warning.

The voice had increased slightly in pitch compared to the previous warnings and sounded somewhat anxious, which Christopher thought was probably appropriate as a Level 4 Warning had never been issued.

After the message repeated twice and then ended with the three closing tones, the marketplace burst into discussion about it. Christopher could hear a man nearby telling his companion that he had thought the previous days' warnings were just the government being overly protective and that the next announcement would cancel the threat, but now he was really worried and thought they were genuine. Christopher understood where he was coming from, but when he looked across the square at Lucas, whose stillness contrasted starkly with the agitation of those around him, he found himself caught between the peace the blind man projected and the concern the warning legitimately warranted.

The food vendors became busier, with people wanting to get enough staples to sustain them through any potential lockdown, whose indefinite length could potentially last for days or weeks. As such, Christopher sold his remaining goods quickly with the help of Ariana, who assisted him as flowers were not as much a priority to the anxious citizens as food was.

They worked well together, as she was familiar enough with his goods from selling them previously to efficiently handle the stressed customers while keeping any worry she might have been experiencing to herself. After his crates had emptied, Christopher pulled her in for a kiss.

"Thank you for your help," he said.

"My pleasure," she responded. Stepping back, she asked, "What do you make of the announcement?"

Trying not to think of Vincent's experience, he said, "Well, we should do what they say and make sure we have enough food in case of a lockdown. I have enough in my cellar, some of which I can sell tomorrow, but let me know what you need and I'll set some aside."

She gave him a squeeze. "Thank you."

With customers not that interested in her flowers, Ariana picked up the baskets with her remaining bouquets and placed them in Christopher's cart as he loaded his empty crates. The two bid goodbye to Martel and left the marketplace together, parting at the split in the road near the blacksmiths' forges that led back to their respective houses. Christopher lightly brushed the hair out of Ariana's face to kiss her goodbye.

He was tingling from their special connection being further realized, and he spent the rest of his solitary walk home reflecting on what might very well have been the perfect day, except, of course, for the uneasy feeling from the latest warning and what Vincent had told him.

Notwithstanding that discomfort, he dutifully worked the orchard and gardens in the afternoon, thoroughly enjoying the physical work that further enhanced his connection to the land and the life that sprang from it. Sitting on the porch later in the waning light, he reveled in feeling more aware of who he really was than ever before, both individually and as a part of the whole landscape.

The crops in the fields, the distant trees, even his humble house itself had taken on a deeper meaning. He now felt he was connecting with them from a heart-centered space with *feeling*, which went beyond understanding them with his mind or seeing and using them as physical objects. Perhaps even the warnings were giving him a new appreciation of his family's property, for if the Territories were really being threatened, then all he had ever known was in jeopardy—the farm, Ariana, the marketplace, and everything in the city, including the cathedral and the statue of the Perceiver.

Despite connecting differently to what was around him, he still had his mental faculties when he needed them, something he had noticed when he was selling his goods and making change. They were available when called upon and used in the moment, but his normal manner of understanding the people, settings, and situations in his direct experience had shifted, and he knew that he could inherently trust this new way of seeing and being.

He sat peacefully, gently rocking in his chair as the streaks of the late day sun bathed the green landscape before him. No task-related thoughts came to mind as they normally would have at this time. Innocence and joy flowed through him like a child seeing the world with new, curious eyes from the safety of a well-functioning family. He surrendered to the wondrous feeling, trusting its movement within him, allowing it to emerge from its hiding place to take a prominent seat in his awareness. He couldn't remember when he last felt this free and unburdened.

As the feeling coalesced to a harmonious intonation within, the words *love and forgiveness are the same* echoed in his head, giving voice to the understanding vibrating in his being. He recognized how he had sometimes held on to old grudges, remembering to have his guard up when dealing with certain people. Those emotional memories and other similar recollections were swept up in the openness coming from his heart, and they disintegrated as he remained immersed in the radiating love he was experiencing for himself and those in his world.

Yet, in the midst of this tranquility, the slumbering snake of self-judgment hissed to life, awakened by the dance of refined energies around its lair. It spat its fiery venom chaotically, trying to land droplets of guilt, anger, and blame wherever it could. For a moment, the drops landed and took Christopher back to when his father had died, burning their way into the scar tissue of his memories with their toxic poison. He doubled over with an intense desire to scream in anger at himself, but what he had felt just seconds before was too fresh, too light, and too forgiving.

"No." The words flew past his lips, and with the exclamation, he sat upright in his chair and focused on the love he had experienced in the artisan shop, the same love he felt for Ariana. In the protected warmth of that space, he realized that it wasn't just loving others freely that he had needed to learn; it was loving himself to the same degree of magnificence.

With that awareness, he turned his love—the universal love emanating from his heart—upon his own being, targeting his self-created mistakes, faults, misunderstandings, and false beliefs, desiring only to see and know truth. And the missing salve for his healing—the deep, true healing that up to this point had so far eluded him—surrounded and bathed him in its light as the serpent dissolved before his weeping eyes.

Basking in the newly-realized, easy freedom from the burden of carrying the beast, Christopher blinked himself back to mindfulness, feeling an expansiveness as if the border of his body had again dispersed itself many feet out from him like in the shop earlier in the day.

He stood, stretched his arms to his side, and took a deep breath of the cool, late evening air, inhaling the loving energy and breathing out any remaining negative emotions, the remnants of which he thought had melted away before. They were like the soot in the chimney of his house that was normally difficult to remove but had been shaken loose by the vibrations of his experiences of the day, and they blew away with his exhalation.

His next breath was clear, pure, and natural, merging with the environment and becoming an integral part of it. It was a holy connection, not just to that which was around him but also to that which was within.

He sat in this peaceful space, rocking in his chair, not discerning that the Wall in the distance had moved once again. It didn't matter, because Christopher knew that everything was right in the world.

Anna

Yay! Anna thought. Christopher had finally realized and expressed his deep love for Ariana. And what a love it was, so pure and genuine and beyond time, like it came directly from the Ancients and their scribbled symbols, passed on through the artisan shop and the old woman who owned it. She hoped someday she could experience profound love like that, whether as the giver or recipient.

With Christopher opening, growing, and moving past some of his old emotions, she wondered if there was a lesson there for her. The idea that who she was, her *being*, was different from what she *did* was a new concept for her, and she found it hard to understand. A person was defined by their actions, or so she had learned in school with her grades and at home with her obedience to her parents' rules. But Christopher, or rather the author, wrote that one didn't define the other. She thought of her father, a constable, who seemed to like to control his surroundings, especially at home. *Is who he is really different from his actions?* She found it difficult to believe.

Still, if she could find a way to forgive her parents for their acts as Christopher seemed to do with his parents, it might help her move forward into adulthood without feeling the influence of those past emotional experiences. Christopher appeared to have shed some of his old emotions in the chapter, and she wanted to do the same, to create a blank slate upon which to write her future. Perhaps when she read the story again, she would understand more about his lesson and how to apply it to her own life.

The higher-level warnings were beginning to make her nervous. She had never heard anything higher than Level 1 before in her world, and it had come just yesterday. From the anxious chatter about it overheard in the streets outside her family's apartment, she couldn't imagine what a fourth level warning would bring.

Her head full of new thoughts and impressions that tied her even more intricately to the tale, she nestled into her pillow and turned the page.

Fifth

The shadows take charge of the drama, each clearly expressing their role as they choose their fates. Separating truth from error, they discern the spectral dance of which they are a part and manifest their power, selecting limits to the reach of the shadowlands.

~

Christopher awakened early with a robust, harmonious clarity and bounced out of bed ready to take charge of the day. Completing his morning routine quickly and effortlessly, he enjoyed a quiet walk with his cart to the city in the emerging light before other merchants busied the road. He felt confident, strong, and capable from the effects of the events yesterday, which continued to linger pleasantly like the brisk, refreshing feeling after a jump in a swimming hole on a hot afternoon.

The marketplace was empty when he arrived, except for Lucas and a young couple nearby setting up their stall of freshly-baked goods like they did every morning. Christopher set down his cart and decided to engage with the blind man before the distractions of market activity began.

Walking over to him, Christopher waved to the couple, and they waved back. He knew them, although not as well as Ariana and Martel, and they had purchased goods from each other on occasion. Inhaling the sweet smell of bread and pastries wafting over the square, Christopher debated whether to treat himself to something, but a quick thought about how he was trying to save enough for his taxes dissuaded him.

"Good morning," Christopher said, standing in front of Lucas.

Lucas looked up with his hazy eyes. "Good morning," he responded.

"Are we going on another adventure today?"

"Would you like to?"

Christopher paused, not expecting the question. This was clearly a shift from the preceding days when Lucas directed their outings, and it was nice to feel that it was up to Christopher this time. He could now see how his previous lack of spontaneity and resistance to change had made him anxious and uncomfortable on their first few excursions. Ironically, a change in routine and getting out of his comfort zone seemed to be exactly what he had needed to break through some of his old, constraining patterns. Now, he felt vastly different than before the blind man had first spoken to him, and even though he thought he had known who he was and what his priorities were just a few days ago, he could see how he had been sabotaging himself with anxious and fearful emotions. He had *believed* too much in feeling limited, and it had reflected in his environment, creating abundant opportunities for him to experience and reinforce feeling powerless on some level.

Today, however, was different. He was feeling good and strong—like his mind, body, emotions, and beliefs were finally aligned—and he thought that another adventure would continue to help him see the world in new ways. His words were clear.

"Yes, I would."

"Where would you like to go?" Lucas asked.

Christopher hesitated again, at first unsure. It appeared he now had to take a more active role in whatever learning was to come.

"I'd like to go back to the cathedral," he declared, trusting in his spontaneous answer.

Lucas stood up and began walking toward the city center. Christopher looked back at his cart and wavered for a moment, then trotted over to the couple with the baked goods.

"Good morning, Eran!"

"Good morning, Christopher," Eran said. His wife smiled.

"Do you mind keeping an eye on my goods until Ariana or Martel get here? They should be coming shortly. I need to go do something."

Eran glanced down the street at Christopher's lonely cart. "Sure thing. No problem."

Early morning activity was primarily made up of the merchants coming into the square anyway, and they all knew Christopher and could identify his setup. They might wonder where he was, but they would watch over things, especially Ariana and Martel, who would be there soon.

"Thanks so much, Eran!" Christopher said and hustled to catch up to Lucas.

Once beside him, the two men began walking together silently down the mostly-empty streets toward the city center, the sound of their steps syncing to sound like one person's. Christopher decided to attempt to engage in a personal conversation to try to understand more about the blind man and to get to the bottom of the quest, which he knew Martel would be asking about later.

"So, where are you from originally?"

Lucas said nothing for a few steps before answering. "We are from the same place."

Christopher, at this stage recognizing there was likely a hidden meaning to yet another cryptic response, smiled and played along.

"And where is that?" he asked.

"When you figure out where you are from, you'll know."

"But I know where I'm from," Christopher said.

Lucas turned and looked directly at him, still walking, his eyes no longer cloudy but the deep orbs of blackness he had seen a few days before. "Do you really?"

Christopher felt something pop in his head, and his mind went fuzzy for a moment, almost like he was about to pass out. He stumbled for a step before regaining the steady pace at which they were moving. They strode silently for a minute.

"Perhaps maybe I don't," Christopher said, feeling there was still much to understand. "How long have you been sitting in the square?" he asked, hoping that would reveal more.

"Longer than you can imagine."

Another evasive answer, Christopher thought. He decided on a different line of questioning. "How were you blinded?"

"Do I act like I'm blind?"

"No."

"Do you think I'm blind?"

Christopher thought for a moment before answering. He remembered Lucas's comment the other day about his blindness, that sight could go beyond form.

"No, but perhaps physically, yes. Why do your eyes sometimes change?"

They walked a few paces again before Lucas answered.

"Their changing reflects the world I choose to see."

"I don't understand," Christopher said.

"You will," replied Lucas.

Like his father's statement long ago and what the loving shopkeeper in the artisan store said yesterday, it was a reply that left him wanting. *Another "someday,"* he thought.

They continued strolling up the hill toward the center of the city as stores began to open for business and people emerged from their dwellings to start their day. Christopher noted the increased activity by the city's uniformed constables coming in and out of the Department of Enforcement of Government Operations building as they passed. Clearly, the warnings had the constabulary busier than usual. He overheard some yelling inside, something about how could they have *lost* the woman when she was locked up, and he wondered if they were talking about the unstable woman from outside the antique store they had apprehended a few days ago. It briefly made him think of her personal warning to him and the elusive ring she had mentioned.

The two men maintained their progress down the street and turned the corner to the vast, cobblestone plaza housing the cathedral. As they approached, Christopher looked up at the towering spire, thinking about his recent, profound experience with the Perceiver. A knowing washed over him when he reached the base of the grand steps. He stopped, and Lucas stopped with him.

Surprising himself, Christopher said, "I . . . I don't feel the need to go inside. I've already seen what I needed to." He looked at Lucas, who said nothing.

Confident and guided by what he was feeling, Christopher said, "We need to go back . . . now," and he turned to retrace their steps with Lucas trailing behind. For some reason, he was experiencing a sense of urgency to return, like a knowingness that went beyond his physical senses, and he honored its call.

Coming around the corner from the central plaza and nearing the detainment center again, Christopher could see the top of the building's dark façade beginning to capture the morning light. With the sun on it, he noticed its color was a very dark blue, a heavier version of the brighter blue painted on the cobblestones in front of the building's door that looked like a large, cobalt carpet, scuffed and dirty from the grime of the streets and the many who tramped in and out of the structure.

Close to the building, he saw three uniformed men escorting a large, muscular man toward the entrance with his hands secured behind his back. He recognized Vincent.

"Vincent!" Christopher cried out, rushing forward to meet the group, stepping squarely in the center of the worn, blue rectangle in front of the door. "What's going on?"

One constable put out his arm to move Christopher out of their path. "Out of the way, sir," he commanded.

Christopher, in his self-assured space, didn't move, and it surprised him. Normally, he was a strict follower of the rule of law, but this was his friend, and something wasn't right.

Vincent was clearly upset, his eyes wide open and exhibiting uncharacteristic fear. "I don't know what's happening," he said. "I was on my way to —"

"Stop talking," barked one of the other men, who tried to guide Vincent forward past Christopher. He had flaming red hair and was a little older than the other two, and Christopher could feel the man's anger simmering under the surface, begging for an excuse to be released.

Christopher held fast. "No, there must be some mistake. What is this man accused of?"

"I don't have to answer to you," said the man, starting to push Christopher out of the way.

"You have to tell him what he's charged with. That's the law," Christopher said fearlessly. The situation that would have normally made him nervous was noticeably missing that feeling.

"You have no power here!" bellowed the constable.

Christopher stood firmly in place as Lucas silently watched the scene unfold. The redheaded constable was now even more agitated, his deep-rooted anger overflowing whatever internal, insubstantial container that held it. "You need to move, NOW," he shouted, "or you will be arrested too!"

Christopher looked at Lucas, who turned to him as his milky white eyes turned black. Christopher hadn't seen them in the process of changing before, but they did so right in front of him, appearing as dark shadows crossing in front of pale moons. Words echoed in his head, and he knew they were from the blind man.

He has no real power over you.

Whatever inner clarity and strength Christopher was experiencing instantly multiplied. He felt certain in his discernment about the situation, that he would escape safely from this confrontation if he was careful, although he was unsure about Vincent's fate.

He looked at the constable and calmly asserted, "If you don't tell this man what he's being charged with, I'll make sure you get written up. What is your insignia number?" *So much for being careful,* he thought.

All three uniformed men stared at Christopher with a combination of disbelief and defiance. The redhead let go of Vincent and with a look of rage grabbed Christopher by the arm.

Just then, an officer of the detainment center emerged from the building. He had a different uniform than the others and his right cheek sported a thin scar.

"What's going on here?" he demanded. He was older and Christopher could tell he had more authority and experience than the other three. The two columns of buttons on his coat and four bars on his chest clearly trumped the one and two bars the other three sported next to their coats' single column of buttons.

Christopher spoke quickly before the others could respond. "This man is being arrested and has not been informed why, which is the law. Isn't that right?"

The redhead holding Christopher screeched, "This man is impeding an arrest! He needs to be detained too!"

The officer looked both Christopher and Lucas up and down, locking eyes with Lucas for a moment, whose eyes had returned to their cloudy state. The officer's authoritative demeanor morphed into what Christopher felt was a little bit anxious.

"Are you getting in the way of our enforcement?" the man asked.

"No, sir," Christopher said. "I know this man, and he is a fine, upstanding citizen."

The officer looked at Vincent. "We'll see." Turning back to Christopher, he said, "Why are you here?"

"We're on our way back from the cathedral." He didn't need to mention that they didn't go inside.

"A bit early for that, isn't it?"

"It was an early trip before I have to start selling in the marketplace."

"Mmm. So, you're not here to obstruct us doing our job?"

"No, sir. Of course not. I saw my friend and am wondering why he's being detained." The redheaded constable tightened his grip on Christopher's arm, and Christopher was now less certain about feeling that he and Lucas would be able to avoid trouble.

The redhead stared at Christopher and said, "He got in the way of us bringing this man in."

"Is that true?" asked the officer.

"I only stopped to ask why he was being arrested."

The officer took a deep breath and let it out. "You realize we don't have to tell you that. You see, once we get to a certain warning level, the applicable laws change. Since we are in an increasingly threatening environment and have gotten to Level 4, we no longer need to inform a person, or their family or friends, of the reason for their arrest."

Christopher now recalled that the manual about the government announcements stated that constables had more discretion when applying laws under the elevated warnings. He mentally kicked himself for not remembering, for it had put him in a precarious position with the authorities. He supposed it made sense that the government needed to be able to have some flexibility in times of threats, like now, but it didn't make sense why they would apply it to a good citizen like Vincent.

"I apologize for not knowing that," Christopher said, hoping his admission would allow them to leave without incident. "I must have misunderstood the manual."

"Indeed," the officer said, eying Christopher and then Lucas, seemingly evaluating his options. After a few seconds, he gestured to them and said to the three constables, "Let these two go. Yes, let's call it a misunderstanding. People get anxious and excited about the warnings. We do our best to help them understand the changes to the law. After all, we're here to protect you." He said the last sentence very seriously while staring at Christopher.

The constable holding Christopher's arm released it with a shove.

"Thank you," Christopher said. "I'd like to ask why this man is being taken in. Even though the law only recently changed, certainly he deserves to know." He normally would have left before continuing to engage in a situation like this, but he felt bold, clear, and confident in his communication and intent to understand.

The officer examined him for a moment before looking at the three men in uniform, who still wore masks of varying degrees of anger and contempt. "Go ahead. Tell him."

One of the three stepped forward and said, "I don't think we should, sir."

"Tell them!" the officer barked, causing the man to step back with a shudder. Christopher was surprised at the officer's quick change in character. Clearly, he needed to retain his authority over the constables.

"Uh," the man stammered, "we were told by a Governor to pick this man up and detain him until further notice." He gestured to Vincent, who had remained quiet since being commanded to. "That's all we know."

"So, nothing specific?" the officer asked.

"No, sir. Nothing specific."

The officer nodded with finality and turned back to Christopher and Lucas, looking warily at Lucas. Christopher *knew* this was related to what Vincent had overheard at his worksite the other day, and there was nothing he could do about it. He had done all he could. Vincent seemed to recognize this and gave Christopher a slight nod, accepting his fate.

"I will tell you that your friend here will enjoy the benefit of the doubt under any questioning," said the officer, who flicked his head toward the door, which prompted the redhead to shoot Christopher a malicious look before roughly shoving Vincent forward toward the door. The other two constables followed.

Christopher and Lucas watched them enter as Vincent gave one last, over-the-shoulder, concentrated look at Christopher that said, *Don't share what I told you or you'll wind up here with me.*

"Thank you for your time and adherence to our laws," said the officer before he turned and disappeared into the building after the others.

Christopher stood there. He had tried to help his friend, even at risk to himself, and he was lucky to have at least gotten some information about Vincent's detainment, even if he hadn't been able to get him released. He couldn't exactly tell the constables about Vincent's inadvertent eavesdropping or that the warnings might be false, because accusing the heads of the government would certainly have implications. As much as the constabulary was beholden to follow the laws and the information it was given, it would always defer to the words of the powerful Governors over the words of a farmer.

An angry face with a mop of red hair appeared in the window of the building, directing its ire toward the two men still standing outside.

"It's time to go," Lucas said. Christopher agreed, knowing that they risked another encounter if they remained, and they continued back to the market.

~

Upon their return, the blind man sat down again in his usual space, and Christopher was about to go to his cart but decided otherwise. Instead, he turned and walked back to the antique store on the corner.

The shop was still closed when he tried the door, so he peered in the window. He had only been inside a few times before, the last time years ago before his father had died. From what he could see, it looked like it hadn't changed much, with piles of old items haphazardly scattered about the tables and shelves.

There was a jangle of keys behind him and a "Good morning!" from the owner, who had come up behind him.

"Good morning," Christopher replied, stepping back from the window.

"You can see better from inside," the bespectacled, rotund man said, smiling. He unlocked and opened the door, and Christopher followed him inside, the bell above them announcing their entrance.

"Actually, I was looking for you," Christopher said.

"Oh?" said the man, who went behind the counter to drop his satchel. "What can I do for you?"

"Well, did you see the tall woman with messy hair a few days ago? She was acting kind of strange. She came out of your store several days in a row and tried to talk to me."

"Yes, I did." His words were careful, measured.

"Do you know her?"

The man paused, looked down, and shuffled his feet. When he brought his head back up, Christopher held his gaze and waited.

"Yes," he finally said, "a little bit."

"Who is she? Where is she from?" Christopher asked, eager to discover something about her and why she had accosted him.

Again, the man looked down and shuffled his feet, but Christopher wasn't going to let it go. "Please," he said.

The man looked up. "She's an old friend. She might seem strange, but that's only when she's here."

"What do you mean?" Christopher asked. "When she's visiting your shop or . . . is she not from around here?"

The shopkeeper looked nervous. He glanced out the front window, swallowed, and coughed slightly. Turning back to his

FIFTH231

visitor, his demeanor softened and the eyes behind his glasses relaxed. It was only for a few seconds, but like with the woman in the artisan shop, Christopher felt like he had just been assessed in some way.

The shop owner sighed in resignation, and Christopher didn't know whether he had passed the evaluation or if the man didn't have it in him to resist his questions.

"No, she's not from around here. She comes from . . . from outside the Wall."

"What!?" Christopher exclaimed. "She's one of the foreigners about to invade us?"

"Shhhh!" The man hushed him and glanced out the front of the shop again. "No, no, no. Nothing like that. She's not a danger to anyone."

"But she accosted me outside your shop a few days ago, spouting nonsense."

The man tilted his head down and peered over the top of his glasses. "Nonsense? Are you sure about that?"

"Um, no, but it didn't make any sense."

"Mmm, yes. What she says can be puzzling at times, but it usually bears itself out."

"What do you mean?"

"She speaks the truth, even if it's ambiguous or sounds outlandish."

Christopher tried to wrap his head around what he was hearing, adding it to the already confusing messages the woman had given him and what Lucas had said about her. *Truth?* he thought. *So, I'm going to die if I'm not ready?* It took a minute for his mind to stop spinning long enough to formulate his next question, something he desperately wanted to know. "How did she get past the Wall?"

The shopkeeper eyed Christopher, seemingly contemplating what to say. He broke his gaze and looked at the wall behind Christopher—a distant look that went far beyond the shop's wall—then back at Christopher. "She has an ability to get herself here. I don't know how. She comes to this shop because it's safer than most places."

"What do you mean, 'safer'?"

"Well, it's difficult enough for her to be here, so she needs to know the destination she's arriving at is safe and secure." He opened his arms wide. "This is a safe place for her."

Christopher thought of what the blind man had said, that she had trouble here and that she was better off in another world. Maybe he meant the world outside the Wall, which perhaps wasn't as dangerous as Christopher and everyone in the Territories had been led to believe.

The shopkeeper continued. "Being here shifts her personality some. That's why she seemed strange to you."

"Like's she's in a different world," Christopher said softly to himself, trying to make sense of what he was hearing.

The man's expression glowed, like they were finally on the same page and understood each other. "Yes!" he exclaimed. "Now do you understand?"

"No, not really. So, if she's from outside the Wall and she's not a danger, she and her people aren't trying to invade the Territories?"

The man laughed a full belly laugh that Christopher might have thought was mocking if it wasn't so genuine.

"No, no," he said as his laughter tapered off. "Of that I am certain."

Christopher didn't know what to think about all this new information. It was challenging his beliefs about the Territories more than even the incident with Vincent or what the gang leader had told him about the discharged criminals.

"Did you see that she got arrested a few days ago?" Christopher asked.

"Yes, but she'll be fine."

"Really? How? I need to know because my friend just got detained, but he didn't do anything. What can I do to help him?"

"Oh, I'm sorry, but it's not like that. There's nothing I can offer that would help."

"But how will she be fine?"

The man took a deep breath. "Trust me, she'll be okay."

"I heard something about a woman being *lost* in the detainment center. Could that have been her?"

"Maybe," the man said as he tried to suppress a grin, but it was clear he was pleased to hear that.

The bell above the door rang and a customer entered. The shopkeeper gave Christopher a firm look, which sent a clear message: *Keep this between us.*

Christopher nodded and said, "Thank you for your help," and exited the shop. He walked back past Lucas to his cart in somewhat of a daze, trying to process what he had learned. There were a few customers in the square but none near him or his friends, who had arrived.

Ariana stepped forward and hugged him. "Where did you go so early?"

"I decided to get an early start on the quest so you and Martel wouldn't have to cover for me," he said.

"And did you find out anything new?" Martel asked.

"Well," Christopher said, "I now have more questions than answers." He leaned forward, beckoned them both towards him, and in a hushed tone said, "Have you ever questioned the government's accounts of things? You know, like do you totally believe everything they say?"

Ariana and Martel looked at each other. Ariana spoke first.

"I have no reason not to. They've kept us safe from outsiders. My grandparents said they successfully repelled an attack on the Wall in their time."

"I heard rumors over the years but never really got into them," Martel said quietly. "Everything works around here, and I like when things work. Plus, you know it's illegal to discuss this stuff."

"Yes, I know," Christopher said, "but I seem to keep coming across things that make me think that the government is not quite like what we've been led to believe."

"What do you mean?" asked Ariana.

"Well," Christopher said, "they just arrested Vincent, and there doesn't seem to be a reason why."

"What? The stonemason?" Ariana said. "Why would they do that?"

Christopher didn't want to share what Vincent had overheard and potentially put them in jeopardy too, so he was vague. "I don't know, but the government seems to be nervous about something."

"Uh, yeah, the invasion," Martel said. "You heard the warnings."

"Yes, but it's something beyond the announcements," Christopher said. "I don't want to get into details, but I believe that," he paused and looked around, "that the Governors may be manipulating us by not always telling the truth." There, he said it.

"Why? About what?" Ariana said.

"I'm not sure, and I don't know the extent of it yet, but I'm trying to find out. I have a feeling that I'll learn more if I can get to the other side of the Wall."

Ariana looked at him in disbelief. "What? You realize that even if you could get outside the Wall, which you can't, there's an army of foreigners on its way to attack us."

Christopher paused and looked at her with a raised eyebrow. "Is there?"

"Do you want to take that chance?"

Christopher took a deep breath. "No, not really? But there's something about that Wall . . ." He trailed off.

Martel chuckled and shook his head. "You understand you're talking about going through or under or over or around the Wall. Even if there wasn't an army of depraved, vicious attackers out there, how are you going to do that? It's impossible. Many have tried—I'm sure you've heard about them—but none have made it."

"Yes, I've heard," Christopher said, "but I can't get past this idea that that's where the answers are, to the quest and all the questions that have come up around Lucas. I feel the truth is out there, regardless of what the government tells us."

"Meanwhile, we've had four warnings indicating an impending attack, and we need to prepare," Martel said. "What are we supposed to do, ignore the warnings?"

"No, no, we need to listen to them," Christopher said, "because I'm not saying they're wrong. I'm just saying I have some questions, and there are times the government may not be being forthright with us."

More people were now milling about the market, and a constable was slowly strolling nearby. Christopher nodded over at him and said, "To be continued," which made the three stop their risky conversation and go back behind their goods to begin attending to customers.

~

The day progressed like any other, except for scattered talk about the warnings and the fearful manner of many in the market. Christopher sold well, his crates of canned and jarred goods emptying before the crates of fruits and vegetables. Many tried to engage him in conversation about the announcements, and he responded that just following the government's instructions should take their worry out of the day, for when has the government led them astray? Every time he said it, however, he felt a little pang of guilt knowing he had his own unanswered questions, and he wondered if he was misleading them. Nevertheless, they left with their goods and seemingly in a less troubled manner than when they had arrived, and he was happy for that.

Still, the incident with Vincent weighed on his mind, and he was considering what else he could do to help. But the answer that kept coming wasn't in his head. It was a *feeling* that everything would be okay, that doing nothing, letting time pass, and simply desiring Vincent's safe return was the best course of action, and he trusted that answer from within. An opportunity would present itself; he just didn't know when it would come or what it would look like.

Early in the afternoon, the rare sound of the clip-clop of a horse's hooves on cobblestones echoed across the marketplace, and everyone in the square turned to see who was approaching. Everyone except Lucas, that is. Christopher hadn't seen a horse in years, so he, too, was staring.

It was a high-ranking government official, and he trotted past the antique store and dismounted, handing over the reins to an attendant accompanying him. He was dressed pretentiously, wearing a black, square-shouldered suit with a dark blue, gold-trimmed sash across it on an angle, a black, silk top hat, and a garish bronze buckle on a wide belt that couldn't contain his considerable belly. His chest seemed unnaturally thrust forward, as if attempting to prominently display the bulky pendant of the Perceiver hanging from the heavy, gold chain around his neck and the ornate patch near his shoulder that was given to high government officials. People around him gave him a wide berth as he slowly lumbered his way up the street, his heft heavily holding him to the earth. The attendant followed with his horse.

The strange silence that had permeated the marketplace upon his arrival began to break as he continued, the conversations and activity slowly returning to their previous levels. The man approached a few merchants, evaluating their goods disinterestedly, then came upon Ariana, who curtsied politely. He nodded in acknowledgement, staring at her longer than he had at any other vendor. When he got to Christopher's cart, he paused and surveyed the fresh produce.

These officials were rarely, if ever, seen in the market. Normally, they had others do their shopping for them, but Christopher could tell this man wanted to be out and about to gauge how people were reacting to the announcements. Apparently, he decided to engage with the farmer.

"Sooo," the man began, "what are people saying about the decrees?" He picked up an apple for inspection. Christopher hadn't heard the warnings described that way before.

"They say they're worried, but I tell them they really don't need to be too concerned at this time." Christopher's words and energy were clear and unambiguous, like his voice and bearing earlier in the morning in front of the detainment center.

Surprised, the man looked up from examining the fruit. "Really? Why do you say that?"

"Because we're only at Level 4. As I understand, there's no *imminent* danger."

The man eyed Christopher suspiciously. "Yes, but the danger is coming, and we must remain vigilant and prepare for the worst."

"Of course," Christopher said, "but we can do that and not worry about it."

The official, whose face reflected no lines to indicate he had ever smiled, lifted his chin and frowned, looking down his nose at Christopher while he shifted his weight.

"Well, I hope for your sake we don't get invaded. I'd hate to see what the evil, immoral foreigners would do to you," he snapped.

Without missing a beat, Christopher responded, "Do you not have faith in the Grand Wall and our Grand Army? If we do get invaded, do you not trust them to do their job and keep the foreigners out of the Territories?"

The man scowled and almost said something but stopped himself. It was clear he was not used to being questioned.

"Who do you think you are?" he demanded when he regained his voice, leaning over the cart in an attempt at intimidation.

Christopher stood confidently and calmly said, "I'm a farmer who supplies fruit and vegetables to the good citizens of the city. What do you do?"

"I keep you safe," the man growled, turning away and expecting the end of the conversation, but Christopher hadn't finished.

"But since the Wall has never been breached, what is it you *really* do?" he said.

The man turned back, his face red. "I keep you safe!" he shrieked, unable to control himself, his voice cracking. Half the people in the square turned to see what the disturbance was.

"Okay, then thank you. Keep up the good work. Next!" Christopher said, dismissing the man and looking directly at the woman behind him whose bulging eyes and open mouth reflected her astonishment at hearing Christopher talk back to such a man of influence.

Insulted and with eyes ablaze, the official snorted and stared at Christopher in an attempt to bully him into obedience and surrender, but today was not the day to engage Christopher's newfound sense of power and discernment. Unfortunately for the official, he was at a severe disadvantage before he had even stepped up to Christopher's cart.

Christopher shifted his eyes from his next customer back to the man and stared, seeing that the thin veneer of the official's heated emotions hid many fears, the greatest of which was a fear of losing authority and control. His words had made the man feel threatened and anxious, and it was not something the official was used to or knew how to handle.

Finally, fuming, the man yielded his gaze and muttered, "You better watch yourself." He looked down at the produce and said indignantly, "And your fruit has spots," and he turned and waddled off, followed by his attendant and horse.

Christopher watched him leave, not considering the last, petty comment because he knew his fruit was good. He wondered, however, if the official would have him arrested for no reason, like Vincent had been, something he hadn't thought of while engaging with the man.

Martel, Ariana, and a few others had witnessed the entire conversation. Ariana was looking at him with alarm and Martel was laughing nervously.

"Are you kidding me?" Martel exclaimed. "That was brilliant!" He slapped Christopher on the shoulder. "I couldn't have said it better myself." He then added more seriously, quietly, "But like he said, you might want to watch yourself. You don't want to tangle with those who hold power."

"I'm not sure what they have should be called true power," Christopher said, thinking that what he had opened up to and learned this week had a soft, subtle, lasting feeling of genuine power compared to the quick, angry burst of forceful energy the man expressed. "There's a difference between power and force." Hearing himself say the words and knowing that he wouldn't have been able to perceive the difference in those two terms just a few days ago, he realized that he might have sounded just a little bit like Lucas.

Ariana came over from behind her flowers and hugged him. "Please don't do that again," she said. "I don't want you taken away, or hurt."

"Everything's going to be okay," Christopher said, hugging her back. And he sensed it. Despite his confronting the constables earlier and challenging the government official, he felt a strength—a power, a *rightness*—in what he had said and done. There was an underlying clarity to the feeling that everything was going to be all right no matter what the repercussions.

What he had expressed had come naturally, an instinctive reaction centered more in his heart than in his head. In fact, the whole day he had surrendered to this feeling, which had driven his actions from his decision on where to go with Lucas early in the morning, to his decision to turn back without going into the cathedral, to his questioning the constables outside the detainment center, to the words offending the official.

For the first time, Christopher felt fully present and in control of himself, but not in a dramatic, self-centered way. This was different. He was allowing life to unfold around him rather than devoting mental and emotional energy into what had previously been an *effort* to decide or do things, which often felt forced and drained his energy. When he could feel present, clear, and strong while minimizing those efforts, why wouldn't he do so? He was beginning to see all his busyness and work on the farm in a new light and recognized that perhaps the old, lingering emotions he sometimes felt challenged by came from his own stubborn will to control the situations around him.

Before this day, he could see that he normally attempted to accomplish things through thinking, feeling, and following up with action—chores, selling, exchanges with Ariana, farm work, conversations, everything. Even if minor and requiring little energy, these interactions with the world came from a place— namely his mind or emotions, or a combination of both—that was not fundamentally *who he was*. They were just the surface of his core essence that he was now just beginning to experience through the lessons with Lucas this week. And this shadowy specter of his personality reflected the world around him more than the truth within him, which he was now beginning to recognize, trust, and *know*. He felt confident that by allowing it to come forth unimpeded by his thinking and temperament that everything around him would be able to flow more smoothly and naturally. He no longer had to *carry* the stones of his responsibil- ities but rather could allow them to roll alongside him with minimal effort. Still, however, the stones remained.

Christopher locked his gaze on Ariana, looking deeply into the blue-green kaleidoscope of colors in her eyes, and repeated very slowly and clearly, "Everything is going to be okay."

Ariana stood up a little straighter, composed herself, and said gently, "Yes, I believe you. Everything is going to be okay."

Christopher smiled, feeling a warmth inside from knowing that she trusted him and that their connection brought her comfort and support. It certainly did to him, and it made him

A TALE OF AWAKENING

start thinking about what life on the farm would be like with her by his side.

As if to challenge that very thought, the loudspeakers screeched awake with three rising tones. Ariana, still in Christopher's strong arms, suppressed a gasp as they both looked up at the speaker on the corner. Christopher genuinely hoped it would be an announcement that the threat was winding down, for it would relieve him of his conflicting thoughts about the government's intentions, at least in the short term, giving him more time to get answers to his questions and to figure things out. But it was not to be.

This is a Level 5 Warning by the Council of Governors. The enemy force is two days away from reaching the Grand Wall. As stated in your zone's manual, all citizens must report to their designated shelter in the city within thirty-six hours, and martial law will be declared at that time. Anyone outside their assigned area after that time will be arrested. Please see your zone's manual for your sheltering instructions. This is a Level 5 Warning.

"Hmm," Christopher grumbled.

Hearing him and seeing his disappointment, Ariana looked at him intensely. "And you said everything was going to be okay."

"Um, yes, it will be. I was just hoping the threat was winding down. We'll be fine if we follow the government's instructions. In the history of the Territories, have the outsiders ever breached the Wall?"

"No."

"Then we'll just follow the manual and instructions, and everything will be fine after a temporary interruption to our lives," Christopher said.

Ariana pulled him in for a hug.

Christopher was more worried than he let on. Besides the disruption in tending to his crops, going to a shelter would make it difficult, if not impossible, to make enough money to pay his taxes. Also, he had never known the Territories to be under such a threat, and even his parents hadn't seen this level before.

He meant what he had said though, but as much as he had these many questioning thoughts about the government—from what Vincent had overheard and from what the gang leader and antique storeowner had told him—it was difficult to ignore the very real possibility that the Territories were about to be attacked. He could feel increasing apprehension spread throughout the square with the warning, and its tangible, visceral impact on him made it exceedingly real, more so than the previous warnings. In addition, prior to his excursions with Lucas, he had been a very pragmatic person, and such a long-standing operating habit was hard to repress given the announcements and reactions from his fellow citizens.

He sold out quickly, as everyone seemed frantic to stock up on whatever they could find, and he began packing up to head home. Ariana still had some bouquets left.

"Hey," he said to Ariana, "I need to go back now." He was feeling an internal urge like early in the morning outside the cathedral, and he wanted to honor it.

"Okay, I'll come with you," she said and picked up her baskets.

"No, my dear, stay and finish selling. Please don't take this the wrong way, but I need to do something on my own. I'll see you later, though." He didn't know exactly what he needed to do or when or where he would see her later, but it felt true.

She looked at him with mild disappointment, but said, "Okay."

He kissed her, nodded to Martel, and began pulling his empty cart home.

It was a solitary, introspective walk back, his mind spinning, trying to reconcile his thoughts and feelings about the government, the warnings, the Wall, and Lucas. Now, with a deadline before the required sheltering, he had limited time to figure things out. *Thirty-six hours*, he thought. *Nothing like pressure to get something done.*

Thoughts about the Wall soon elbowed out the other concerns, and he felt that that was what he needed answers to more than anything else. Something inside was pressing him toward it, and the only thing that was going to satisfy his curiosity was to physically go to the Wall. The feeling became so compelling as he traveled the dirt road that he was getting excited just thinking about it; the curious child was ready to explore. He figured he could spend some time by the Wall before it got dark.

Once home, he stored his cart, grabbed an apple and a drink of water, then set out for the West Wall. The need to go to it felt more important than even working the fields to prepare for tomorrow, which indicated its importance to him. As he walked towards it, he could see that it was further away than when he had seen it the other day.

Following the same road and paths he had taken previously, Christopher soon stood again in front of the great stone edifice. It had undeniably moved since his previous visit and was now apparently dissecting a large grove of birch trees on a hillside. He touched it, feeling its cool, damp strength, and began walking along its length, dragging his hand along the ridges in the rough exterior.

He continued for what seemed like an hour, communing with the Wall, inviting its secrets to be revealed. He thought about what the antique storeowner had said about the woman who had accosted him, the outsider somehow being able to cross the barrier, but also that she had trouble inside the Wall. Something about it seemed false or magical to him because it didn't make sense. Then again, neither did the properties of the Wall.

He could see how the barrier would repel foreign invaders, as it appeared to be impenetrable. But despite what he had heard about it being impossible to get past, or deadly, he now knew from his earlier conversation that there *was* a way, however mysterious it might be. This confirmed what his heart was telling him, that it was somehow achievable and something he was feeling increasingly compelled to attempt.

At some point, Christopher turned back the way he came and dragged his fingers across the stones as before, looking for any perceivable weakness or hidden passage. The Wall, however, would not give up its mysteries. Its rough face stood firm, expressionless, and unmoving, not unlike the demeanor of the blind man, and both were inherently challenging him to overcome the confines of who he thought he was.

He noted that he wasn't feeling frustrated at not learning anything new on this excursion to the Wall; rather, he felt a certain sense of peace in knowing that he had followed the inner call to take the trip, and that was enough. If it didn't result in any new understanding, then so be it.

Returning to his starting point where the fresh path and the Wall met, Christopher sat leaning against the cold, hard surface, enjoying its shade. His thoughts emptied and, weary from his early start to the day and his walk along the barrier, he dozed off.

~

He awoke in the middle of a flat, grassy field. The sun streaked through the large, billowy clouds that dotted the sky. Insects buzzed about but didn't bother him. Looking around, he could see that the horizon extended as far as he could see in all directions. There was no Wall.

Not feeling surprised, he extended his arms out to his sides and took a deep breath of the fresh, clean air, feeling a freedom he hadn't felt before, like a bird being released from its cage and spreading its wings to fly for the first time.

He started walking in no direction in particular and soon heard a low rumble. Behind him, an enormous, dark, towering structure moved slowly in his direction. Confused at the change in scenery, he stood and watched it for a minute. It didn't look like the Wall he had been leaning against; it was curved outward, extended higher than he could see, and had little definition except for different shades of gray. It looked like a giant storm cloud but denser than it had any right to be, and it moved toward him like a dark, heavy thunderstorm across the plains.

Suddenly feeling confined, Christopher turned and tried to run, but his legs moved sluggishly, barely able to take a step. It wasn't like they were stuck in mud with his feet anchored to the ground; he just couldn't get his legs to move at anything resembling normal speed.

With the ominous, shadowy structure bearing down on him like a slow-moving predator, he panicked, struggling to put distance between himself and the menacing, malevolent darkness, but he could barely move. He was caught, trapped like a helpless animal waiting for its demise at the jaws of the massive, gray beast.

As the shadow approached, the feeling of evil overpowered him. His breathing shortened further and further as the air was sucked out of his body and replaced with blackness. He tried to scream for help, but no sound came forth. Fighting to move with no success, the weight of the destructive force slowly rolled over him, crushing the last life from his lungs and decimating the landscape with darkness.

Waking with an anxious breath, Christopher scrambled to his feet, gasping and clutching his chest. It was a dream, or more appropriately, a nightmare. It took a few minutes for his breath to return to normal. When it did, he sat down again against the Wall, exhausted despite the brief sleep.

What are you trying to tell me? he thought. The dream was a continuation of one he had had a few times previously, but never to completion and never with this intensity. Before, it had always ended with the dark cloud still in the distance and him feeling only slightly immoveable—he was still able to run, albeit slowly. Still, he woke up from those precursor imaginings feeling artificially restrained and with a weight on his chest, but nothing compared to what he had just experienced. Surely, something was coming to his awareness that begged for attention, and to be dealt with. If he couldn't outrun the darkness, he at least hoped he would be able to handle it and accept that what was on the other side of the emotions was worth the struggle.

After reflecting for some time, he stood up, took a deep breath, and patted the Wall. "See you later," he said softly, and he proceeded back down the path toward home.

~

Ariana was waiting for him on his porch when he got back, sitting in one of his chairs. She waved as he approached.

"You're in my chair," Christopher said as he climbed the stairs. Ariana smiled and stood up, and they embraced.

She had left the city soon after he did, had gone home to take care of some things, and then had walked to his place. She knew where he lived, as she and her family had come by to offer condolences after his father had died, but now the circumstances were entirely different . . . for both of them.

The evening was a blur. They snuggled first on the porch, enjoying the sunset, and then moved inside, making up for time that seemed like it could never be recovered. Their connection was profound and palpable, on the surface a culmination of years of knowing each other and finally accepting their fated union, but more deeply a remembering of a blessed bond that transcended time itself.

"So, where did you go after the market?" she asked once they had settled inside on the old, straw couch his grandfather had made.

"I went to the Wall," he said. He had no desire to hide the fact.

She looked at him disapprovingly.

"I couldn't help it," he continued. "There are some things I'm being drawn to discover, and I believe the Wall is key to them."

"And what about the invasion? You told me this afternoon that we just need to follow the instructions and everything will be okay."

"Yes, and I believe that. I just need some answers. There's a part of me that doesn't trust what the government is telling us. I mean, have you ever questioned why the stories of the Grand Army repelling the invaders seem so . . . thin?"

She gave him a quizzical look.

"The old tales talk about how the Grand Army saves us from the foreigners beyond the Wall, but from what I heard from my family, details are always scarce, and the Grand Army continually remains unseen, even just before and after a presumed attack. Where are the personal accounts of the battles besides the government versions of them?" His question made them both pause.

"We shouldn't be talking about this," Ariana said, but she continued anyway. "The Grand Wall is what saves us. The Grand Army doesn't do much because the Wall is so impenetrable."

"It may be impenetrable, but I heard of someone who was able to get into the Territories from outside the Wall. I don't know how, and it sounded mysterious, but I believed it."

She eyed him skeptically. "That's impossible. How come we've never heard about it? There's no way. How? A secret tunnel?"

Christopher shrugged. "I wish I knew. I'd like to confirm the government's accounts of what's going on."

"So, you don't trust the government, but do you trust me?" Ariana asked.

Christopher was surprised at her switch to something personal. "Of course," he said.

"Well, I know that we've never been invaded, so the government has been doing something right. And if we *don't* believe them and the foreigners actually *are* able to breach the Wall, then we wouldn't be protected at all."

"I agree," Christopher said, "which is why we should follow the manual's instructions to be safe."

He rose and walked to a shelf nearby, pulled a hide-bound book from among a stack of books and papers, and returned with it to the couch. He flipped it open and began to scan the pages, summarizing as he went.

"Let's see . . . Level 5," he began, flipping to the fifth sheet and running his finger down the page. "Increased vigilance . . . no unnecessary travel . . . constables have more discretion in applying laws . . . prepare for sheltering by packing food and water in case of invasion . . . follow instructions as they are announced . . . and there's an address for sheltering. That's it."

He closed the book and tossed it to an empty space on the couch.

"I have enough food stored in the cellar for both of us to bring to the shelter—cans, jars, and dried goods. So, besides packing provisions and preparing for sheltering, I have, what, a little over thirty hours to try to figure some things out?"

Ariana nodded. "Um," she drew a finger up his arm and looked him in the eyes, "you said, 'for both of us.' Should we say we now live together so we can shelter together?" She gave him a goofy, flirty grin.

Christopher smiled and nodded, and she nestled into his arms.

"I don't want to over worry," she said, "but I'm concerned about the warnings because I care about you and us and the Territories, and I want us all to be safe."

"You are safe. We are safe. The city is safe. The Territories are safe within the Wall," he said tenderly. "Everything's going to be okay. I've got you."

She snuggled into him more deeply, as if his words and comforting embrace were a warm blanket that would protect her from her own, chilly thoughts.

He was encouraged by how the day had unfolded, trusting his feelings and impulses despite the uncertainty of several situations. Consequently, he felt more in charge of his life than ever before, which gave him the strength to feel that he could take care of her and keep her safe even if the foreigners actually attacked, breached the Wall, and invaded the lands.

However, right now his heart and mind were being pulled in another direction, away from her and the manual's instructions. Despite what he was feeling for her and his concern about the possible attack, he suspected his inner longing to find answers was going to spirit him away from her very soon.

But for now, he was holding the woman he loved—tightly, lovingly—and she melted into him, and he didn't want to let go.

~

"What do you want to know?"

The voice was back, as clear and as deeply resonant as its prior appearance.

"Ask."

It wasn't as surprising as before, and Christopher felt the lightness in his chest again. His throat didn't feel constricted, and his head was jumbled but more liberated compared to last time. He didn't want to squander another opportunity.

"What do you want to know?" the voice repeated.

Christopher began to feel some clarity. It was elusive, but an energy was building inside him that began to focus his thoughts. The many questions in his head tumbled over each other for placement but faded to the background as his mouth opened to speak with a power of intent he didn't know he possessed.

"Everythi—"

Before the single word could fully escape his lips, his chest and head exploded in a dizzying surge of energy, expanding him beyond form and scattering his awareness into the far reaches of the universe. He passed out.

Bolting upright in bed, Christopher's heart beat powerfully and rapidly in his chest. Ariana stirred beside him but didn't wake. It was the middle of the night and dark outside.

He turned and sat on the edge of the bed, breathing heavily but without the choking feeling from the previous time he had dreamed of the voice. The feeling of expansion lingered, and he observed it slowly trickle down to nothing many minutes later as he felt himself come back to fully reinhabit his physical form. His mind was spinning, going nowhere in particular except for incoherently trying to piece together what had just happened. As before, even though it was just a dream, it felt real.

Breathing normally and with his heartbeat back down, he lay back and closed his eyes. He needed to get some rest because he could sense that something dangerous yet extraordinary was coming that would have an enormous impact on him and his life with Ariana, and he didn't know if it related to the invasion, the Wall, the quest to understand more about Lucas, or something else. But as the unstable woman outside the antique store had said—and he had the overwhelming feeling that she had spoken the truth—he needed to be ready. His life depended on it.

Anna

Yes, *everything!* Anna thought as she finished the chapter, her heart beating heavily in her chest like Christopher's in his dream. Despite being thrilled he was spending the night with Ariana at last, she *really* wanted him to learn all that he wanted to know and was finally able to ask. *Everything.* It excited her that it might actually be within his reach. However, she was sure he would have to undergo a last test or two before he got there. All good stories had something like that to build to a good climactic ending.

But this was more than just a story; it really seemed true. From the description of the Territories, to the cover of the book she held in her hands, to the depiction of the antique shop and owner she was so familiar with, Anna was getting the feeling that except for the blind man's mystical qualities and the woman from outside the Wall, everything in the tale at least had the *potential* to be true.

A few things about the world in the story stood out to her, as they made her think of how they might cross over into her world. The angry, redheaded constable sure sounded a lot like her father—which was curious to see in a story—but that didn't make sense because it was written so many years ago based on what the owner of the antique shop had said and by the style of writing and appearance of the pages. She also wondered if it was the same shopkeeper she knew, just younger in the story. She made a mental note to ask him about it the next time she was there. And she wanted to be able to explore the city to try to find the artisan shop with all the paired figurines because it sounded so wonderful and loving and she might be able to have an experience like Christopher's in it.

With how Christopher had handled himself outside the detainment center and in the square with the official, although it was nerve-wracking for her to witness as a reader, she now felt inspired to do the same, to stand up for herself and for what was right. Her father immediately came to mind as she glanced up at her portal "to another world," and she found herself caring less about whether or not he would be angry about it. Whatever his reaction, she resolved that it was going to stay this time.

She really hoped Christopher would learn the secrets of the Wall. She could feel the oppressiveness of being forced to live within its imprisoning boundaries, its heavy shadows ebbing and flowing across the landscape with the movement of the sun, and she wished he could escape it and find the freedom he so desperately desired. It mirrored the suffocating rules she lived under, ones she couldn't wait to put behind her, not to mention feeling some level of the same confining feeling of living within the Wall's physical boundaries. If Christopher could learn the secrets that would carry him past the limitations in his world, then maybe she could do the same. In this, they had a common goal.

Compared to Christopher's story, hers was still being written, but she felt a kinship with him and his journey to try to go beyond his world, to not just understand what was out there but to *experience* it. There was power there, power that she was beginning to feel inside. And while Christopher had Lucas to help him see with more clarity, she didn't have anybody like that to assist her. She did, however, have this manuscript, which was already exposing her to new ways of seeing her world.

Anna snuggled further into her pillow, giddy in anticipation of the last few chapters that she was sure would bring fresh insights and revelations. She hoped Christopher would find success—at whatever he put his mind to and wherever the pages took him—for she suspected it would give her the confidence to do so herself on wherever her own journey led. As she had progressed through the tale, she felt increasingly that her fate had become intertwined with his, this unknown farmer's, and that his accomplishment, or lack thereof, would help set the stage for the rest of her life.

With that thought, a twinge of worry floated into her awareness, because if she identified with Christopher and his journey, what if the ending of the tale was tragic and the people in the story she had come to know and love died horribly at the hands of the invading foreigners? She shivered at the thought, sincerely hoping there would be a positive outcome to Christopher's quest to understand the Wall and what his father had said to him about Lucas when he was a boy. Her worry, however, lingered uncomfortably beneath that hope.

Now, feeling guardedly optimistic about Christopher's journey, as well as her own through her connection to him, she glanced up again at her portal on the wall and turned the page.

Sixth

The shadows perceive beyond their roles and view the stage from above,
seeing what can be known, and the curtain rises to expose the masquerade
to the eye of truth.

~

The dawn light illuminated the sky outside the window as Christopher rolled over and put his arm around Ariana. She gave a sleepy groan and stretched before turning onto her side to face him.

"Hi," she said, smiling broadly, wrapping herself around him.

"Hi," he replied, beaming back.

"What time is it?"

"Time to stay in bed." He didn't like the concept of a clock or timetable just then. She chuckled, resting comfortably in his arms. Although unplanned, he thoroughly welcomed her presence in his home. It felt natural.

After a few minutes, he extricated himself from their entwined limbs, went to the window, and peered into the distance.

"I think the Wall moved again," he said.

He paused, thinking about the Wall and its mysteries, then quickly dismissed the thoughts. It was too early in the morning, and he had an unexpected guest.

Ariana leaned up and tried to look out the window but didn't put much effort into it and collapsed back down in bed.

"I know we shouldn't talk about it, but what do you think of the Wall moving?" she asked in a hushed tone as if one of the Territory Governors was in the room eavesdropping. "Do you think it's the foreigners preparing to attack or the government doing something that makes it move and, like you said, maybe lying about it? Is that one of the things you want to figure out?" Apparently, *she* didn't think it was too early to talk about it.

Christopher nodded. "Are the warnings because of a legiti-mate threat or were they made because the Wall moved, or both . . . or neither?" he added.

She turned on her side to face him again. "Well, the first warning came before the Wall moved the first time, so some-thing else triggered it."

Christopher nodded. "Like information about outsiders getting ready to attack."

"Yes, right, so the threat is real."

"Unless the government isn't being truthful with us and something else triggered its movement," Christopher said. "Or maybe it's only a threat to the government but not to us, but they want to make us *think* it's dangerous to us."

"What do you mean? Why would they do that?"

"I don't know. Maybe something is happening that threatens their power, and they don't want to lose it, so they get us all riled up to keep us from questioning what's going on. Then they can hide behind the warnings."

She paused, and it gave Christopher a chance to reflect on what he had said, as he had only just thought of it.

"But what about the Wall then?" she asked. "I mean, its expansion has got to be either magic or a strange science we don't know anything about, like the loudspeakers, or you're right, that something else causes it to move. I just can't believe it's random, or unknown. Someone knows." She sighed. "But we can't do anything about it anyway so . . ."

Christopher had thought long and hard about what might be generating the Wall's movements, but now, with her questions and comments, he made a vague connection. Looking at the past times the Wall had moved during his lifetime—as a child, a teenager, and its expansions these recent days—he realized that its movements always seemed to come after he personally experienced some kind of revelation or emotional clarity that made him more present to his surroundings. Obviously, that was a coincidence, though. He pushed the feeling aside, but something made him follow up on his previous line of thinking, and he said, "Maybe the Wall is the only thing the government *can't* control."

"Ugh, my head hurts thinking about it," Ariana said. "The laws against talking about it are probably in place to prevent just this sort of crazy speculation."

Christopher smiled. He was encouraged that she held similar questions about the Wall, but he was glad the conversation about it seemed to be ending. He didn't want to talk about his greater pull toward it yesterday, what the latest events meant for him and their relationship, and what he could feel coming, things he still didn't yet understand.

He crawled back into bed. "Like I said, time to stay in bed." And he distracted her with a kiss.

~

Under the diminishing pink morning sky, they walked together with their goods toward the city as they did most mornings, but today was different. This time they undertook the journey together, in more ways than one.

Ariana had gone back to her place earlier to prepare her baskets of flowers, and Christopher had met her with his cart at the fork in the road by the blacksmiths' workshops. They were running later than usual due to lingering in bed and enjoying the early morning together, and when Ariana left, Christopher worked furiously to gather some fruits and vegetables from the fields and canned items from the cellar for the day's market. By the time they met at the crossroads by the blacksmiths, the forges were blazing and the hammering of metal echoed in the street.

Christopher had noted on his solitary walk to meet her that he wasn't as stressed as he normally would have been getting a late start to the morning. With the past few days of revelations and Ariana's presence, the changes to his routine that normally would have enhanced his anxiety hadn't done so. Surprisingly, he instead felt more relaxed and secure in the feeling that whatever circumstances were thrown at him, life would go on regardless, and having some variation in it wouldn't be as disruptive as he would have anticipated in the past. Perhaps over the years he had misplaced his priorities by trying so hard to do things the way they had always been done, when in reality it was variation that had created the wonderful opportunities he had experienced this week, first with Lucas and now with Ariana.

He easily pulled his cart with her by his side, her baskets sitting among the limited crates of produce and nonperishable items he was able to collect. With room in the cart, he had insisted he carry her load, and she hadn't protested much. She swung her arms freely, appearing to enjoy relief from her usual burden.

He was in good spirits thinking about how wonderful it would be to have her so close every morning, but his mind kept drifting to the Wall and the questions it brought up, which distracted him from her radiant company. He also thought about what the unstable woman had said about the ring and being ready, but more about what life or death situation she had said would be coming. He wondered if her eccentricity disguised madness or prophecy. He hoped the former, but from what the antique shopkeeper had said and what he felt in his gut, it seemed it might very well be the latter.

His attention remained split for the rest of their trip into the city, even though he and Ariana engaged in light and joyful conversation. When they arrived at the marketplace, Martel and the other regular merchants had already been there for a while.

"You two seem to be in good moods," Martel said with a wink, greeting them as they approached. Ariana blushed while Christopher shot him a look. Martel gave a slight nod and said nothing more.

Under the Level 5 warning, things were even busier in the market than the previous days as the city's residents now had a deadline within which to be sure they had the supplies they needed for sheltering. With customers lining up consistently, Christopher did a robust business, but Ariana did not, only selling a few bouquets to familiar patrons, as few were interested in her flowers given the circumstances. She soon moved her baskets close to him and assisted his efforts. Throughout, they snuck furtive glances and smiles at each other.

Christopher noticed that the reactions of different people to the government warnings were quite diverse, with some incredibly anxious, some concerned, and a few simply taking it in stride and accepting what they needed to do with little emotion. He wasn't of the first category but rather the second, or maybe a combination of the second and third, concerned yet practical in handling the information.

There was something else happening. Christopher's mind and body were engaged in dealing with his customers, but some aspect within him was sensing something more, like he was witnessing himself playing out the role of a farmer and merchant instead of just being *in* the role. It didn't affect what he did and what was going on around him—he was still able to peddle his goods—but he saw himself above and somehow removed from the physical activity.

He observed something similar with Ariana but less mentally and more emotionally, seeing their incredible physical and loving connection as exquisitely beautiful and destined but also as being limited in expression in the material world. He could feel, almost see, that there was so much more, which made it increasingly difficult to engage with her normally as the morning progressed.

After a few hours, the number of people in the market began to dwindle, and Christopher pulled Ariana in for an embrace. The physical touch with her still felt natural to do. He just couldn't figure out why it seemed less than enough.

A woman approached and, scanning Christopher's goods, said, "Can I get a jar of carrots, jar of beans, jar of peppers, and half a dozen apples, please?" Christopher wasn't surprised she mostly wanted canned items.

"Of course," Christopher said, as both he and Ariana pulled the items together for her and placed them in the basket she had brought.

"You don't remember me, do you?" she said as she handed over some coins.

He looked closely at her. She was thin, with dark hair tied back under a lilac-colored kerchief, and she seemed familiar, but he couldn't place her.

"No, I'm sorry. Have you bought from me before?"

She smiled. "No, this is the first time. I want to thank you."

"Thank me? For what? I hope something good," he joked, smiling back.

"For seeing me," she said.

He stared at her, and it struck him that this was the woman who was with the bearded, tattooed gang leader a few days ago on his second outing with Lucas. She looked *very* different with her head held high and her shoulders and face appearing more relaxed. She also *felt* very different, less anxious and infinitely more confident.

"Yessss," Christopher said slowly as he replayed the scene in his head. "I remember you now. Good to see you out and about." Initially, he didn't know why he said that, as he thought it sounded inappropriate, but she didn't take offense.

"I no longer associate with him," she said. "You helped me see myself more clearly, and I just couldn't be with him anymore after that."

"But I only asked if you were okay."

"You were the first person in my life to really *see* me." She emphasized the word, and he knew what she meant. They had shared a very brief yet intimate connection, one that transcended the circumstances of their meeting, and it had made a lasting impression on both of them. Apparently, he wasn't the only one who had benefited from his excursions with Lucas.

"And that was enough, so thank you," she said with a depth that Christopher could feel in his bones. After glancing quickly at Ariana, who was observing their interaction, she walked away.

He watched her leave, admiring how she had transformed.

"Who was that?" Ariana asked, giving him a hug. For a moment he thought she might be jealous, but the notion left as quickly as it came because what he felt from her conflicted with it.

"Remember earlier in the week when I didn't want to talk about some of the things I experienced with the blind man?"

She nodded.

"That was someone I met during one of those times, when I saw the leader of the gang." And he proceeded to tell her everything about the incident as they helped the next few customers.

She took it all in, and when he was finished, she said, "I'm not surprised. You have that effect on people." He smiled and squeezed her hand in response.

Looking past her through the remaining people in the square, Christopher caught a glimpse of three uniformed constables come around the corner by the antique shop, walking with purpose directly toward him. As they approached, he recognized them as the men he had seen in the heart of the city, the ones who had arrested Vincent. Sensing what was about to happen, he turned to Ariana and said, "Can you take over? I have to do something."

His tone or demeanor must have expressed some worry because she said, "Is everything okay?" He heard her but had already started walking towards the constables.

He met them in the middle of the square with a greeting of "What can I do for you fine gentlemen today?"

The redhead and one of his companions forcefully grabbed Christopher's arms and put them behind his back. The third commanded, "You need to come with us," as onlookers moved away from the commotion.

"Why?" Christopher asked calmly, not resisting.

"Because I said so, that's why," the man said, his lip curling in anger.

"Am I being arrested?"

"You're being detained," said the man in front of him as the two other constables bound Christopher's wrists. Having secured him, they turned to walk back the way they came, roughly walking him with them.

Ariana had run over to the men and grabbed Christopher's arm. "What's going on?" she asked worriedly.

"Ariana," Christopher said in a slow, resonant tone that spoke to her beyond what just saying her name could express. "It's all right. I'm going to be fine."

"Yeah, we'll see about that," said the redhead, who had a firm grip on his elbow. "Ma'am, let him go." He pushed her arm away and continued walking Christopher out of the center of the market.

As he was marched down the street, the question, *What do you see?* resounded in his head, and he looked over and Lucas was staring directly at him with his black eyes wide open. Holding his gaze for a moment, Christopher felt a strange comfort despite the circumstances, and any remaining fear about his situation vanished.

Before turning the corner, he took one last look back at Ariana, who was standing in the same place where she had grabbed his arm, and he tried to convey what he had just felt from the blind man. Even if just a fraction of what he was feeling connected with her, she would understand more than what she observed. He could see she was agitated and confused because he knew that *she* knew he hadn't done anything wrong. He hoped that when their eyes met for that brief moment that some of her concern would be alleviated.

Once out of the square, Christopher walked easily with the three uniformed men, a slight grin on his face as Lucas's question resonated in his head. He couldn't help it; he found the dramatic actions of the constables a bit humorous compared to the strangely mundane feeling he was having about the situation, even though a part of him knew it was anything but ordinary.

He observed his surroundings as when he walked the same route with the blind man the other day, but this time feeling even more detached from the hustle and bustle around him. He was also seeing his life more clearly, and from a greater context. The situation he was in was simply one of many moments that passed that could be dramatized, taken more seriously than needed, and he didn't want to believe in or accept that approach anymore.

"What are you smirking at?" growled the redheaded constable, noticing Christopher's expression.

"Oh, just the movement of life," Christopher replied absentmindedly, like an old man sauntering down the road with all the time in the world.

"Oh, yeah," snarled the man. "Enjoy it now. Where you're going, there won't be a lot of movement for you."

"Or life," said the constable on his other side, and the two chuckled gruffly.

Christopher looked directly at the redhead and smiled. "I suppose I'm not worried about it."

Hearing that and seeing Christopher's serene composure, the man reacted angrily. "Well, you should be!" he said, annoyed that his intimidation hadn't worked. In reality, it had the opposite effect. He lifted Christopher's elbow to an uncomfortable height behind his back, and Christopher involuntarily winced and bent forward with the physical pain, which seemed to somewhat satisfy the redhead, so he lowered the arm.

Christopher looked closely at the man—through and into him somehow, seeing beyond his appearance—and felt compassion. He could see, could *feel*, the anger and pain that led to the man's outburst and the negative experiences that had shaped his worldview. He recognized how the constable framed everything he saw through a tainted lens, one filtered by experiences and an upbringing no one should ever have. The world was a dangerous place to him, and the only way he knew how to survive was to exert control over it or to lash out in reaction to it. There had been very little love, if any, in this man's life. And underneath the anger, Christopher sensed a palpable sadness, a heart breaking with loss, which just fueled the resentment and antagonism the man felt toward others.

In his head, Christopher's thoughts went to a place he didn't know he possessed, but they were more than thoughts; they were a connection between his heart and his mind that held a knowingness that went beyond logical understanding. He held the man's pain in his sight and spoke to him silently.

May you be restored to the perfection in which you were created. Let the world behold your true nature expressed in form.

Christopher, surprised by the words himself, could sense a crack in the man's temperament, but he couldn't tell if it was physically visible or not.

And then he said, out loud this time, "You will see her again . . . someday." He didn't know why he said it or where it came from, but he could feel its truth.

Apparently shocked, the statement caused the blood to drain from the redhead's face as he stared at Christopher for a few steps. Once the man had gathered himself, he said, "What did you say?" trying to sound angry, but Christopher felt it come from a place of fear. The man looked away, no longer able to hold the farmer's peaceful gaze, and he quietly and blankly stared ahead, trying to suppress his emerging emotions. Christopher felt no need to respond.

Still walking together, Christopher disengaged his focus from the constable and went back to surveying the streets and people they passed. With the increased warning levels, there was more scurrying about than usual, and he was able to take in information on a much deeper level than before, feeling as though he could understand what drove people to do the things they did.

Like with the redhead, it was as though he could peel back the layers of what he was seeing to reveal what lay beneath.

Most of the people he directed this new, refined sight upon had a palpable fear of the impending attack by the foreigners, but underneath it were differing reasons for the concern: worry about keeping children and the family safe from harm, anxiety about going to a shelter, apprehension about having enough provisions for a long lockdown, anger at the outsiders for launching an attack. But he could also discern *beneath* those layers and get an impression of *why* they were feeling the way they did, like the mother who he could tell grew up being overprotected by her parents and wanted to do the same for her family during this time of crisis, and the middle-aged man who lived in the same house he grew up in and the idea of staying at a place different from his familiar home filled him with anxiety.

Beyond how Christopher could now understand the people he passed, he could also see how it all fit together as a whole. His comment to the constable on the movement of life took on a more profound meaning. He saw life's progress and change being embodied through individuals, groups, departments, industries, functions, and lands encompassing everything at all levels and in all systems within the Territories. Nothing and no one was excluded and all participated, whether they were aware of it or not.

And at that moment, Christopher knew that he had to get to the other side of the Wall, that it was inevitable, and that it was just a matter of time before its secrets would be revealed to him. As much as he had grown personally and increased his ability to see and understand during this miraculous past week with Lucas, somewhere out there were the answers and deeper knowledge he sought, and going beyond the shadows of the Wall was the key that would open that door.

As the three constables led him onto the street where the detainment center was located, Christopher remained in this heady, visual space. Approaching the building's entrance, the door opened and the officer with the scar on his cheek emerged, the one who had questioned Lucas and him the previous day.

"What do we have here?" asked the officer, stopping in front of the group of four.

"Another troublemaker, sir," said the man who led them.

Christopher looked over at the angry redhead to whom he had sent both the healing words and the unexplained statement, and the man was staring straight ahead, his face still ashen. Something was softening in him.

"You again?" the officer said, moving closer to Christopher. "Is that true? Are you causing trouble?"

"I suppose that depends on the definition of 'trouble,'" Christopher said with a grin.

The man who led them snarled while the officer presented a controlled smile, apparently appreciating Christopher's wit given his circumstances. The smile quickly melted away and his demeanor stiffened as his eyes focused past Christopher.

Glancing over his shoulder, Christopher realized that Lucas was standing right behind him. Even though he was seeing things differently and accepting what was happening to him, seeing the blind man was a relief on some level.

"You shouldn't be here," said the officer coolly to Lucas.

"I'm not interfering," said Lucas, "but aren't you forgetting your role here?"

The officer lifted his chin and took a deep breath. He switched his focus to Christopher.

"Why is this man being taken in?" he asked, looking at Christopher but directing his question to the three constables.

"I don't know, sir," said the one who had led them. "It's like the one from yesterday morning. We were told to pick him up for questioning."

Pondering for a minute, the officer sized up Christopher. With a glance back at Lucas, the officer stated emphatically, "Release him," and turned to walk back into the building.

While the three men stood dumbfounded, Christopher asked, "And what about my friend from yesterday?" He half-turned so his bound wrists faced the men, who were still standing there stunned at the turn of events.

The officer nodded toward Christopher's wrists, indicating to the men to release the binds. The redhead, still in a somewhat distracted state, began to untie them.

"You *are* a troublemaker, aren't you?" the officer asked. It wasn't as much a question than a statement, with no expectation of response.

Christopher was happy to answer anyway. "Only good trouble, when it's the right thing to do."

The officer smirked. "I can see why you spend time with him," he said, nodding toward Lucas. Turning back to the door, the officer added, "Release him too, the man from yesterday."

"But sir—" one of the constables began to retort, but he was cut off immediately.

"Do it now!" the officer snapped. "We're about to be at war and we have a city to defend, and we don't have time for this!" He glared at the constable, who took a step back, and then proceeded into the building.

Having released Christopher's wrists, the formerly angry redhead stood in front of Christopher and tried to resurrect his former attitude by saying, "This isn't over," but it collapsed like a crumbling wall, coming out weak and broken, like the false bluster of a bully who's been called to account.

Christopher looked deeply into the man's eyes and said, "I hope you stay safe during these times and that you find it in your heart to trust that everything is okay." The words, once again, felt guided by an unseen hand.

The man took a step back and reactively sneered, but what Christopher could see with his eyes contradicted what he could feel underneath the man's bearing and expression. He knew the man's life was going to change.

"I'll wait here for my friend," Christopher added.

The three constables gave him one last irritated look and marched through the large door and into the building. Christopher turned around to thank Lucas for his presence, but he had disappeared. A few minutes later, Vincent emerged looking haggard and sleep-deprived.

"What? Did you do this? Did you get me out?" he asked.

"I merely asked them to do what's right," Christopher said as Vincent enveloped him in a great bear hug.

"Thank you, my friend. Thank you," Vincent said.

Together, they began walking back to the marketplace, the big man leaning on Christopher for support.

~

The two men came around the corner of the square and walked past Lucas, who looked like he hadn't moved in days. Vincent had straightened up and was walking without assistance by then, although he still appeared disheveled. Ariana saw them coming and ran up to them, giving first Christopher and then Vincent a hug.

"I heard about what happened to you," she said to Vincent. "Are you okay? Are both of you okay?"

"Never better," said Vincent, forcing a smile.

"Yes, never better," repeated Christopher. Vincent may have been joking, but Christopher, for the most part, was not.

They walked back to Christopher's mostly empty cart, and Christopher gave Vincent some water and fruit.

"Thanks," Vincent said, devouring the food and gulping the water.

When he was finished, Ariana said, "We should get you home."

Vincent nodded and stood up. "I can make it myself. I'm fine. No need to bother. You've done enough for me already."

Christopher and Ariana protested, saying they were heading home anyway, and Christopher consolidated his few remaining goods into a single sack he had stored in the cart and loaded his empty crates. Ariana placed her baskets on top, and the three left the square to walk the road home.

They walked quietly, seriously, down the road out of the city and into the countryside, each lost in their own thoughts. It was clear Vincent didn't want to talk about the experience, something Christopher completely understood. Like his own experiences recently, he knew it would take some time to fully understand. Words couldn't do it justice now.

With the three walking slowly, Christopher welcomed being closer to nature and away from the noisy vibrations in the city, especially after the announcements had induced an increased level of anxiety in the throngs of people there. He was still trying to understand his surroundings with a newly acquired vision and could now apply that sight to the natural environment around him without the city's heavier distractions.

Appreciating his expansive connection to the earth and his place in its diverse systems brought his thoughts back to the Wall, and he began to feel constrained, as if he were choking in a non-physical way. Looking around and connecting to what was around him in the environment—the stoic magnificence of a tree providing shade on their walk, the uncorrupted wind blowing across a field, the soft, ceaseless power of the stream beside the road, the lighter-than-air birds that chirped at the group's passing—he could feel that he couldn't relate to them as deeply as he knew was possible. Something was limiting his new, open manner of seeing and understanding the world, and he found it suffocating.

But he also knew that a journey was before him, one that would once and for all release him from such suffering . . . if he could survive it. And he knew that transcending the Wall was essential to that journey.

~

Vincent lived close to the forges, so when he, Christopher, and Ariana arrived at the split in the road there, Christopher reached for the sack of remaining goods in his cart and gave it to the stonemason. Not having the energy to object more than once, Vincent thanked him profusely and turned onto the smaller road that led to his house while Christopher and Ariana walked back to Christopher's farm together.

As they approached his property, the wonderful feeling of her presence beside him was suddenly replaced by a heavy, sinking emptiness in his body. He initially couldn't identify its source, but sure enough, when he saw a scroll tucked into the handle of the door of his farmhouse, he knew exactly what it was.

He climbed the steps to the porch and picked up the rolled paper, which sported the large, wax seal of the government.

"What is it?" Ariana asked.

Christopher sighed, thinking this couldn't have come at a worse time. With Ariana there, he certainly couldn't keep it from her, so he just handed her the document. "Go ahead. Open it."

She broke the seal and paused to look at him. He nodded for her to continue, and she unrolled the paper. The official stamp of the government's tax office was at the top, with the large, formal text of a decree below it.

DECREE. We do hereby decree and proclaim that the property owner of the sixth farm on the right south of the intersection of the North-South Road and the Cross Territory Road in Zone Seven is delinquent on taxes and the property will be seized if said taxes are not fully paid by the end of business three days hence. Signed, Territory Governors.

Ariana gasped while Christopher just stared at it. He had feared this was coming, but seeing it now, the reality of it hit him: he was going to lose the farm.

"Didn't you make enough this week to cover it?" Ariana asked. "Business was good with the warnings, right?"

Christopher shook his head. "Good, but not good enough." Even if he hadn't spent some of his proceeds on the wooden statuette for Ariana, he would have needed another week to earn the amount needed, but with the Territories about to be in lockdown, that wasn't going to happen. His thoughts about it a few days ago had been too optimistic.

"Well, take what I made, and I can get a little more from home." She reached into her pocket, pulled out a small pouch, and held it out for him.

He didn't take it but rather folded her hand back around the pouch. "No, that's yours."

"It's *ours*," she said.

"I can't."

"Yes, you can."

"I won't," he said firmly. He knew she helped support her aunt, and he wasn't going to take that away from her. Plus, he still felt he needed to resolve this on his own.

She stared at him as he took the document from her and went inside. She followed, saying nothing. He poured two glasses of water, handed her one, and stepped back outside to sit on the porch. She again followed, pausing before sitting in the chair next to him.

"I'll figure it out," he said, finally breaking the awkward silence.

"How?"

"There's more than the farm at stake here. Let's focus on what's more important right now: preparing for sheltering."

"I'm worried about you," she said, her voice rising. "You're ignoring the decree, you're about to lose the farm, an invasion is almost upon us, we're about to be in lockdown, you just got arrested, and you don't seem bothered by any of it!"

"Almost arrested. You see, I figured a way out of it."

She looked at him sternly.

"Okay," he said, "all those things have affected me, are affecting me, but so much has happened this week that has given me perspective on all of it. I feel there's something else I need to do that could help solve everything, including saving the farm and finally figuring out the quest."

"The quest! The quest is nothing compared to the rest of what's happening." She couldn't suppress her annoyance.

"But that's just it. I really believe they're all related in some way."

"And you're going to just figure it out? Even if it costs you the farm?"

He slowly nodded.

"So, what is it you need to do that's going to solve all these problems?"

He looked deeply at her, hoping she would understand. "I need to go the Wall."

The urge that had been building up within him was making his heart and mind ache for it. In some strange way, the attempted arrest by the constables and the mounting threat from the foreign invaders had only increased his desire to understand more. And now that he was almost certainly going to lose his family's farm, he had to do *something*. He had already resolved he had to try, whatever the consequences, even if he ran into the foreign army.

She clenched her jaw and stared at him, her cheeks flushed.

"The Wall! In the middle of all that's going on? You're about to lose your house, the farm! And besides, there's a serious threat out there!"

He was trying not to feel guilty for putting her through these emotions, and it dawned on him that they weren't his to bear. He was being honest, and her reaction was hers, not his. That didn't mean he couldn't feel her distress, though.

"I know, but it can't wait. And it's not just going to the Wall. I need to try to get to the other side," he said.

Her tone switched from anger to concern. "I can tell you what's on the other side: a wicked army, a wasteland, and certain death. I know you know the stories."

"I do, but it's not something I can ignore anymore. This week, with what I've experienced, this is the next thing, the only thing I feel is left." It was heartfelt, and he hoped it came across that way instead of imploring.

She leveled her gaze at him. "We just found each other. I don't want to lose you."

"And I don't want to be lost, but despite all that I've learned and how much I've changed, I would be lost if I didn't go."

"What about us, about me?"

"I love you and want you to be safe, and I feel that *us* would be stronger than ever once I do this."

"If you survive," she added. "And the warnings? I know you question them, but what if foreigners really are out there getting ready to attack?"

"I have to take the chance that they're not."

"And the environment outside the Wall, what about that?"

"I'll take provisions."

"How are you going to get to the other side?"

"I don't know."

He could tell she knew he was serious, as he had an answer to everything, even if some of the answers admittedly lacked detail.

"There's nothing I can say that will change your mind, is there?" She sounded disappointed and exasperated, like she had lost the battle.

"I have to do it . . . for myself, for you, for us, for everyone." He wasn't sure why he added the last word.

She took a deep breath and stared at him. He leaned over, took her hand, and kissed her head, and repeated what he had said the previous day, "Everything is going to be okay."

She took a moment before responding. "Good, because I'm going with you."

He was not prepared for that, and he sat back and gawked at her, tongue-tied. A quick internal check with himself told him that it wasn't a good idea. This was his journey to take, alone. He finally spoke.

"It's one thing for me to risk, but I can't put you at risk as well."

"But it's my choice, and you said everything is going to be okay."

"Everything is going to be okay with you protected in the shelter," he clarified, "not accompanying me to an unknown and dangerous land. This is something I must do alone." His tone was deadly serious.

"What about your gift, the carving? That's us and our love for each other. Aren't we that deeply connected? What happens to you also happens to me."

"Yes, we are connected, which is why I must take this journey on my own. You, too, will be affected by what I discover."

"Or hurt by what happens to you," she added.

She had a point, but he knew what he had to do, and nothing she could say could change that. He didn't respond.

"Well, maybe I won't be here when you get back, *if* you get back," she said, releasing his hand and standing up.

Hearing her words, or more accurately *feeling* them, his heart sank. He rose and reached for her, but she pushed his hand away. The gravity of her resistance was more than he had anticipated, and he didn't know what to say. This was not how he had pictured the conversation going.

As she stood there on the verge of tears, a distant loudspeaker creaked to life, and the now familiar rising tones blanketed the landscape. It was far away but still clear. Ariana stiffened as the announcement began.

This is a Level 6 Warning by the Council of Governors. The enemy force is within a day of reaching the Grand Wall. As stated in your zone's manual, all citizens must report to their designated shelter in the city within twelve hours, and martial law will be declared at that time. Anyone outside their assigned area after that time will be arrested. Please see your zone's manual for your sheltering instructions. This is a Level 6 Warning.

After it repeated two more times followed by the three tones, the speaker crackled off.

"You realize you'll probably get arrested before you even get to the Wall," Ariana said blankly.

"I've already been arrested. It wasn't so bad," he teased, before realizing that it wasn't the right time for humor.

She looked at him, clearly frustrated. "I don't want you to leave, and I don't have to like it, but I understand you have to do this."

He nodded.

"Then there's something I must do." She suddenly seemed sad. Christopher's pulse quickened.

"I thought you found what you were looking for, but I see that's not the case. It's clear to me now that we have different priorities for our lives."

He didn't like where this was going.

"I can't be here to watch you throw your life away. After sheltering, I'm going home. This . . . this was a mistake." She leaned in and gave him a hug and quick kiss on the cheek. "Goodbye, Christopher." And she turned and walked down the steps of the porch.

He was stunned, his emotions swirling. "Wait! What? Don't leave. Please!"

At the bottom of the steps, she turned back briefly and said, "I hope you can remember that I love you," and she followed the path away from the house.

Shocked, Christopher's mind buzzed with confusion and regret as she walked off, not knowing what he could have said differently or what he could say now to try to change her decision. It blended with what he felt was her emotional turmoil about the risks he was taking—not just for himself but for their life together—for something whose results were so undefined.

She was almost off the property when he found his voice and shouted after her, "I love you, too!" through his tears.

She didn't turn around.

~

Ten minutes later, having gathered supplies for the journey, Christopher set off toward the Wall.

Heartbroken, he had watched her depart, remaining on his porch until her figure faded into the distance, her last words giving him courage yet also generating sadness and guilt. He hoped she would eventually come to understand, really understand, where he was coming from and where he was going.

With the Level 6 warning present in his mind, he was ready when he encountered a young constable on the road to the Wall.

"Where are you going? Didn't you hear the latest warning?" the man in uniform snapped.

"Yes, sir, I did. I must go this way first to acquire something before going to the shelter, but rest assured, I'll be on my way presently," Christopher said, navigating a fine line by telling the truth obliquely. He could see that the young man was a little nervous about either the increased warnings or being in a new position where he had responsibility, or both.

The man looked at him warily, squinting as if he could discern Christopher's trustworthiness, while Christopher held the man's gaze confidently.

The constable stepped back and said, "Okay, then. Go on and be quick about it," and waved him by.

Christopher nodded and resumed his journey. He wasn't worried. He knew he would get to the Wall. He just didn't know what would happen when he got there.

In the distance, he could see that it had moved again and was even further away. Not just undeterred but excited and inspired, he smiled to himself, convinced that its expansion indicated he was getting closer to its mysteries.

Navigating his previous route, he again slipped off the road onto the well-worn path hidden by the bushes and walked the trail until it became less worn. Reaching the birch grove where he had experienced his recent nightmare, he paused to take a break.

There was a wide line where the Wall had been that was devoid of trees, but young shoots of vegetation were already growing through the soil's surface. He continued to the edge of the grove where he could see the Wall in the distance and sat on the ground beneath a large, sturdy birch, leaning back against the trunk. The barrier seemed far away, perhaps an additional thirty-minute walk he estimated.

Closing his eyes, he put his hands into the dirt at his sides, feeling the energy of the earth through his palms. His breathing slowed and entrained with the environment, the natural world enveloping him in its arms. He sat there, hands on the ground and leaning against the tree, feeling the oneness that he had glimpsed throughout the week. This time, however, it was more natural, pure, and complete, uncontaminated by the presence of others. With no one to distract him, no work to do, and being away from the heavier vibrations of the city, his mind and heart were at rest, and he merged with his surroundings.

~

He surfaced from his reverie slowly, gently, perhaps an hour later during the sun's descent in the sky. He had fallen into a kind of half-sleep, a trance-like state where the physical world faded, yet he felt more aware of it and what lay beyond it than ever. He emerged refreshed on all levels and ready for the adventure ahead. Standing and picking up his provisions, he started a new path toward the distant Wall.

Eyes on his destination, he continued his walk down a valley, up a small hill through another grove of trees, down into a field of indigo wildflowers, then over a stream and into another woodland, this one with maple and oak trees. He wondered if he was the first person ever to set foot there, as it appeared to be new and untouched ground, formerly hidden by the great stone structure.

Up another slope with the trees thinning, he stopped at the top of the rise where he had a clear view down into the barren, sandy valley and beyond. He could see the Wall in the distance, further away than he had thought, and it stretched to both sides so far that he couldn't see it curve around to know that he was enclosed within it, although of course he was. It wasn't possible not to be.

With the sun setting, he sat on a large stone and watched the colors in the high clouds change to pink with veins of lavender over the desert terrain before him. Abstract thoughts filled his mind, coming through a place between and just above his eyes. He felt an odd kind of pressure there and had a feeling that anything he wanted to understand could be known. It was just a matter of concentrating, trusting, and knowing it was reachable. Indeed, this was what he was doing on this journey.

But he could tell his focus wasn't pure, and it inhibited touching into the knowledge he knew he might be able to access if he had no distractions. As much as he had an intense desire to go beyond the Wall, the warnings of the impending attack, worries about losing the farm, Ariana leaving him, and his concern for her safety distracted from that goal. *What if the foreign army really is there in the morning?* he thought. *Then what do I do?* He stopped himself from thinking of it further, as he didn't want to flush it out to any upsetting conclusions, which would only divert his focus even more.

With the approaching dusk and darkness on its heels and seeing no place to take shelter down in the sandy valley, Christopher backtracked to a spot of flat ground surrounded by some larger trees and found a place to bed down for the night. The adventure, the mystery, and the danger could wait until tomorrow.

Anna

*N*oooo! Anna thought. *Not a breakup! They just got together and now this? Why didn't he fight for her more?* She shut the book, threw it off her lap, and stood up, clenching her fists.

This wasn't the first time she had had an intense reaction to a story. It indicated how much she identified with the characters and how invested she was in the tale, which she could tell was now heading into its climax. With Christopher's many questions and the challenges before him, he was facing a mountain of trials that seemed impossible to overcome.

Pacing around her small room to try to release some of her anxious energy, she thought about how she still identified with Christopher. His strength of knowing what he had to do was admirable, but at what cost? Everything good in his life? It put some of her own struggles into perspective. She wasn't willing to risk her life to escape her limiting world like he was, at least not yet, but it certainly gave her the courage to stand more squarely in her beliefs and face some of her fears.

She found it interesting that the woman from the earlier chapter with the gang leader had come back into the story, and it reminded Anna of also wanting to be seen like that, to be accepted for *who she was* rather than for what she accomplished through her routines, rule following, and academics.

She was worried when Christopher was arrested but glad he had avoided Vincent's fate in the detainment center. There was something strange about what the government was doing, but at least the officer with the scar on his cheek showed some sense and released both of them. Clearly, the potential attack on the Territories took priority over the Governors' seemingly petty accusations. Maybe some in the government weren't so bad after all.

Christopher's enhanced ability to see fascinated her. She wished she could have sight like that and be able to see why people did what they did, although sometimes she suspected their motives anyway. Maybe she'd be able to understand her parents better if she had that ability.

She stopped pacing and looked down at the three spirals on the book's cover. She had to finish the tale now. There was too much left unresolved. Christopher leaving behind everything in his life and venturing forth into the unknown was exciting, and not just for the story but also because she desired the same for herself and wanted to take the journey with him.

She sat back down on her bed, made herself comfortable, and flipped through the pages to find where she had left off.

Reading the next chapter title, she thought, *Christopher better know what he's doing.*

Seventh

The abiding light reveals the shadows and bears witness to the destruction of the stage. The theater reopens to the illimitable whole that is, the shadows being born no more to bind themselves to the masquerade. And the shadowlands, and everything that dwells within them, are eclipsed by the light, never to be seen again.

~

Christopher woke around dawn by the faraway sound of three rising tones. The land was still in shadow, but pink streaks of morning light were beginning to marble the high, white clouds above him.

The announcement was faint when it came. He was surprised he was able to hear it given his distance from where he thought the closest loudspeaker was, but the government always seemed to have ways to make sure every inch of the Territories was within its reach, apparently even the land that had previously been outside the Wall.

This is a Level 7 Warning by the Council of Governors. The enemy force is at the West Wall and is preparing to attack. You must proceed to your designated shelter immediately. Although we have full confidence that the Grand Wall and Grand Army will keep us safe from the foreign invaders, do not leave your shelter under any circumstances or you risk a horrible death at the hands of the enemy. This is a Level 7 Warning.

Before it repeated, Christopher rubbed his eyes, stood up, and stretched, feeling stiff from sleeping on the firm ground. He listened carefully to make sure he had heard it correctly as the words reached him two more times.

A pang of worry struck—about Ariana, his friends, the farm, the safety of the city and surrounding lands—and it intermingled with the desire and belief that had led him there, as well as with what the gang leader, Vincent, and the antique shopkeeper had shared. Amid all the swirling, competing thoughts and emotions, he closed his eyes and tried to go back to the feeling that told him that things were going to be okay regardless. He was only partially successful.

He reached into his pack of provisions and took out a strip of cured meat among the jumble of dried fruit, bits of preserved game, and beeswax-wrapped apples in his pack, then sat on the ground listening to birds in the cool, morning air while he ate. Surrounded by trees and with no one nearby, he felt vastly disconnected from the city, and even from his farm. As the treetops began to glow in the morning light, he breathed in the serenity of the scene, which helped him relax into the present, largely away from his tumbling thoughts and the warning. *What peace can be found in nature*, he thought.

After eating and taking a drink of water from a large, leather flask he had brought, he packed his belongings and walked to his viewing spot from the previous evening to see if he could observe the Grand Army or the invaders at the West Wall. When he arrived, what he saw was not what he had expected.

There was nothing, only the desert from the prior day stretching endlessly before him—no West Wall, no army, no foreigners—just barren, lifeless sand. As the rising sun crept upwards behind him, Christopher strained to find any details that could help him make sense of what he was seeing, but none

appeared. He was looking at a wasteland. The rumors, about the
land beyond the Wall at least, were true.

He didn't know how long he stood there, his mind spinning
with questions—most prominently, where was the Wall?—but
eventually his thinking gave way to the inner drive to discover
that had built up all week. His goal had not changed.

He took a deep breath and began to walk down the slope,
feeling the dirt beneath his feet become less sturdy by the step.
By the bottom of the hill, his gait had changed as he was moving
entirely on sand, something usually only found in the far south
of the Territories. Nevertheless, he continued forward toward an
uncertain destination, although one he still trusted would satisfy
his longing to comprehend.

After a few hours, the going became difficult. Christopher's
muscles weren't used to walking in loose sand, and it fatigued
him quickly, especially as the cool breeze and shade from early
morning were replaced by direct sunlight and hot, dry air. He
tried to make himself more comfortable, covering his arms and
head with spare fabric from his pack, but it wasn't enough. The
elements were beating on him. Still, he labored ahead, possessed
by a determination that went beyond the physical discomfort.

That resolve carried him through the day in fits and starts.
When questions or worries arose, he was only able to occasionally move past them by going within to the knowingness that had
directed him to undertake the trek in the first place. It was calm
and peaceful there, like a clear pond with no ripples agitating its
surface, a mirror to his true nature that he was seeking to understand. But sometimes he just couldn't get there as the intense
physical effort created doubts, questions, and fears about his
choices. When he did revive the inner strength and focus to find
that space, however, he was able to enter it to escape the
torments of the energies that scattered his mind and emotions,

of which there were many as he trudged forward through the sand with great effort.

He was exceedingly thankful when the sun began going down and the temperature dropped late in the day. Tired and sore, he didn't know how much ground he had covered, not that it mattered; his quest was something that went beyond physical distance. He had tried to travel in a straight line, which was difficult to manage during the middle of the day with the sun overhead, but now it generously offered a bearing upon which he could focus.

He struggled a bit further in the waning light, mildly energized by the cooler temperature. Eventually, he decided enough was enough, and he stopped to rest for the night.

Digging into his provisions, he pulled out the flask and gulped down a few mouthfuls, careful to ration it as he had done throughout the day. He took a few bites of the dried meat and removed an apple from its tightly-wound, beeswax wrapping, which had gotten very soft in the heat but not quite to the point of melting.

Sitting on the sand and enjoying his meal as much as possible given the circumstances, he wondered what the next day would bring. His mind, however, filled with competing questions, concerns, and speculations, followed his exhausted body and shut down quickly, and he was soon falling asleep as the starry light began to paint its glimmers on the dark canvas above him.

~

Christopher awoke stiffly with the dawn light directly on him. There was no shadow from the Wall obstructing the earliest rays. He took a swig of water from his flask and ate some dried fruit before starting off again, travelling directly opposite the rising sun. He wanted to cover ground before the heat of the day became too intense.

He walked steadily, if not awkwardly, in the sand. Over the mostly flat desert he traveled, occasionally encountering great dunes that rose off the uniformity of the landscape like massive, sleeping beasts. They were a struggle to climb but less effort than trying to go the long distances around, so he summited them.

At the tops of the dunes, he looked ahead for anything that would indicate a break in the monotony of his surroundings but never found any. He continued forward anyway, knowing that the answers were out there somewhere in front of him. *They have to be*, he told himself.

Not having seen any foreigners or army outside the Wall, or any sign of life thus far in the desert, he no longer worried about running into anyone dangerous. He did, however, occasionally think that perhaps they had attacked a different part of the Territories and he had simply been lucky to bypass them, so his concern for Ariana and his friends remained. Having not seen the Wall at all yesterday left him wondering if it was now gone forever, which would leave his homeland open and unprotected, something he shuddered at the thought of.

In the heat of midday, he stopped to restore his energy with some food and water, covering up as best he could from the sun directly overhead and from the occasional gust of wind that blew sand into his eyes. His flask was being depleted fast, so he took only a sip to save some for later, or for the next day if necessary. Without water, he knew survival would be impossible.

After a long and difficult afternoon, as nighttime fell again, Christopher collapsed, exhausted. Another full day under the hot sun had drained him, and with rationing water, he wasn't able to fully replenish what his body had lost. Nibbling on some dried meat, he tried to get some energy back, but he knew he needed more water to help wash it down, as it was devoid of moisture, so he didn't eat much.

He slept deeply that night under the stars, dreaming of a future with Ariana on the farm.

~

Waking early again with the morning light, Christopher stood up shakily, his whole body crying out with aches. He picked up his pack and started walking, saving whatever little water he had left, despite his parched throat. He was still being driven by his quest to understand, which transcended the physical suffering.

Step by step, the walking slowly broke him, and many hours later he collapsed in a heap on the sand like an old rag doll thrown neglected into the corner, his perseverance bested by heat and fatigue. He lay on his back, arms outstretched and breathing hard, questioning if he had made a colossal mistake.

He closed his eyes and thought of Ariana and what they could become together if she came back to him, of Lucas and whether he would be disappointed in Christopher's choice to undertake this journey after all had learned from him, of Vincent, Martel, and his other friends. *What have I done?* he asked himself, defeated, as the warm wind pelted him with grains of sand.

He lay there facing upwards for only so long because the sun was searing his face. When he couldn't take it any longer, he sat up and looked around. Nothing had changed. The desert still appeared limitless in all directions. The Wall, the foreign invaders, and the answers he was seeking were nowhere to be found.

He took his pack off his shoulders, found the flask, and drank whatever was left, which wasn't much. He savored the last few drops, feeling as if each was a mouthful.

Still, he needed to go on. He had traveled too far and didn't have any more water, so he wouldn't be able to make it back to the Territories alive. The only possible direction was forward.

Upon standing, he looked around and felt a sense of dread. The blowing sands had erased his footprints and he didn't know in which direction to continue in the largely featureless land. The sun was overhead, so he couldn't use it to help orient himself, and it didn't feel prudent to just stand there waiting in the heat to figure it out. After just a moment's reflection, he decided to give himself over to providence, and he chose a bearing and starting walking, marching forward in the best straight line he could muster into the desolate and inhospitable void.

Weary but carrying on, he thought of his friends again, his home, the farm, relaxing with the view from the porch. They all passed through his mind as he searched for something that might ground him in the formidable environment. But nothing fulfilled the hollowness he was experiencing. He felt lost, abandoned, ashamed of his selfish decisions that would hurt so many people if he didn't return, which was looking more and more likely.

The day dragged on with every step, the sun's rays crushing his will to continue. Nonetheless, he found the kernel of desire within that had initiated the journey in the first place, and he fixated on that.

Soon, however, the going became so difficult that he had to trick himself into thinking that each next step forward in the soft sand would end his suffering and bring him the awareness he sought, but his accomplishment was always just one step out of reach, an attainment as elusive as the land before him was endless.

Exhaustion and thirst began to overtake him, and he knew that delusions would not be far behind. Soon, even the desire and goal with which he had started the journey disappeared, and the only thing left was simply putting one foot in front of the other. He was reduced to every movement forward being a test and every completed step a grand achievement. That was what his world had been reduced to.

This went on until his legs gave out, and he dropped to the sand like the dead weight he was. In his current condition, the great dune in front of him was insurmountable. He was done walking. The journey was over.

As he knelt with his eyes closed and body parched, thoroughly drained on all levels, he had a vision. It felt real, but he wasn't entirely sure in his disoriented state.

He was seated at a long table with many other guests with a bountiful feast displayed before them. Water and wine flowed freely, and all were partaking spiritedly in the spread. Christopher reached for a glass of water and tried to bring it to his lips, but someone's hand arrested his arm holding the cup. It was the officer he had seen twice in front of the detainment building, the one with the scar on his face who had released him and Vincent. He was smiling.

Leaning in, the officer said, "We want you to have that, but you have to agree to join us first."

Christopher looked at him blankly, not understanding, but then noticed that all the other guests at the table were in the various uniforms of government authority. Christopher needed water but somehow could feel that if he took a drink, he would indeed be joining the service that had detained Vincent and had almost detained him.

And then he saw that his arm holding the cup of water was clad in the same style and colored fabric as the officer's. Looking down, he realized he was dressed identically to the man. Shocked, he stood up and pushed away from the table, dropping the cup and shouting, "No! No! No!"

Christopher's parched lips scratched out an audible "No" before he opened his eyes. It was a hallucination.

Almost tasting the water he didn't drink in the vision, he lifted his head and looked at the large dune ahead of him. Squinting, he thought he could see something on top of it. He tightened his focus and saw that it appeared to be a figure beckoning him forward. Muddled with fatigue and confusion, he moved forward on his hands and knees, slowly crawling up the sandy slope, half sliding backward with each foot of progress.

It took an hour, or so it felt, until he got to the top, and he put his hand forward once more and it landed on the bare foot of a woman. Looking up slowly, there stood Ariana looking down on him, as beautiful as ever, wearing a flowing white dress glowing with the sun's rays.

Christopher thought he had died and seen an angel. Tears of joy streamed down his cheeks, and he reached out for her hand but grasped only at the air. He blinked, and the apparition was gone.

Frantic and confused, he turned in all directions, certain she was still there, but his gaze only met the blowing sand.

Then he heard her voice in his head. *Your journey is over. Trust me. We can be together now. Come to me.* The voice was guiding him forward, and he saw her again, floating in the air before him.

You came back! he thought. *I knew we were supposed to be together!*

He crawled a few feet toward her but then stopped. He noticed that the dune had a steep, cliff-like side to it, which dropped off directly in front of where he was kneeling.

Come to me. I will bear you up and welcome you home, she beckoned to him.

He no longer knew what was real. Attempting to scream in frustration, no words came forth, and he buried his head in his hands.

You are safe. Everything is going to be okay. I've got you, Ariana's voice said.

And with that, Christopher snapped to attention. Something felt different, discordant, and he realized that those were words *he* had said to *her* and that they were not something she would normally say, so it broke the deception. His purpose came rushing back into his mind, recognizing now that she was an illusion.

Still kneeling, he straightened up and tearfully said, *No,* clearly and resolutely in his head, and he could feel the energy of the hallucination leave as her image dissolved in the sunlight.

He took a deep breath, hoping the air would clear his mind and at least anchor him in the dismal reality he was facing, but he wound up coughing from the blowing sand that hit the back of his throat. As he knelt atop the dune trying to reclaim his physical and mental functions, high, incoming clouds brought welcome shade. With his mouth closed this time, he breathed in the cooler air through his nose, bringing a trace of relief to his hot lungs.

The clouds preceded a storm that was brewing behind him, and they were becoming thicker and heavier by the minute. Glancing back at it, Christopher saw deep, broad, dark gray storm clouds quickly rolling toward him, consuming the desert.

But that wasn't all. The sky had suddenly become darker all around him, even where it was cloudless. He looked up and saw a shadow moving in front of the sun, an ominous sign that certainly couldn't portend anything good for him. The momentary wave of relief he felt at being protected from the sun's rays dissipated quickly as he digested the weight of such a powerful omen, and with the sandy wind assailing his body, he was reminded of where he was and what was bearing down on him.

He knew he didn't have the energy to go far, but there was a cliff in front of him that could at least provide some protection, if he could only get to the bottom of it.

He stood up and took a step to the right, with the idea of going down the soft, sandy side of the dune, but he could barely take another. He was too weak. Either he had to jump off the cliff or withstand the storm where he was.

Not willing to risk a potentially deadly leap in his debilitated condition, he turned and knelt to face the ominous weather that was almost upon him. Even in his weakened state, he was determined that the tempest would not best him. But as it got closer and the winds blew harder, stinging him with flying sand, he began to question his choice, for he knew the ferocity of these end-of-season storms and realized their power would be that much greater in the desert.

The storm intensified quickly as the light around him faded, and he was trapped, not able to move and barely able to breathe. The pressure of the gale on his dry throat and lungs suffocated him, and he could hear nothing but the roaring wind. This was not how he wanted to go, at the hands of the elements. He felt deep down that his journey wasn't over, yet the fierce storm bearing down on him would almost certainly end his life.

Christopher steeled himself as the dark cloud enveloped him, the violent winds pounding his body with sand. He closed his eyes as tightly as he could.

And Lucas's voice pierced the sound and fury, signifying hope.

I can stop this, it said.

Well, then stop it! Christopher shouted in his head, wanting to escape with his life.

What will you do for me? the voice asked.

That didn't sound like Lucas, and it surely wasn't the time for a lesson, but Christopher was desperate.

I'll continue to learn from you, he responded in his head, *every day if I must.*

You've learned enough, the voice said. *Will you use what you've learned to rule the Territories with me? Together we will lead it to kingdoms never before reached.*

Confused, his body buffeted hard by the high winds and sand in the intensifying gloom, Christopher didn't know how to respond. This was not the Lucas he had spent the past week with, the mysterious blind man who had brought him on adventures that had opened him to inner landscapes he had no idea existed.

I will stop the storm, the voice said.

Given Lucas's apparent mystical abilities, Christopher believed the blind man could stop it. And the idea of using what he had learned to rule was enticing. He would be able to elevate his station from farming to a position where he and Ariana could have the life they could only dream about. He would also be able to teach others what he had learned from Lucas, showing them the increased perception that lay within everyone as the Perceiver had shown him.

But something about the blind man's words felt hollow and empty, and a small, quiet voice inside called him inward. He followed it down, despite the powerful forces in the increasing darkness around him, to the calm and peaceful place where his knowingness slept, and it came to life and spoke truth. The words came with a soft power that was as strong and impenetrable as the Grand Wall.

No, Christopher said, *I will do it myself.*

And with those words, he summoned all his remaining strength and concentration into focusing on the peace of that sacred space, and he brought forth an indescribable stillness that cracked open the heavens and manifested into form, calming the air around him.

Within that pocket of tranquility, the assaulting wind and sand no longer affected him. He was in the middle of the storm yet untouched by it, contained within a bubble of peace and serenity of his own creation, except that it wasn't his; he was simply the vessel for it.

As he expanded the feeling further and further from his center, around him the winds diminished and the clouds broke, revealing once again the unforgiving landscape in the inexplicable, midday darkness. The storm had dissolved, but day had become dusk in the desert.

Relieved at having quelled the storm's fury, it took him a few more minutes to realize that he might have just traded one kind of demise for another, for he was still alone and without water in the barren wasteland.

Physically and mentally exhausted, he slumped over, still on his knees, his head and shoulders limp. Fully spent, he didn't have any energy left to even think, let alone bring forth another miracle from within, even to save his own life.

He finally willed himself to look up to where the sun was supposed to be and saw the image on the cover of the book of forbidden parables hidden in his boyhood room, the thin crescent that was left of the sun being devoured by shadow, just as his life was being extinguished by the desert. At this point, he wished he could crawl up and through the shadow to the light beyond it to escape to another world.

With difficulty, he opened his pack and tried to get a few drops of any remaining water from the flask. Finding none, he dropped it in the sand and strained to look out into the distance in the fading light. There was still nothing to be found. It was over, this quest or whatever it was he had undertaken.

His body relaxed as he accepted his fate, but then he noticed something in the flat area directly below him near the bottom of the cliff, what appeared to be someone kneeling in the freshly-blown sand. Blinking and rubbing his eyes to make sure his mind wasn't playing tricks on him again, especially now in the dim light, the figure remained.

Excited but cautious, Christopher stood up and tried to shout but couldn't produce any sound with his parched throat. Somehow finding the physical strength, he picked up his pack and stumbled down the side of the dune in the implausible twilight, tripping and rolling most of the way. Crashing at the bottom, he crawled forward toward the form, still trying without success to vocalize to get the person's attention.

It appeared to be a man, and he was kneeling, not moving, and facing away from Christopher with his head hanging down, a ghostly apparition on what was increasingly like a moonless night. Christopher wondered if he was dead.

Crawling slowly around the stranger to get a better look, his eyes wide in anticipation, Christopher got within an arm's length, close enough to see the man's chest moving, which meant he was breathing and alive. He inched closer and tentatively reached out and touched the man on the shoulder. The man turned his head slightly, but it still hung down and Christopher couldn't see his face.

Believing the man needed water, Christopher realized that even though he had emptied and discarded his flask, he might have something in his pack that could help. He quickly opened it, reached in, and found an apple wrapped tightly in beeswax, the last item he had that wasn't dried, and something he had overlooked in his delirium. Unwrapping it, he found it warm, soft, and wrinkled, but at least it was something that had some moisture.

He gently took the man's leathery hand, turned it upward, and placed the apple in it. Despite the increasing darkness, all of Christopher's senses were attuned to what was before him, so he could see just well enough.

The man's fingers slowly, tenderly, grasped and felt the fruit as if trying to figure out what it was, and his head came up and turned toward Christopher. The stranger's clear, blue eyes opened and met Christopher's gaze. Christopher, in his compromised but elevated sensory state, stared at the familiar face until he realized he was looking at Lucas.

Shocked, especially given the condition he was in and what he had just experienced with Lucas's voice in his head, he scrambled away quickly, staring at the man in disbelief. The blue eyes made him look vastly different, yet in some way even more wise, and it was clear that any trace of sightlessness was gone; the blind man could see *everything*.

"What . . .?" Christopher managed to croak out as the darkness around him reached its peak.

Lucas looked at him peacefully, his kind, lucid eyes twinkling with a wisdom far greater than Christopher could comprehend. He stood up, walked over to the shaken journeyer, and held out his hand, his head haloed by the impossibly missing sun behind him that had turned into a glowing ring.

Christopher, unsure, looked at Lucas's hand suspiciously at first, doubting its reality, but still he reached out. And the moment he touched it, his life as he knew it was over.

~

As Lucas helped him to his feet, the light of the sun burst forth from behind the shadow to nearly blind Christopher with its brightness, and his thirst and all physical discomforts suddenly vanished. He blinked until his eyes could fully open, and he saw that he had indeed traveled to another world. The desert was no longer there. It had transformed into a cathedral of light, and he and Lucas stood in its center as a powerful wind gusted through the crossing.

With the blind man radiating the surrounding light, Christopher began to dissolve. Everything he knew, everything from the realm he was so close to, so invested in, was falling away.

His shoulders relaxed as the burdens of the world lifted. Any worries he may have had about the farm, Ariana, Vincent, the government, or about anything in his life simply thawed and dispersed into the brightness around him, carried away on the beams of light emanating from the shimmering, iridescent walls. His back and hips relaxed, loosening and unwinding so that he felt as if he stood ten feet tall.

Every minute fragment of his body sped up with energy, pulsing, spiraling, spinning out the last, heavy remnants of the life he thought he knew, the life he thought he wanted. Vibrations of what seemed like all frequencies reverberated around him and through him, shaking loose the detritus built up over years of living within the Wall. He saw the debris as chunks of blackness coming out of his body, cracking and turning to dust before his eyes as it encountered the intensity of the light around and within him.

His body burst forth with a boundless power that reached to the edges of the universe, dissolving itself into a unity with the ocean of light everywhere. He saw—he felt, he *knew*—that this had always been in him, had always *been* him, and everything that had occurred in the life he had known scarcely registered in its insignificance compared to it.

He had never before felt anything remotely like this. The entirety of his physical being was at total and complete ease. And beyond what was happening to his body, he could barely understand, let alone describe, the other aspects of what was emerging.

As his form came into actualizing its flawlessness, his mind expanded with the power of a thousand suns. All he had experienced with Lucas—back from when his father had helped him give his first apple to the blind man to his recent outings in the city—came into perfect focus, and he saw the deeper, more profound meanings of the week's lessons. None of them had been an accident.

The first day accompanying the blind man to the brothel was a lesson about connection, belonging, creation, and the feeling of freedom and unity the expression of those things brought forth. The creative force was not something Christopher had felt strongly before then, but he could now feel and appreciate its power as he touched into its connection with all things, sourced from the common wellspring of life-giving energy he was feeling from the light around him.

The second day, the tense interaction with the leader of the gang held an experience in realizing his individuality. Because he recognized that all people were fundamentally the same, being different or holding different views simply added to the beauty and color of individual expression in the world. He found self-empowerment that day and learned that he could choose whether he wanted to be caught up in appearances and observable actions or live from a deeper level, one that he had customarily dismissed before.

On his third excursion with Lucas when they went into the center of the city to the cathedral, he felt the beginnings of awakening to something beyond himself and the world around him through his connection with the Perceiver. His intuition, something he had generally bypassed in favor of managing his life in a more physical, practical manner, had expanded and enabled him to better understand his surroundings based on the inherent qualities that he could *feel* rather than simply see on the surface.

On the day he went to the artisan shop while walking with Lucas the fourth time, his heart opened and he could finally truly feel deep, genuine love for others and, more importantly, was able to trust and find love for himself. He recognized that forgiveness and love were equivalent in their expression, because having one inevitably brought forth the other. The experience enabled him to accept that his connection to what was beyond his physical existence in the world had become real.

When he took it upon himself to go to the blind man on the fifth day of their engagements, he enthusiastically had taken charge of his life instead of allowing what was around him to dictate it. The ensuing experiences—speaking fearlessly with the officer and constables at the detainment center when Vincent was taken in, and later with the official at his cart—had surprised even him in their clarity and confidence. He was able to communicate in such a way because he was discerning his environment and making decisions more lucidly, feeling the innate power he was now experiencing even more completely.

The following day, the sixth one after having been struck senseless on the road into the city, his arrest and ability to see and *know* beyond what his physical surroundings presented brought him to an understanding that with a focused intent, anything was possible, like the transformation of the constable's painful and distressing emotions and now finally getting answers to his many questions, which were resolving themselves at this very moment as the experience continued.

All those days with Lucas had been both a progression and a concurrent opening of his senses that brought him beyond the world he knew. Now, the beauty and brilliance of those lessons anchored in him and expanded, giving clarity to all else in his past as he fell into the whirlpool of what was emerging.

His memories of his mother and father, of Ariana, Martel, and the other merchants in the marketplace, all the good and bad he had ever experienced fit impeccably into the beautiful tapestry that was woven around him in gossamer waves of light. From the timing and deaths of his parents—which had set him up to feel abandoned, sad, and anxious heading out into the world as a young adult—to his difficulties and delights running the farm, to his interactions with Ariana, his great love, and Martel, who had befriended him and supported his challenging and unusual quest, to what he had been confronted with internally and externally this week, he saw that all these experiences had been his teachers on the meandering path that had brought him ever closer to understanding the unknown shadows of his life, a life of perfect failings.

He could see that his father, although he hadn't known that what Christopher was now experiencing would happen, knew that there was something special about his son and that consistently nourishing the blind man would help it be realized. Even the unstable woman outside the antique shop had been there to help feed his deep need to understand and be ready for what was now occurring, and what she had said to him had indeed come to pass.

He realized that even when he had felt helpless and depressed in the past—such as when his mother and then his father had left the physical world—even those times had been exquisite in the precision in how they affected his life, providing a particular path of thoughts, emotions, and actions that had brought him to what he was experiencing now. All those dark and anxious periods following challenging events had been gifts, although unknown to him at the time and thoroughly rejected. But they had all unfolded in divine order, as this was now unfolding.

These lessons that life had brought him were the fuel for this journey he was on. Everything he had gone through in his life was a perfect dance of circumstances, relationships, situations, and experiences, all coming together to draw him forward to this moment to reveal what he possessed even before life began.

Everyone had this within them; there was nothing special in him that others did not have or could not realize. A simple nudge was all that was necessary to kindle the desire to understand more, and the path to recognizing lessons sprouted from there. That's what had started it for Christopher. At the time he hadn't known where it had come from, but his altered state on the road to the city over a week ago was but a droplet from the source he was now bathing in, and it was all contained within him from long before that, from the beginning.

And Christopher knew, finally, the answer to what had perplexed him since he was a boy, the treasure at the end of the quest. He knew it beyond all rational thought, a recognition with absolute certainty felt with his entire beingness with all the energies around him. *Someday* had arrived. And the answer—the words, the *feeling*—echoed unambiguously and assuredly in his head more forcefully than if he had shouted them from the heavens. He could finally put the enduring question to rest.

Father, I understand.

Tears of sadness, of relief, of joy, of knowingness cascaded down his face. He was feeling himself—his old self, the Christopher others knew—for the last time. Death had come for him, not in the form of earthly, physical passing but of ideas, emotions, thoughts, and personality. Everything he had been he no longer could be, and everything he was remembering he now could realize in its wholeness.

He became consumed by an all-encompassing feeling of love. It washed over him in tender, angelic waves, carrying away the last vestiges of his old existence and resurrecting the pure being that lay beneath. Its unconditional nature was so complete that duality ceased to exist, and he was left bathing in the energy, awareness, and feeling of unbounded oneness with all that lived.

Nothing of a negative nature existed, as everything had its place in the divine order, playing out lessons over and over again to get to precisely *this* point. Even so-called positive emotions couldn't survive this state because it was so completely infused with unconditional love that everything else diminished to nothing. Assessments and contrasts did not, could not, exist in any form. Even happiness had no place, as it was a state of comparison to that which was not happy, and both states vanished into the all-encompassing and overwhelming power of the one love he was experiencing.

He hoped for nothing and feared nothing. Those sentiments were not a part of him anymore, and he knew they never truly were. They, and all emotions, were creations of who he had been inside the Wall, a manifestation of a lower self that used them to survive the three-dimensional world, shadows playing upon a shadow. They were no longer needed.

Nothing of that world continued here, now, where the possibilities—the *potentialities*—were limitless. His whole being was remembering, for the first and ever-present moment in time, his innate freedom, completeness, and unity with all that existed as he immersed himself in the clarity and understanding of those who had walked the same ancient path he had just traveled, his brothers and sisters in the world of light.

Christopher looked at Lucas and saw his being of light reflected above his head as a glowing, golden-white halo like the ring Christopher had just witnessed in the darkness of his earlier life. The glaring brightness of the blind man's form then diminished just enough to reveal the face before him—perfectly joyful, peaceful, and loving—seeing him as he was originally created. He was drawn into the depths of the cool, blue eyes before they began to change, as did the face, slowly morphing into a largely featureless surface that reminded him of the weathered appearance of the Perceiver. The transformation continued until he realized he was now looking into familiar eyes, only clearer and wiser, and a reflection he knew all too well: his own. *He* was the king in the cathedral wearing the crown of light.

In that recognition, the light the two radiated grew brighter, and Christopher's arms spontaneously stretched out to his sides to open himself to embrace the brilliant figure that stepped toward him.

Except there was no embrace. The figure simply moved *into* him to occupy the same space, and Christopher's arms stretched further apart as he accepted and allowed the intense energy of the being to settle in his form.

He heard a murmuring in a language unfamiliar to his ears but familiar to his heart, the language of the Ancients, as the beautiful words swirled around and encompassed him in a resonance that carried understanding beyond what simply hearing them conveyed.

Together, the two beings merged into one column of light so bright that had he been seeing with his physical eyes he would have been blinded. But this light neither pierced nor hurt his vision. It was as soft as it was bright, as compassionate as it was powerful, and with his eyes wide open, Christopher could finally see Truth.

With his body of light, he found himself in a magical garden oasis bursting with the vibrancy that created and sustained life. The cathedral—a self-created construct based on his previous perceptions of belief and faith—had dissolved along with all the other remnants of his preconceived illusions.

He could see the desert landscape he had traveled through beyond the garden sanctuary crackling with energy. What had previously seemed so vacant of living things brimmed with life, from the miniscule bugs crawling on grains of sand, to the small animals who fed on them, to the rainbow of colors around the plants, trees, and flowers in the garden around him, to the wholeness of what the desert was in its entirety. All of it was bright, alive, and in perfect order, and Christopher understood how he could not have seen it before.

LIFE! It was all around him, in this one present, connecting in relationship, as that was the only way for the unimaginable oneness to express itself. Differences in form—the shadowy actors that temporarily occupied the theater within which he thought he had understood life—were necessary to experience the beautiful, varied expressions that sprung from the source from which all originated.

He knew that his blindness to understanding in his previous existence was part of what he had needed to struggle through; he had to be sightless to expose how to truly see. Lucas had shown him that. Christopher felt an overwhelming gratitude to the blind man, his brother of light, for revealing the path.

He took his first few steps as a new being, fully accomplished and wholly present. With each footstep he engaged completely, feeling the direct relationship with his new environment—the path beneath his feet, the fresh air in his lungs, the fragrant flowers around him, the calm pool of water in the center of the oasis, the magnificent apple tree next to it abounding with ripe, luscious fruit, the entire landscape even beyond his field of vision. He was both connected to all in his surroundings and one with them, the boundaries of his body seemingly optional depending on how and where he placed his vision.

Walking to the pool of water, he looked down at his reflection, a face recognizable but so very different from who he was before, its past gone and its source revealed. Beyond the surface, sitting at the bottom of the pool, he could see the stones of the thoughts and emotions he had carried that had created waves in his life, having splashed into his consciousness with a force that left ripples lingering for years. Yet long after the surface calmed, the stones remained, irritating his tender feet when he strolled through the shallow depths upon feeling the resonance of similar obstacles. He now could see they were not the foreign objects he had thought they were that needed to be disavowed and removed; rather, he saw and accepted them simply as pieces of the whole of his existence, elements welcomed into a warm embrace within which their hard exteriors became forgiving. The stones endured, but only as experiences and no longer as uncomfortable inflammations to his previously fragile, earthly personality. They transformed into soft sand upon which he could walk freely and easily now, seeing and understanding the struggles of the past yet unburdened by them.

He bent down and dipped his cupped hands into the cool liquid, brought the life-sustaining fluid to his lips, and drank. Refilling his hands, he lifted the blessed water up and dribbled it over his head, anchoring the whole of the transformational experience he had just beheld, for it washed away the idea that he, or anyone, could ever have erred in thought, word, or deed.

He stood and looked up at the grand apple tree next to him, its sturdy branches reaching skyward and dangling their tempting, red gifts. He paused, smiled, and took one in his hand, gently plucking it from the sacred tree's grasp. Its firm, smooth surface couldn't contain the energy bursting from within, and as he sank

his teeth into the crisp exterior to meet the sweet flesh, his awareness connected and extended into and through the tree and
down into the roots where it spread to encompass the entire
garden oasis. He felt the refreshing groundedness of earth's
bounty infuse his being, and all the knowledge in the world was
his, with the recognition that there was nothing that ever needed
to be redeemed, for everything was clear, true, and unencum-
bered by the whims of personality and the trivialities of the
physical world.

Looking around and smiling with contentment and understanding, he gave of himself to his surroundings with the awareness that it would be reciprocated in that moment, in each and
every moment, for all time. Thus was the nature of relationship.
He knew that in his giving was receiving, because one could not
be separated from the other, as all were connected. He took a
few steps into the enchanted garden, shared his loving, enlight-
ened state with his environment, and became the love that he
bestowed.

Joyfully experiencing the purity of the abundance that flowed
through him, he accepted his role as a creative vessel to manifest
from the oneness he now knew, a role he had always played
despite being oblivious to it. All beings that walked the earth
couldn't help but be the channels for the blessings and all the
good in the world, and he had always been among them.

He had been given a divine gift: the awareness of this
ceaseless power of creation. One's energy was the collective
combination of the conscious and the subconscious, the seen
and the unseen, the known and the unknown. This energy
attracted itself and reinforced the vessel that expressed it, and it
happened faster than time could move. But every moment
contained a choice to experience and create anew—from the
source of the oneness within—to fundamentally change the

vessel itself, something so often rejected for a stagnant life beholden to the past. He was beyond that now, creating as one with all that surrounded him with the wisdom and love coming from the wellspring of all creation.

Life was not meant to be static; it was meant to change, to grow into uncovering that which made all people—indeed, all things—the same. That's how individuals could experience the divine, how they could feel and understand the incredible connection Christopher was now feeling within himself and his surroundings. Life, in all its perceived ups and downs and twists and turns, unfolded throughout time to bring this inner knowing to the surface, a passage to another world that lay within, at the center of being. He saw and knew that everyone needed to suffer these perceived shadows of form in order to escape them. And he knew that all would, eventually, even if it took lifetimes.

After a few more steps, he found himself inexplicably on the road to his house, and it was the most natural thing in the world. The desert had vanished and was a distant memory, as was the Grand Wall. His mind didn't need to make sense of it because he had grown past it. There was no need to labor anymore, physically, mentally, or otherwise.

He sauntered down the road, feeling the joy of a child curiously exploring nature in the spring. Disbelief didn't exist in his state of connecting with the trees, birds, insects, and earth, for he and they had an unmitigated commitment to the sincerity of life, which danced around and through them all in a harmonious ballet of unity.

Approaching his farmhouse—oh, how he loved that house!—Christopher saw Ariana emerge onto the porch with her magnificent beauty shining from within and without, and his heart leapt. An old, faraway part of him recollected something about losing both her and the farm, but the energies that had created those situations were gone now, and he no longer had a need for what they had brought. They, and other remembrances, had been of his own making, and he now chose to be beyond their shadows, so he knew that somehow the government would not take the farm and that he and Ariana would be together. He didn't know how those outcomes would come about, and it didn't matter, only that any other results were not possible anymore.

He ascended the stairs to the porch and embraced her, and their energies combined into a unifying whole, a perfect, merged radiance that could not be put into words. It was a glorious addition to what they each possessed individually, which remained undiminished.

Holding hands, they sat down and gazed into the distance. Christopher looked at the horizon, the true horizon, because there was no longer a wall that could contain him. In truth, there never really was. The limitations and barriers in his body and mind were gone now, so their manifestations were no longer necessary. The realm he now dwelled in was boundless.

Ariana looked over lovingly at him, squeezed his hand, and said, "Are you okay? You seem different."

He looked at her with his new eyes, seeing beyond her appearance to the depth of her being that mirrored his own. Nothing about either of them was out of place or wanting for anything, for the entire world, all worlds, were contained within them.

Christopher responded with the only thing he could express right then, the only thing that indeed meant anything in the limited language of the physical domain they both inhabited. And as the words emerged from his lips, for that unceasing instant, he was the universe and the light and all the impossible things he could now understand.

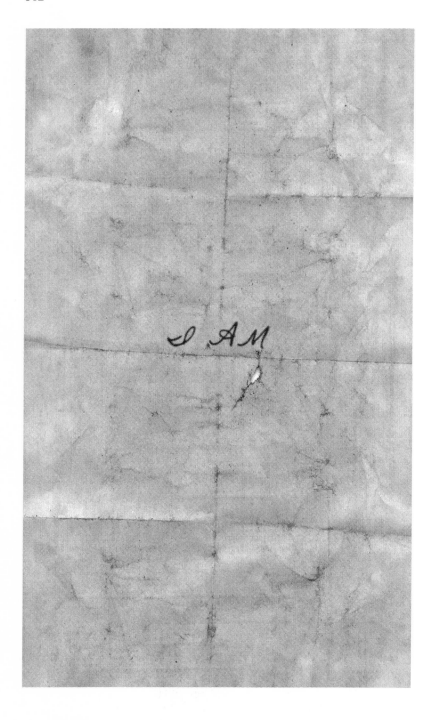

Anna

Anna sat staring at the last, creased, faded page, her body tingling with goosebumps at the two words. The time had passed quickly and her eyes were tired, but more notably, the story had moved her to her core and had caused her to have trouble thinking. It was like she was above and beyond her mind, and she couldn't process what she had read with what she was feeling.

She looked up at what she had drawn on the wall, her portal "to another word," then read the two words on the page a dozen more times. Something deep inside her was opening, like she had been given the key to the rusty lock on an old door she could now open and peer behind to reveal the birthday present within.

It took some time for her to regain her faculties and feel physically lucid again. When she did, she felt strong and confident.

When her mother called her to remind her of the afternoon birthday gathering she was running late for, she bounded out of her room holding the leather-wrapped book.

"Mom, it was *soooo* good!" she shrieked. "Best story ever!" Then, taking a more serious tone, she asked, "I wonder if it's true."

"Well, honey, it doesn't matter, if you believe it to be true," her mother said, which sounded surprisingly familiar.

Anna smiled, grabbed her coat, and ran out the door.

~

When she arrived at Melissa's, Laura was already there. True to her word, Melissa had made sweet biscuits, a few of which had already been eaten. While it was Anna's special day and her friends were excited for her, she had trouble focusing because she was thinking about the story. It had touched her profoundly, even though she had a feeling there was much more in it that she didn't yet grasp. One thing she knew was that she couldn't wait to get home to read it again.

She eventually managed her exit after her friends celebrated her birthday with a song, the delicious treats, and some good-natured laughing and teasing. She appreciated it and played her part, but her attention was elsewhere.

Once she was finally heading home, the closer she came to her house the more she experienced a feeling of unease. And as she turned the last corner onto her street, she knew something was very wrong. The fear rising within was palpable, as though a shadow had taken beastly form and would devour her if she continued. Like Christopher perceiving things beyond what his physical eyes presented him, she *knew* she was walking into danger, but also like Christopher, she couldn't ignore the feeling of needing to keep moving forward.

Bracing herself and drawing strength from Christopher's courage in the face of adversity, she approached her house and opened the main door, her hands almost shaking. She progressed up the inside steps, treading softly, alertly, scrutinizing her surroundings with all her senses. The air outside her family's door was thick with a combination of fear and anger, the sharp-toothed, predatory jaws of the beast ready to crush not just her life but her spirit as well. And she wasn't wrong.

When she opened the door, her father stood glowering in the entryway, gripping the precious, handwritten pages in his fists, the leather covering open and on the floor. Her mother stood behind him with her head bowed.

"What in the devil's name is this?!" he bellowed, shaking the papers, his face contorted in anger, the color of it matching his red hair.

The old Anna knew better than to answer, but the newly-emboldened Anna, the reader of the tale, couldn't stop herself.

"It's a story, and I like it!" she retorted.

"I will not have this in my house!" her father yelled.

"It was *my* birthday present! It was a gift. You didn't even have to pay for it!" Anna shrieked.

"This is blasphemy!" her father shouted, holding up the papers, his strict, religious upbringing revealing its unsightly face. Hot with rage, he stomped to the terrace doors and threw them open. Anna followed, her legs somehow able to move.

"Not in my house!" he thundered, looking back at her.

He stepped to the railing and flung the manuscript off the balcony. The papers dispersed and fluttered down into the busy street. Storming back inside, he leaned over her and glared. In a low voice, he said ominously, "If I see anything like that again, you'll be next."

Shocked and speechless, Anna pushed by him, ran to the balcony, and looked over the railing. The pages were scattered about the street, getting kicked up, torn, dirtied, and trampled by people walking back and forth who barely registered the commotion.

One man, however, was standing motionless in their midst and reading one of the sheets from the story. She could tell because the tale's final page was easily identifiable with its creases and wrinkled, weathered appearance. The man folded the piece of paper, slipped it into his pocket, and looked up at her.

When their eyes met, Anna felt a wave of calm flow over her, instantly reducing her fear of her father and anger at the loss of the manuscript. For the few precious moments they stared at one another, she experienced but a fraction of the feeling she had read about in the mysterious author's handwriting.

And she knew everything was going to be okay.

Epilogue

Sitting at his desk, the old man's steady fingers hovered over the last words after writing them, the only two words on the page. The story of his former life was finished. The rest was for others to tell. He put his quill down and gathered all the papers together, the top one reading, *A Tale of Awakening by Erich Evepret.*

It was long ago and a different existence, but all true as he remembered it. He had far outlived the other individuals in the story, so no one could corroborate his account, but the old man did not need validation; he had lived it.

His life since those times had been both ordinary and extraordinary, spent in a state of joy, love, and connection with the livingness in all things. He lived with these expressions of who he was, knowing they could be found in every experience, even in those that appeared dark, distressing, or otherwise mundane. The present moment had become an ongoing gift to him, as it was to all who recognized it.

He stood up, thought for a moment, and sat down again. Opening a drawer full of miscellaneous papers, he rummaged through them, finding an old, faded, and creased sheet with the same two words he had just written. He smiled, feeling as if the universe were winking at him, and remembered how the page had come to him so many years ago, falling at his feet like a gift from heaven, as indeed it was. He lifted his stack of papers and replaced his last written page with the old, weathered sheet.

The old man closed the drawer, opened a different one, and pulled out a faded, leather cover with three spirals on the front. Opening it, he placed the finished manuscript with its timeworn final page into it, tying the covering together with the frayed, rawhide straps. He left it carefully on top of the desk, stood up, and strolled outside.

Making his way off the porch and up the small hill behind the house, he approached a lone basswood tree guarding a fenced-in plot with several old, family gravestones on one side. The other side held a solitary wooden marker securely wedged atop a rare, white stone taken from the fields. The oak plank, chosen by Ariana and bearing her name, was beginning to wear from the elements after so many years, the letters starting to smooth and flatten from their original, carved height. She had learned much from him in her long life but had understood it would take additional time to fully absorb the lessons, time that she had run out of in the physical world. She had known what she needed to do, though, and knew that it had to come after the ground had reclaimed her body. "Before my grave marker fades," she had said, "I will understand."

He stood before it, not needing to bow his head or kneel as was customary; rather, he stretched out his arms and took a deep breath, inhaling the abundance of the natural world around him of which she now was a part, at least physically. He felt some of the deepest gratitude he had ever experienced at that moment, for everything.

The old man returned to the porch and sat in the chair that fit him so intimately. The cool, evening air blew a refreshing breeze as he enjoyed the uninterrupted view he had seen almost every day for well over a century. He thought about how the city had grown over the years, now expanding as far as the black-smiths' workshops that used to be the midpoint of his walk to the marketplace. It was a slow-moving creature, the sprawl from the heart of the Territories, but one that now flourished, just like all who lived within its reach.

There were no longer any constraints. The Grand Wall was now just something in a story that parents told to their children, and the constabulary was so rarely needed that it had been greatly reduced in size and was only called upon when true, physical threats presented themselves, which wasn't often. The dangerous foreigners of the past were no more, if they even existed in the first place.

It was another world, one that extended to the ends of the earth, for nothing could contain the expression of the people anymore. They were free to explore, free to create, free to travel, free to think, free to believe, free to love, free to surrender, allow, and perceive, free to know endless possibilities—free to truly *live*.

The old man, and Ariana to a lesser degree, had existed in this manner before the natural world had reclaimed her body, spending the days in that free state doing whatever needed to be done, because it no longer mattered how they spent their time as long as it genuinely came from that sacred place within. The old man couldn't help but live from there, while she had had to be taught how.

She had learned much from her beloved's teachings to the crowds that had once gathered for his talks, but there was so much more that he hadn't been able to convey to her no matter what methods he tried. She would have needed the direct experience herself to truly understand. She would, someday, just as others would.

He knew it was time for those who had studied with him to take the next step, to learn to elevate themselves instead of looking to him for their salvation, which only served to delay the personal experience they desired anyway. As such, he had decided to stop teaching. His words would live on, however, in the hearts and minds of his students—some of whom would continue teaching—and in any written accounts of the lessons.

He was aware of one such text, but he didn't know the details except from whom it originated. Anna had been one of his most ardent and astute students, and he trusted that her writings would speak truth to those who read them, as she had grown into an effective teacher herself. He knew her words would sprout in the fertile mind fields that had been properly cleared, for awareness grows abundantly once buried obstructions are identified and brought into the light to be defused. He didn't know what had become of her writings, but it didn't matter. Truth would arrive to those who sought it when sufficiently desired.

Sitting in his chair, the countryside stretched before him, unimpeded, for as far as he could see, the long shadows of the perfectly imperfect earth reaching for him across the fields like a desperate victim pleading for help. Even as they grew, he knew they couldn't grab him—not anymore, not since that day beyond the Wall—for the shadows lived and died in the world of form, a world beyond which he now existed.

He smiled and closed his eyes, knowing he had completed what he had come to do. It was time.

When he opened them, Lucas stood at the foot of the steps to the porch, ageless, his eyes clear and blue and looking as peaceful as ever the old man recalled. Saying nothing, he walked up the steps and took his place in the empty chair. The two shared a knowing glance and sat silently together as they watched the sun gradually slip below the horizon to extinguish once again the self-created shadows of form.

Acknowledgements

I would like to acknowledge and thank my beta readers and editors for their feedback and editorial contributions, including Jonathon Calloway, Ruth Santos, and Gina Ottoboni, among others. I would also like to acknowledge and thank Rev. Penny Donovan, Donald Gilbert, and the Sacred Garden Fellowship community and teachers for helping reframe many years of spiritual study into an understandable whole; Barb Cove for her timely and perceptive guidance; my non-physical teachers and guides for never losing faith in me even when I lost faith in myself; and everyone I've interacted with in my life—friends and foes, passing acquaintances and family—whether it was for five minutes or fifty years, for assisting and guiding me in becoming who I am today along the path of learning, loving, and seeing truth, setting the foundation for the expression of this book.

About the Author

Peter Santos has been studying spirituality and healing for over three decades while balancing a varied and successful career using his left brain. His extensive travel to sacred sites around the world, including walking the Camino de Santiago in Spain and trekking to sacred Mt. Kailash in Tibet, has grounded the spiritual wisdom he has received, and he is happy to be able to share what he has learned through his writing and teaching. He lives in Vermont.

If you enjoyed this book, please consider leaving a review, as reviews can meaningfully support independent authors like Peter. In addition, you can stay updated on Peter's writings, events, and other projects at www.peter-santos.com and on Facebook at www.facebook.com/petersantosauthor.

Made in the USA
Middletown, DE
09 May 2023

29853115R00191